Praise for *The Moonshine Shack Murder*
and the Southern Homebrew Mystery Series

"*The Moonshine Shack Murder* is a charming cozy mystery that will warm you from the inside out and keep you guessing till the end!"

—Kate Lansing, author of *Mulled to Death*

"A creative storyteller, the author quickly builds a delightful and engaging community . . . Kelly skillfully devises an intriguing mystery . . . The Southern Homebrew series starts with a 100-proof story." —Fresh Fiction

"The mystery is captivating, the characters are a delight, . . . and the author's trademark humor brightens up even the most stressful scenes." —Open Book Society

"This series is off to a fantastic start . . . I can't wait to return to Chattanooga and The Moonshine Shack for a sample or two and whatever trouble Hattie gets herself wrapped up in." —Escape With Dollycas Into A Good Book

"I loved everything about this book—the characters, the moonshine, the animals, the quick wit and snarky dialogue." —Storeybook Reviews

"Fast-paced, clever, and filled with humor."

—Socrates' Book Reviews

"Family pride, friendship, romance, and a little hooch make *The Moonshine Shack Murder* a fun start to a new series."

—Cozy Up with Kathy

The Proof Is in the Poison

A Southern Homebrew Mystery

DIANE KELLY

BERKLEY PRIME CRIME
New York

BERKLEY PRIME CRIME
Published by Berkley
An imprint of Penguin Random House LLC
penguinrandomhouse.com

Copyright © 2022 by Diane Kelly

ISBN: 9780593333242

First Edition: June 2022

Printed in the United States of America
1 3 5 7 9 10 8 6 4 2

Book design by George Towne

The Proof Is in the Poison

Chapter One

Thunk. The sound of my cat's front paws hitting the wooden floor of our rustic cabin woke me from my slumber. Smoky had been snuggled up against me in bed all night, but he'd decided that breakfast was more important than sleep now. He'd also decided he wasn't going to wait for me to rouse myself. He issued his breakfast order with an insistent chitter that said I'd better get to it if I knew what was good for me.

My demanding feline friend was named after the Smoky Mountains that rose into a mysterious gray mist near our hometown of Chattanooga, Tennessee. Until recently, I would have described the cat as aloof. Things had changed after a killer had forced Smoky and me off a winding mountain road. Together, we'd survived a harrowing rollover in my secondhand van and an ensuing pursuit through the woods by a man intent on silencing me for good. Since the terrifying ordeal, Smoky came around more regularly

and expressed real affection, purring and encircling my an-
kles, even swiping my cheek with his sandpaper-like tongue
once or twice. He'd never be the cute and cuddly type of
kitty, but at least he now let me know he loved me—even if
our relationship would always be on his terms.

I glanced at the clock on my bedside table. 6:48. *Ughhh.*
Though my alarm wasn't set to go off for another forty-two
minutes, I supposed it couldn't hurt to get moving. I had a
busy day ahead of me. Sighing, I deactivated the alarm,
threw back the covers to climb out of bed, and addressed
my demanding cat, who was eyeing me with a grumpy
glower. "Don't get your fur in a fluff, boy. I'm coming."

I followed Smoky's swishing tail to the small kitchen,
which was adorably outdated. The round-cornered mint-
green Kelvinator refrigerator had stood in place since the
late 1950s. My determined and resourceful granny always
managed to rustle up the hard-to-find parts to repair what
she called her icebox, once even driving all the way to Tallahassee, Florida, to get a new thermostat. She'd passed
on ten years ago, but she'd left me with lots of wonderful
memories, including that fun trip to Tallahassee, as well as
a head covered in dark curls, just like she'd had when she
was younger.

My grandparents had lived in this cabin all of their married life. After my granny headed on to heaven, my grandfather had continued to reside here until he decided to move
to the retirement home. He'd offered me the cabin. My sib-
lings and cousins had no interest in the small, no-frills house
that was too far from the city, schools, and stores for con-
venience yet too close to the city to constitute a real get-
away. I, on the other hand, had been thrilled to move into
the place. The cabin might not be much to look at, but it
was peaceful and quiet. What's more, the home played a

significant role in the scandalous history of the Hayes family. My great-grandfather's old moonshine still remained hidden in the trees out back, though the apparatus was now covered with rust and vines. The also rusty Ford flathead V8 that Eustatius Hayes had used to outrun law enforcement during Prohibition likewise sat in a shed behind the cabin. No way would I let my family's ancestral home be sold off. I'd paid my grandfather what the cabin was worth, which wasn't much. Although the porcelain bathtub was chipped, it worked just fine for a quick shower or a relaxing soak, and I didn't need the latest in kitchen appliances or countertops to be happy here.

I opened a can of whitefish pâté and upended it in Smoky's bowl. The food slid from the can with an unappetizing *sluck*. Not that Smoky seemed to mind. The instant I set it down in front of him, he dug in, gobbling his breakfast as if he hadn't eaten in weeks.

Now that my chubby charge had been fed, I set about taking care of my own needs. Hot coffee. A warm biscuit. A steamy shower. T-shirt, overalls, and comfortable sneakers, a must for all the walking I'd be doing today. After brushing my teeth, I slapped on a little makeup, dabbed some hair product into my hand, and ran my fingers through my shoulder-length curls to wrangle them into submission. *Ready to go.*

Smoky, who was employed as my Moonshine Shack's unofficial mascot, was ready to go to work, too. He'd already lain down in his extra-large plastic carrier. I fastened the latch, grabbed the handle on top, and grunted as I lifted my precious cargo. I carried him out front and set him down next to the rocking chair on the porch while I locked the door. The mid-June sun hovered just over the ridgeline above, the rays penetrating the thick forest and creating flashes of light around us. When we returned home tonight, the fireflies would do the same, lighting up the dark yard like a neon-green disco ball. Speaking of neon green, such was the color of my brand-new custom-painted van, which I'd recently bought to replace the one that had been totaled in the rollover. The color went along with my moonshine brand logo, which featured two fireflies with bright behinds.

Once we were in the van, I headed down the curving road into Chattanooga. My first stop was at a gas station, where I topped off my tank. My second stop was at the Singing River Retirement Home. Granddaddy waited out in front of the one-story stone building for me, sitting on his metallic red scooter, one arm crooked cockily over the handlebars as he chatted up a couple of the ladies who lived in the home with him. Granddaddy's hair might be white and sparse, and his weathered skin might have the texture of beef jerky, but these traits were offset by the spirited glint in his eyes and the broad smile made extra bright by freshly polished dentures. He wore his usual scuffed boots, a lightweight plaid shirt under denim overalls, and the black Stetson cowboy hat my granny had bought for him years ago. The hat had been a perfect gift for him. Granddaddy might be pushing ninety, but he was still the same irascible rascal he'd always been.

I unrolled the passenger window and called out to him. "Mornin', Granddaddy!" I raised a hand and gave a friendly nod to the ladies. *What are their names again? Selma and Louetta? Velma and Lucille? Thelma and Louise?* Heck, I couldn't remember. I supposed it didn't much matter. Granddaddy had no intentions of ever replacing Granny, but he wasn't above a little flirtation if it earned him a casserole or a slice of pecan pie. Besides, I'd seen these same two ladies working their feminine wiles on the other gentlemen in the home, too. They weren't looking to replace their husbands, either, only going for a little fun and companionship. No harm in that.

"Mornin', Hattie!" my granddad called back, his smile and eyes bright.

I climbed out and circled around to the back of my new van, where I lowered the ramp so we could load the scooter into the cargo bay. He motored up to the bottom of the ramp and climbed off the scooter, retrieving his cane from the basket. As he made his way to the passenger door, I climbed onto the scooter and drove it up the ramp and into the van, ducking to make sure I didn't hit my head. I pulled the ramp into the bay, closed the back, and retook my place in the driver's seat.

As we pulled away from the home, I cast a look at my grandfather. "You're looking extra chipper this morning."

"It was doughnut day in the dining hall," he said. "I'm hopped up on sugar." He reached into the front pocket of his overalls, pulled out something round wrapped in a paper napkin, and held it out to me. "Snatched one for you. Blueberry cake."

"My favorite! Thanks."

I ate the doughnut on the drive to my Moonshine Shack, popping the last bite into my mouth as I pulled to a stop in the small parking lot behind my store. I brushed crumbs from my lap as I slid down from the driver's seat. Once I rounded up my grandfather, his scooter, and my cat, I unlocked the back door and stepped into the combination office and storage room at the back of my shop. With the air conditioner set to eighty degrees to save electricity, the place was warm and stuffy. I nudged the thermostat down to a more comfortable temperature and released Smoky from his carrier. He sauntered out, performed a full-body stretch, then continued on into the shop, hopping up to take his usual place in the front window where he could keep an eye on Market Street and cast condescending glances at passersby.

Granddaddy carefully drove his scooter into the maze of stacked cartons in my storeroom and disappeared behind a wall of boxes. But while I could no longer see him, I could hear him. "You've been busy!" he called from behind the wall.

"Sure have!" I called back. With competition from microbreweries and other local craft liquor producers, my moonshine shop hadn't exactly taken off like a rocket when it opened in late spring. But traffic to the shop had picked up after recent, crazy events. Catch one killer and suddenly the media that has been ignoring you and your moonshine business wants an exclusive feature in their news reports. But, hey, I'd take all the free publicity I could get. That publicity had brought customers to my shop.

Yep, things were looking up for my Moonshine Shack. I'd hired a woman named Nora to help out at the store on weekdays while her children were in school. Nora had proven to be a responsible, diligent worker with a sunny disposition that made my customers feel right at home. I'd added two new products to my shelves, too, a candy apple moonshine flavor suggested by Officer Marlon Landers, the hunky cop I was dating, and 'shine sauce that combined my granddaddy's traditional moonshine with barbecue sauce produced by a local restaurateur. I'd even ordered my grandfather one of those power recliner chairs, the kind that would also tilt forward and stand a person right up with the push of a button. Like Smoky, Granddaddy enjoyed hanging out at my shop, but he tended to doze off. Falling asleep in a rocking chair out front could be dangerous. He might slide off the seat and hit his head. I'd surprise him with the new chair once it arrived. It was the least I could do for the man who'd not only taught me how to make moonshine but who also assisted me in selling the stuff in my store. He worked the register, made flavor suggestions to the customers, and served as a mascot of sorts, sitting out in front of the Moonshine Shack and attracting the attention of tourists and locals alike with his folksy charm, far more effective than any inflatable tube dancer or sign spinner.

Having help in the shop allowed me to focus my efforts on marketing rather than routine store operations. One of my recent efforts had paid off. The Chattanooga Choo-Choo Model Train Convention would kick off at 10:00 this morning, a little over an hour from now, and continue through Saturday. Yours truly had convinced the manager of the convention center hotel to hold a Monday Moonshine Mixer in the bar. It would give the conventioneers a reason to gather and spend their money, which would benefit both the bar's bottom line and mine. I'd offered the manager a good price on my Southern homebrew in return for him allowing me to post promotional signs and offer the crowd discount coupons if they came down the street to my shop to purchase a jar or two of my 'shine. It was a win-win. I figured model train people were a nostalgic bunch, and they might find my folksy wares and rustic shop to be right up their alley.

Granddaddy took a seat on a rocker out front, and set to whittling a little block of wood. He made all kinds of cute little critters, and I'd even given him some space on a shelf in my shop to sell them. They made a nice supplement to his social security, and gave him a little extra spending money, most of which he lost in poker games at the retirement home. The man couldn't bluff to save his life, and I knew from playing a few hands with him myself that he had an unmistakable tell—he wiggled his ears when he had a good hand.

Meanwhile, I plopped down at my desk in the back corner of the storeroom and spent a few minutes updating the shop's financial records to account for the weekend's sales. I'd sold nearly three grand in moonshine on Saturday and Sunday combined. *Not bad. Not bad at all.* Of course, business was much slower on weekdays. But with any luck I'd entice some of the conventioneers to come down to my shop this week.

My bookkeeping complete, I logged off the computer, gathered up the stack of flyers I intended to distribute at the model train convention, and slid them into a tote bag. I added promotional coasters, discount coupons, and even a few T-shirts printed with my logo. I stepped to the front door and called to my grandfather. "Time to load up, Granddaddy."

My grandfather used his cane to push himself up from the rocker, barely retaining the muscle strength to manage it. Even so, he got around darn good for someone his age. Naturally, Smoky had by now abandoned his spot in the front window and settled atop the cases of moonshine I'd set aside for tonight's event. He stared me down as I approached, as if daring me to move him. With a groan from me and a growl from him, I picked up my cat and carried him to his padded bed atop my desk. But Smoky wasn't about to accept being put in his bed lying down. He reached up and swatted one of the curls that bobbed around my cheek, letting me know he was the one who was really in charge here.

I groaned again as I stacked the two cases of my fruit-flavored moonshine on a dolly. I'd expected running a store would be work. I hadn't expected it would also be a workout. I was building my muscles right along with my customer base. Meanwhile, my grandfather tucked six earthenware jugs of his Granddaddy's Ole-Timey Corn Liquor into the basket on his scooter. "You sure six jugs is enough?" he asked.

"The mixer is only for two hours," I said. "Six jugs should be plenty."

He sent me a sour look that said he disagreed, but at least he didn't argue with me.

I slung my tote bag over my shoulder and admonished Smoky to "Be a good boy while I'm gone."

The cat raised a furry shoulder as if to shrug and say *Maybe I will and maybe I won't.*

Following my grandfather's scooter, I rolled my wares out the front door of the Moonshine Shack and onto the porch, turning back to set the alarm and lock up. My kitschy storefront façade was made to look like a hillbilly cabin, with boards nailed together in a purposely slapdash pattern. I'd furnished the porch with two rocking chairs, a swing, and a table with two stools for customers to play cards, checkers, or dominoes. The effect was charming and rustic.

My store secured, Granddaddy and I headed up Market Street, enjoying the fresh summer morning. My grandfather whistled as we went. I recognized the tune. It was the classic moonshiner song "Good Old Mountain Dew." The song was originally written in the 1920s by an attorney who'd represented many a client charged with violating laws relating to the production of distilled spirits.

Yep, the history of moonshining in the region was a long and sordid one, starting when Scotch-Irish immigrants first introduced whiskey making to the Southeast's backcountry folk in the eighteenth century. One of those Irish immigrants was my ancestor. In fact, one meaning of the surname Hayes meant "fire" in Gaelic, so it seemed only fitting that the Hayes family produced a product that caused a burn.

Speaking of heat, another week or two and the summer sun would kick in full force, sending residents and tourists alike to the area's swimming holes, such as the North Chick Blue Hole, Deep Creek, or Foster Falls. Summer also provided residents many opportunities for backyard cookouts or relaxing on decks and porches. A drink with a splash of moonshine in it could make those summer evenings a bit more enjoyable.

I raised a hand and waved to a barista through the window of a coffee shop I frequented. She waved back. The enticing aroma of coffee tempted me, but I'd have to do without today. I'd need my hands free to pass out my flyers, coasters, and coupons.

As the main thoroughfare in the city's riverfront district, Market Street was lined with restaurants, bars, shops, and entertainment venues, many of which had yet to open for the day. To the north, Market Street extended over a bridge across the Tennessee River and continued on the other side. Lodging was centered around the convention area a few blocks south, on the same side of the river as my shop.

In no time, my grandfather and I approached the rear of the hotel. He rolled up on his scooter as I pushed my dolly behind him. Rather than circle around to the main entrance at the front of the building, we seized the opportunity to scurry up a back walkway and enter an auxiliary door on the heels of a guest who'd gained access with his room key. The man glanced back as we followed him inside.

No doubt he'd consider an octogenarian on an electric scooter to be harmless. I gave the man a smile to let him know I was harmless as well. I gestured to his blue and white striped overalls. I, too, wore overalls, though mine were solid blue denim. *Looks like we had the same sense of fashion.* "You must be here for the model train convention," I said.

"Sure am," he said. "Came all the way from Arizona."

"Arizona?" Granddaddy repeated. "Boy howdy, that's quite a trip."

It's also a perfect segue. "After all that traveling, you'd probably enjoy a nice drink." I pulled one of the flyers off the stack on the dolly and handed it to him. "We're holding a moonshine mixer tonight in the hotel bar. You should come by. The bartenders will be making all sorts of fun cocktails."

I'd worked with the bartending staff to devise train-themed drinks for the event. We'd concocted one called a clown car, which was a nickname for a caboose. The drink included cherry moonshine mixed with ginger ale, and was garnished with a cherry to resemble a clown's rubber nose. Another we'd called the brass collar, a term for bigwig railroad representatives. It was made with cola and two shots of my granddaddy's 'shine, and garnished with an orange slice to represent a train wheel. The derailment, the strongest of the specialty drinks, included two shots of my blackberry 'shine mixed with lemon-lime soda and garnished with fresh blackberries and a mint leaf. As its name implied, too many of the drinks could knock someone off track. Fortunately, with the majority of the conventioneers staying in the hotel, overindulgence was less of an issue. Still, the bartender and I would keep an eye on things, make sure people paced themselves.

The man perused the flyer and said, "Sounds fun. Count me in."

"Great!"

He peeled off to head down another corridor, while my

grandfather and I continued on. The doorknobs on nearly all of the guest rooms sported a door-hanger style advertisement from a pizza place down the block. Apparently, I wasn't the only one looking to cash in on the model train convention.

As we made our way, shouting from farther up the hall caused me to slow my steps and my grandfather to roll to a stop on his scooter. A large middle-aged man towered in the doorway of one of the guest rooms ahead, looking down his bulbous nose and wagging a meaty finger at a frail housekeeper who cowered behind her cart. The woman's back-combed bouffant hairstyle was maple syrup brown, with a quarter inch of silver roots in need of a touch-up. Her dated hairstyle and loose, papery skin said she was a senior citizen, and the fact that she was still working past retirement age told me that life had been hard on her, just as this jerk was being now.

The enraged guest pointed to a sign hanging from the doorknob. "That do not disturb sign is there for a reason!"

"I'm sorry, sir!" the woman cried. "I didn't see it behind the pizza ad!"

Next to me, Granddaddy scoffed. He shook his head and muttered under his breath. "Seems odd that a man who doesn't want to be disturbed has no problem hollering at the top of his lungs in a hotel hallway."

I had to agree.

Though the housekeeper's explanation had been reasonable, the man continued to berate her. "Nobody touches my train controller! Nobody!"

She apologized again. "I didn't touch your controller. I only touched the cord, sir. I unplugged it so I could run the vacuum."

He stepped out into the hall. "I'm reporting you to the

manager." He turned his back to her and stalked off toward the front of the hotel.

The woman's shoulders slumped in defeat for a moment, before she straightened them and snatched a bottle of spray glass cleaner from her cart. The cleaning liquid was a vivid blue, what an artist like my friend Kiki Nakamura would call cobalt. The woman aimed the spray bottle at the man's broad back as he grew smaller down the hall. She tugged the trigger twice and made a sound to imitate gunfire. "*Pew, pew!*" She punctuated the sound effect by calling the man a very dirty word. At least she had plenty of bite-sized bars of soap on her cart if she decided to wash her own mouth out as penance.

By then, Granddaddy and I had reached the woman and her cart.

I greeted her with a smile and a "good morning."

She started and put a hand to her chest just above the name tag that read *Martha*. "I didn't hear you two coming up behind me."

"That's no surprise," Granddaddy said. "Who could hear anything over that blowhard? Someone must have peed in his cornflakes this morning."

She smiled back at us, seeming to appreciate our support. Her gaze moved down to my dolly. "Y'all with that moonshine outfit down the street?"

"We are. I own the shop. My name's Hattie Hayes." I hiked a thumb at Granddaddy. "This is my grandfather Ben." I reached into my tote bag, retrieved one of the flyers, and handed it to her. "You should come by the hotel bar for a moonshine cocktail this evening. After taking all that guff, you've certainly earned it."

She read over the flyer before handing it back to me. "As tempting as that sounds, it's probably best if I lie low."

She had a point. The jerk who'd just chewed her out might be at the mixer, and things could get awkward. "I hope the rest of your day goes better," I said, giving her a final supportive smile before setting off again with my dolly and grandfather.

With it being only a few minutes after 10:15, the hotel bar was not yet open, but the woman in charge of the restaurant unlocked the door to the bar's stockroom so we could leave the cases and jugs of moonshine. I left the dolly, too. I'd pick it up that evening when the mixer concluded.

Our business at the hotel finished, Granddaddy and I respectively rolled and strolled across the parking lot to the convention center. An inordinate number of rental trucks were parked in the lot, teams of men carefully removing large model train displays built on bases of plywood. As gingerly as they handled the displays, you'd think they were moving explosives. But it was no wonder they were exercising such extreme caution. The intricate displays must have taken weeks, if not months or years, to build. I looked forward to checking them out once they were all set up and operating.

Though the event had officially kicked off a quarter hour ago, a long line of conventioneers still waited to get in the door and get their name badges. We worked the line as they waited. As I handed out flyers for the mixer, Granddaddy talked it up. "You won't want to miss this event," he said. "Our moonshine is the best hooch ever made."

A balding man cocked his head. "Isn't moonshine illegal?"

His buddy had questions, too. "Where'd you make it?" He snorted a laugh. "In your bathtub?"

Their questions were valid, and Granddaddy gave them a quick lesson in history and etymology. He told them that moonshine originally got its name because it was produced "by the light of the moon," meaning it was made illegally at night, often at stills hidden away in the backwoods of Appalachia. He went on to say that, while moonshine was the most common term for the corn-based mash liquor, 'shine had a whole slew of monikers. "Homebrew is one of 'em. You might have also heard moonshine called rotgut, white lightning, hooch, corn liquor, corn squeezin', bootleg, bathtub gin, and even mountain dew." Of course, the latter name was subsequently appropriated by the beverage company for one of its soft drinks. As far as the Moonshine Shack, we sold the pure stuff in jugs under the brand name Granddaddy's Ole-Timey Corn Liquor.

I chimed in. "The term *moonshine* has evolved over the years. Moonshine is now produced legally and commercially, though many make it at home as a hobby."

The man who'd snorted rocked back on his heels and nodded, seemingly impressed. "You two seem to know your stuff." He exchanged a look with his buddy. "Think we ought to give their hooch a try?"

"Why not?"

Why not was as good a reason as any, I supposed. "See you two later in the hotel bar, then."

Chapter Two

My grandfather and I continued on. Once the line had advanced and only a few people remained, we took a place at the end of it, inching forward as the attendees were processed. A news van turned into the lot and the driver pulled it over to the curb. A reporter in a red sheath dress climbed down from the passenger side and checked her teeth and glossy black hair in the side mirror as her cameraman wrangled his camera from the cargo bay. She turned to the crowd and activated her thousand-watt smile, her white teeth nearly blinding in the morning sunlight. She worked the crowd like I'd done minutes before, making her way along and asking people what brought them to the train convention.

As she approached me, her gaze ran from the top of my head down to the toes of my sneakers and back again. Though she said nothing and maintained her bright smile, it was clear she'd summarily dismissed me. She likely preferred to interview people in train attire to better set the mood, but it was hard not to take the slight personally, as if she didn't think my look would appeal to viewers.

When I reached the registration booth just inside, I paid the fee so Granddaddy and I could attend all six days of the event. In return, the man running the counter handed each of us a lanyard with a name badge hanging from it. We thanked him and edged away from the booth. I slipped my lanyard over my neck before turning to my grandfather. He removed his hat and I draped his lanyard over his shoulders as if I were awarding him an Olympic medal in electric scooter racing. Properly outfitted now, we glanced around, taking things in. A couple of men in uniforms stood near the entrance, chatting. One was a security guard, the other an EMT. I supposed the convention center kept a medic around in case of an accident or medical emergency. In a big crowd like this, you never knew what might happen.

Just as I played old bluegrass and jug band music at my 'Shine Shack to set the mood, so had the organizers of the convention designed a playlist to go along with the theme of the convention. From speakers overhead came Glenn Miller and his orchestra, playing big band music and singing about the Chattanooga Choo Choo, over on track 29. Other noises met my ears, too. The *woo-woo* of train whistles, the *chugga-chugga* of trains moving down the tracks, the *bang-bang* of hammers and the *zzzzip-zzzip* of cordless drills as the conventioneers assembled their displays. The place had a distinctive smell, too, a combination of oil, cleaners, and coffee.

Granddaddy pointed to a display board on which papers had been tacked. "Let's check that out."

We moved a few feet forward and stopped before the board. At the top was an enlarged copy of the convention schedule, including the dates and times of each model train contest. The diesel category would be judged today, while the steam engine models would compete on Wednesday. The winners of the model contests would be announced at a ceremony Saturday afternoon, along with the People's Choice awards, which included various categories. "Favorite Train" was self-explanatory. The Photo Match award would go to the display that most accurately re-created a famous photograph incorporating a train. There was also something called the Thumbs award for the most humorous model. In addition to noting the times for the model judging, the schedule included lectures on such topics as "Adding Animated Features to Your Model Railroad," "Computer Controlled Signaling," "Layout Planning and Design," and "Preserving Natural Scenery." There was even a class called "Size Matters: Choosing the Right Scale for Your Models."

Alongside the schedule was the association's code of conduct that covered judges, contestants, and observers alike. The code required that judges be fair and impartial; that observers remain silent during the evaluation process; and that contestants be truthful, accurate, and behave in a civil manner. Sounded to me like it was a codification of common sense, but common sense was sometimes an oxymoron. Couldn't hurt to make the expectations clear to all involved.

The display included some history and data about model railroading for those, like me, who were unschooled in the hobby. The display noted that models went into production only a short time after real railroads were developed. Models ranged widely in size, but the O, HO, and N scale trains were among the most popular. O scaled models were made on a 1:48 scale. HO scale models, which were the most common, bore a ratio to actual size of 1:87. At the smaller end of the spectrum were the N scale models, which were scaled at 1:160 of an actual train. With my petite stature, I supposed I'd be an N scale if I were a model train. The board noted that, in addition to scale, model trains were also identified by gauge, which referred to the width between the two rails of the track. HO scale trains had a track gauge of 16.5 millimeters.

Having attained this basic education in model railroading, I looked around. Vendor booths formed a perimeter around the exhibit area. The merchants sold everything from classic wood train whistles to new and vintage train sets to the striped hats and overalls nearly everyone there appeared to be wearing. One booth sold assorted plastic structures, including churches; libraries; schoolhouses; fire stations; and long, attached fake-brick buildings with storefronts made to look like old-fashioned Main Streets. Another sold fine gravel in assorted colors for laying realistic-looking ground cover, as well as charcoal-black tape printed with solid white lines along the edges and a dotted white line in the middle to mimic a road. A third booth displayed all sorts of building, cleaning, and maintenance supplies, including special sponges for cleaning tracks, lubricating oil, tubes of adhesive, small plastic pipettes for applying glue, and little bottles of something called smoke fluid. There was even a booth where conventioneers could order custom-made pieces from a craftsman and artist who specialized in making miniatures. I'd love to have a miniature replica of my Moonshine Shack, but I doubted I could afford a custom design. *Maybe I could fashion one myself out of Popsicle sticks.*

My grandfather and I made our way around the vendor area first, as most of them had finished setting up. We stopped at a booth that had displayed several winding foam pieces set up in elongated, repeating S curves. Curious, I pointed to the materials. "What are these for?"

"Building inclines for the track," said the vendor. "We've got sets with two percent, three percent, and four percent inclines over an eight-foot stretch." He pointed to some laminated photos lying on the table. They showed layouts wherein the track ascended to a second level amid hilly scenery before gradually descending to the main level.

"Ah," I said. "Mystery solved." It was interesting to see what lay under the displays, their skeleton foundations. I handed him one of my flyers. "We'd love to see you at the moonshine mixer tonight, if you are so *inclined*."

He groaned. "You trying to drive me to drink with your horrible puns?"

"Whatever it takes." I pulled a coaster from my bag. "Here. Have a coaster."

He took it from me and held it up. "This I can use. Your lame jokes I can do without." His wink told me he was only teasing.

While my grandfather would have loved to spend hours looking over each and every item at each booth, we simply didn't have time to dawdle today. When he stopped, once again, this time to admire a simple wooden train, I said, "I know you want to look at all the train stuff, Granddaddy, but we have to keep moving." I held up a stack of flyers. "We need to distribute all of these today."

He reached out, grabbed a wooden train whistle from the table, and held it up. "Can I at least get this?"

Dealing with him was like bargaining with a child. "Sure," I said, reaching into my tote bag for my wallet. The whistle was cheap and a good compromise for now. "When we come back later in the week, you can spend all the time you'd like at the booths, okay?"

Knowing he'd get more time to browse the merchandise seemed to cheer him up. He gave me a smile before putting the whistle to his lips and blowing through it. *Toot-toot!*

I grabbed three whistles for Nora's children, too. After I paid for the toys, Granddaddy and I continued around the row of vendors before venturing into the rows of intricate model train displays. People, predominantly men, moved about the space, setting up their exhibits. Most were older men, middle-aged or elderly, but there were a few younger men in the mix, too. My guess was some of them got their love of model trains from their grandfathers, much as I'd gotten my love of making moonshine from mine. They were as serious about their craft as I was about mine, too. Their intense expressions as they checked and double-checked their connections and couplings were incongruous with their playful attire but, again, I could relate. Though I dressed like a bootlegger from the backwoods, I took my moonshining seriously.

A few displays in, Granddaddy stopped his scooter before a space marked with a sign that read A3. Noting that his exhibit had attracted visitors, the man setting up the display paused, setting down the sign he'd been about to put on an easel beside the model. Rather than overalls, the man wore a long-sleeved shirt in the traditional hickory stripe pattern for train engineer clothing. He had a thick head of pewter-gray hair and sported a wide walrus-style mustache, à la Nick Offerman.

Seeming to forget my early admonishment about dawdling, Granddaddy retrieved his cane, climbed off his scooter, and ambled over to take a closer look at the model. He squinted at the display. "This setup looks kind of familiar."

I followed him over and ran my eyes over the exhibit. "It does. Hmm."

The exhibitor's mustache rose as his mouth spread in a mischievous grin. "I'll give you three guesses."

Never one to back down from a bet, even one where only pride and no money were involved, Granddaddy said, "You're on!"

The model included a town surrounded by abundant verdant foliage, much of it covering a mountain that rose to the southwest. The city depicted consisted primarily of small, antiquated houses on modest plots, but an imposing three-story brick building rose above them. I still might not have recognized the locale if not for the river winding through the city and the two-story Brown's Ferry Tavern, a pre–Civil War relic of logs and thick swaths of mortar that gave it a striped appearance. While the homes and the brick building no longer stood, the tavern still existed just west of the city and had been designated as a historic site. The place had been owned by a Cherokee leader and marked the boundary of the Cherokee Nation at that time. The infamous Trail of Tears had run along the road adjacent to the property. My eighth-grade social studies class had gone there on a field trip.

A mutual epiphany taking place, Granddaddy and I exclaimed in unison, "It's Chattanooga!"

"You guessed right," the man said. "My display depicts the arrival of the first freight train in Chattanooga from Cincinnati on February twenty-first, 1880. The first passenger car rolled in a couple of weeks later, on March eighth. It was an important time in our nation's history. Joined the North and South by rail."

I knew from my state history classes in high school and local lore that Chattanooga had been a critical hub in terms of rail transportation back in the day. Hence, the classic song we'd heard on our way in. It seemed fitting the guy would have this display here. The level of detail was remarkable. Not only had he included trains, structures, and people, but he'd used natural materials to form a variety of trees, bushes, and ground cover. A steam-powered paddlewheel boat was even docked at a pier in the river. It was intriguing to see what my hometown looked like more than a hundred and forty years ago. The represented time period explained why some of Chattanooga's other famous buildings didn't appear in the exhibit. The Read House Hotel and the Basilica of Saints Peter and Paul, notable historic landmarks, had yet to be constructed in 1880. The same went for many of the bridges that now spanned the Tennessee River.

After putting his informational board on the easel, the man pointed out some of the city's main features from back in the day. "See this here?" he said, pointing to a structure with external pipes and a large water tank. "That's Bluff Furnace. It was Chattanooga's first major industrial site. Tons of iron were made there. The place was abandoned after the Civil War. There's an art museum on that spot now."

I recognized the bluff over the Tennessee River as the current location of the Hunter Museum of American Art. "I've been to the museum."

He pointed out another building, a towering one that featured a clock, a bell tower, and a dome. "And this is the Old Hamilton County Courthouse."

"Well, I'll be darned," Granddaddy said. "I remember my folks talking about the courthouse fire when I was young. They were both just kids when it happened, but they told me they could see the flames from their houses. They were scared the whole city would burn down."

The man pointed to the three-story brick building. "That's

the Masonic Academy. It was built to be a school for girls but was used as a hospital during the Civil War."

My eyes spotted a horseshoe-shaped tunnel. I recognized it from several rides on the Tennessee Valley Railroad steam trains over the years, the first being on my grandfather's sixty-fifth birthday when my own age was still in the single digits. Granddaddy insisted on treating the entire family to the train ride, using up most of his first social security check. We'd even had the chance to see them rotate a locomotive on a turntable. The trip had been a highlight of my childhood. I pointed to the tunnel. "That's the Missionary Ridge Tunnel, isn't it?"

The man gave me a confirmational nod. "You've got a good eye."

"You know a lot about Chattanooga history. Are you a local?"

"I'm from Ohio," he said. "The other end of the tracks. But I performed quite a bit of research to make sure my model was as accurate as possible to the time period."

Who knew there was so much to model railroading? I introduced myself and my grandfather. The man gave his name as Patrick Jaffe, and before we moved on I invited him to the moonshine mixer. "Seven to nine in the hotel bar," I said. "We'll have trivia contests and prizes, too."

"Sounds like fun," Patrick said. "I'll be there."

The reporter and her cameraman walked up to Jaffe's booth as Granddaddy and I continued down the row and circled around to Row B. A few displays from the end, we came upon the back of a large, lumbering man erecting a three-sided plexiglass barrier around his model. He pulled out a triangular ruler and used it to make sure the plexiglass panels stood at exact right angles. Next to the display, a plump fiftyish woman sat in one of those zero-gravity lawn chairs that were basically portable, lightweight recliners. I owned one of the chairs myself. *So comfy.* But where mine was a basic design, hers was the deluxe version, complete with a small side table, cup holder, and canopy to block the sun or overhead lights. Another chair just like it sat empty next to her. No doubt it belonged to her partner.

The woman wore loafers, jeans, and a colorful cable-knit sweater to combat the frigid temperature in the convention space. *That's what happens when men control the thermostat.* Judging from the knitting needles in her hands and the skein of blue yarn in her lap, she'd made her sweater herself. Her name tag lay faceup on her rounded bosom, displaying her name—Dana Gebhardt. Though she'd forgone the frilly petticoats and fussy dresses of the era, she'd given a nod to the glory days of railroad travel by donning a cute and colorful calico bonnet tied in a big bow under her chin. Her chestnut hair peeked out around the edges. But perhaps the most telling thing she wore was an expression of resigned boredom.

Chapter Three

After introducing myself and my grandfather to the woman, I handed her a flyer about the mixer along with a promotional coaster with the logo for my moonshine brand on it. "Good morning, Dana. I'm Hattie Hayes. I run the Moonshine Shack just down the street. I'm making the rounds to invite everyone to a mix and mingle tonight in the hotel bar. We'll have a trivia contest and train-themed drinks, made with my special Southern homebrew."

"Moonshine?" The woman sat up in her chair. "Now that's something I might actually get excited about."

When her companion glanced over at us through the plexiglass, I recognized him as the obnoxious loudmouth from the hotel hallway earlier. Up closer like this, I could tell more about him. He had a bulbous nose and veiny skin, tiny red capillaries winding along his cheeks like a road map. *His blood pressure must be through the roof.* He wrung his hands, applying gel hand sanitizer, as he scowled at me through the glass. "We're beer drinkers." He turned his scowl on the woman. "And if you're so bored, you could have stayed home. You're lucky I let you come along to these conventions."

"Lucky?" She gave him a patient smile before turning back to me and Granddaddy and rolling her eyes good-naturedly. Clearly, she'd grown accustomed to the man's grumpiness and didn't take him seriously. She cupped a hand around her mouth and said in a stage whisper, "If I didn't come to these model train conventions, I'd never get out of Milwaukee."

Milwaukee. That explained the man's comment about being beer drinkers.

As he pulled out a rag and a bottle of blue spray cleaner to wipe his fingerprints off the plexiglass, Dana leaned toward me and said, "Guess where Bert took me on our honeymoon?"

It was an easy question to answer. "A model train convention?"

"Bingo!" She raised an index finger in the air in the universal gesture for you got the right answer. "Guess where we've spent most of our birthdays and twenty-six of our thirty-one anniversaries?"

"Hmm." Granddaddy removed his hat and scratched his head in jest. "Could it be model train conventions?"

"You guessed right, too!" she said. "The National Model Railroad Association has fifteen regions in the United States. Bert insists on attending every regional convention plus the national one."

Dana must have the patience of a saint to put up with her husband and his one-track mind. Speaking of tracks . . . I stepped over to the plexiglass and peered through it, being careful not to touch the freshly wiped surface. Granddaddy left his scooter to take a closer look, too. Though Bert's display had fewer structures than the one Patrick Jaffe had made, it showed a similar theme and dedication to detail.

The exhibit contained the sandy soil Utah was known for, though it appeared to be securely glued down. Tiny bushes dotted the sand, resembling stationary tumbleweeds. Sand was piled in spots to form hills. A steam train identified as Jupiter headed west on the tracks, while the Union Pacific 119 headed east. Dozens of itty-bitty figurines depicted the railroad workers and executives gathered in the center, a few of them on horseback. One of the men held up a bottle of champagne in celebration. Only one or two women, identified by their wide, bell-shaped skirts, were among the group. One man stood atop the crossbeam on a flagpole flying what was evidently the flag of the United States at the time, bearing one star for each of the states in the union then. My quick count told me there were thirty-seven. Two tiny men shook hands over what had to be the last rail to be laid, as it contained a tiny, shiny gold spike.

Bert's display included an easel on which he'd placed an enlarged image of the photograph titled *East and West Shaking Hands at Laying of Last Rail*. His model precisely depicted the image in the photo. *Impressive.*

Noting our interest, Bert proceeded to tell me and Granddaddy about his model. "For short, that picture is sometimes called *The Champagne Photo* or *East and West*." He pointed out various elements of the scene he'd assembled. "See here? That's engineers George Booth and Sam Bradford." He told us that each of the men had broken a bottle of bubbly on the other's locomotive, which stood cowcatcher to cowcatcher on the track. "The men shaking hands are Samuel S. Montague, the chief engineer of the Central Pacific Railroad, and General Grenville M. Dodge from

Union Pacific. A photographer named Andrew J. Russell snapped the photo. He was the only soldier known to have served as an artist in the Civil War."

Dana chimed in. "Russell is considered America's first photojournalist."

Bert gave his wife a nod. "That's right."

I addressed Bert through the glass. "I take it you're competing in the Photo Match contest?"

"I'm not just competing in it," he said, "I'm going to win it."

Sheesh. What the man lacked in couth, he made up for in confidence.

Granddaddy chuckled. "Pretty sure of yourself, aren't you?"

Bert made no apologies for his arrogance. "Darn straight."

While Dana had been making jokes about her husband's obsession only moments before, she beamed now, proud of her spouse's accomplishments. "Bert's earned more trophies and ribbons than anyone else on the competition circuit. Everyone knows his models are the ones to beat." She exchanged a glance with her husband, and he seemed to stand even taller in appreciation of her support. When she turned back to us, her lips quirked in a coy smile. "I feel like the prom queen when I come to these conventions with him. It's been fun to visit different places, too. I've seen more of America than most folks."

Good to know her situation had an upside.

Bert reached into a large toolbox and retrieved a tiny vacuum. He activated the device and it came to life with a soft whir. He bent over and carefully used it to suck up a few particles of sand that had been loosened in transport. He pulled a magnifying glass from his pocket and peered through it like a denim-clad Sherlock Holmes to make sure he hadn't missed a single grain of sand that might remain on the track. The loose sand addressed, he returned the vacuum to the toolbox, pulled out a different bottle of blue cleaner, and spritzed a little on a small rag, gingerly cleaning the track.

"Wow," I said. "I didn't realize these setups required so much maintenance."

"The electric current attracts dust," Dana explained. "If the tracks aren't kept clean, the oil on the wheels can get gunked up. Next thing you know, the train starts jerking and the lights flash on and off. Gotta keep the tracks clean if you want a smooth ride."

"If your husband keeps his trains this clean," I said, "he must be helpful around the house, too."

She snorted. "Bert doesn't lift a finger around the house. But at least I don't have to help him clean his trains. He won't let me touch them."

Dana stepped up next to me and Granddaddy and pointed through the plexiglass. "See that little gold spike? Bert had it specially made. It's seventeen-point-six karat gold, just like the real last spike." She raised her voice so he could hear her over the clear barrier. "God forbid he buys *me* something made of gold."

He ignored her and she chuckled. Seemed the two had fallen into a routine shtick.

On the other side of his model train display was a mobile case with a metal cabinet below, the unit resting on locking wheels. Sitting on shelves behind the glass windows were several vintage model trains, some still in their original packaging. As we gazed into the display, a man who looked to be in his mid-sixties strolled up. He sported salt-and-pepper hair and a trio of dimples—one on his chin and one on either cheek. His name tag read Ronald Wallingford. He stepped up on the other side of Dana, the four of us now crowding the glass.

"Oh, boy!" Wallingford said, sounding like a boy himself as he gazed yearningly at a blue and yellow train car. "That's a 1965 Weaver Norfolk and Western work caboose!" He turned to Dana. "Santa left one of those in my stocking the year I turned eight. I'd been clamoring for one all year, driving my poor parents crazy. I'd collected bottles to return to the store, mowed lawns, anything to save up to buy it, but I still didn't have quite enough. Good thing Santa took pity on me, huh?" A faraway look entered his eyes, as if he'd traveled back in time. "I had so much fun with that caboose." A moment later, he seemed to snap back to the present, standing up straight, his eyes clearing. "I've got the rest of my original set, but not that caboose."

Granddaddy asked, "What happened to it?"

Wallingford snorted softly. "Santa was just as generous the next year. Brought me the puppy I'd been begging for."

He didn't have to finish the story for me to put two and two together. "The puppy treated your caboose like a chew toy?"

Wallingford nodded solemnly. "Broke my heart. Luckily, it didn't break my dog. He'd swallowed a few pieces, but it didn't hurt him none. They came right out the other end with no problem." He looked from Dana to Bert. "Who do I talk to about buying this caboose?"

Bert, who'd been ignoring the man, came around the back of his plexiglass shield to stand beside his display. "That would be me."

The man stuck out his hand. "Ronnie Wallingford."

Though Bert gave the man's hand a shake, he offered neither a smile nor his name.

Ronnie said, "I'd love to take that caboose home. I'll give you two hundred dollars for it."

"No sale," Bert said.

Ronnie gaped. "That was a good offer! One just like it sold on eBay for only one fifty last month."

Bert hiked a meaty shoulder. "Then you should've bought that one."

All of a sudden, Bert was putting the *ass* in *passenger car*, but Ronnie gave him the benefit of the doubt, assuming he was just being a tough salesman. "You drive a hard bargain. I'll give you two twenty-five."

Bert merely snorted derisively and circled back around the shield to continue cleaning the tracks.

Wallingford looked to Dana, his forehead crinkling like corrugated metal. He was clearly flabbergasted.

Dana gave the man a compassionate smile before turning to address her husband through the plexiglass. "C'mon, honey. Ronnie had a caboose like that when he was a kid, but his dog got a hold of it."

Bert dabbed at the track. "Why should I sell that train to someone who won't take care of it?"

Dana threw up her hands. "It was decades ago! He was just a boy then, Bert."

Still holding the rag, Bert crossed his arms and stared Ronnie down through the divider. "I'll give it to you for one grand."

Ronnie made a choking sound. "That's highway robbery!"

"Or train robbery," I said, hoping my joke might break the tension. It didn't.

Next to me, Granddaddy shook his head and muttered something about Bert being *a greedy such and such.*

Dana made one last plea to her husband's seemingly absent sense of reason. "You bought that old train at a garage sale for forty dollars, Bert. At two twenty-five, you'd be making a heck of a profit."

Bert turned on his wife and roared. "Whose side are you on? Stay out of my business!"

Despite the fact that they were separated by the plastic shield, Dana took an involuntary step back. Her shoulders rounded forward, as if she were shrinking inside herself. She might have felt like the belle of the ball a moment before, but now her husband had made her feel as small as the miniature people in his model train display.

Dana might have been belittled, but Ronnie's chest swelled big as he glared at Bert. "I'll get my hands on that caboose one way or another!" His ultimatum delivered, he stalked off.

Making tracks seemed like a good idea. But before I could leave, Dana said softly, "Bert's just having a bad day. He's nervous about the steam train competition on Wednesday."

Those facts didn't give him the right to take out his anxiety on others, but I supposed Dana was in for the long haul and had seen her husband under better circumstances. She could form a more balanced opinion of him, forgive his occasional crankiness. Even so, he seemed a pro at the cranky bit. I had to wonder whether it was occasional or habitual.

As if realizing he shouldn't have snapped at his wife, Bert stepped over to Dana. He didn't offer her a verbal apology, but he did take her hand and give it a squeeze. He held on, as if waiting to feel a squeeze in return. Their eyes met and, a moment later, she accepted his peace offering with a reciprocal squeeze.

As Granddaddy settled back onto his scooter, I raised a hand in goodbye. "See you tonight, Dana!"

By then, it was nearing noon and my stomach was rumbling. Granddaddy was getting hungry, too. We returned to my shop to find Smoky was still lounging in his cushy bed on the desk. He lifted his head an inch or two, telling me in his own lazy way that he was aware of my return and that he might have missed me a little—not enough to get out of his bed to greet me, though, so I shouldn't get a big head about it. I reached over and scratched his ears. "I missed you, too, boy."

The bells on the front door jingled as my new assistant Nora arrived promptly for her shift. She sported a pair of tennis shoes, jeans, and a T-shirt with my moonshine logo on it. Her blond hair was wound up in a cute and carefree twist along the back of her head. She was one of the most efficient and productive people I'd ever met. Having three children in elementary school might have something to do with it. She didn't have time to waste. Although Nora normally worked only from noon to 3:00, she'd agreed to cover the store for me tonight so that I could attend the moonshine mixer. She'd arranged for a babysitter to keep an eye on her brood until her husband arrived home from work. She was doing me a big favor staying late on a school night. I'd reimburse her the cost of the sitter and put a bonus in her next paycheck as well. My good friend Kiki often helped at the store, too, and would keep Nora company in the shop this evening.

I gave Nora a smile and a raised hand in welcome. Granddaddy did the same.

"Hey, boss," she said. "Hey, Ben." She looked from one of us to the other. "How'd it go at the convention center this morning?"

"Great!" I said. "I think we'll have a good turnout to-night. People were still arriving and setting up, though, so we didn't get to all of them. I think we'll head back down to the convention this afternoon if you don't mind watching the shop on your own for so long."

"You're offering me more alone time?" She arched a cocky brow. "You know alone time is like gold to a mother, right?"

"I hope you won't get too much solitude," Granddaddy teased. "Hattie can't make a living without some customers coming into the store."

Before I could even suggest how Nora might fill her time, she'd run her gaze around the shop and identified several tasks for herself. "Looks like the peach and blueberry flavors need restocking. I'll get the clean glasses from the sink and return them to the sample table. Want me to put out the sandwich board, too?"

"Yes, please." I reached out and put a grateful hand on her shoulder. "What did I ever do without you, Nora?"

She smiled. "Happy to help." Her smile turned wry. "And to be appreciated." No doubt her children took her for granted, as kids with a good mother tend to do. I was guilty of the crime myself, and I hoped one day my kids would be just as lucky, to know they had a mother they could count on to make sure their every need was met.

I retrieved the train whistles from my tote bag and held them out to her. "Picked these up for your kids."

Granddaddy brandished his whistle. "Hattie got me one, too." He proceeded to blow it. *Toot-toot!*

Nora took the whistles from me and groaned in mock agony as she held them up. "You bought whistles for my kids? Are you trying to torture me?"

In retrospect, maybe the noisy toys hadn't been the most

thoughtful gift. "I'll pick you up some earplugs next time I'm at the pharmacy."

Nora disappeared into the storeroom as a clop-clop-clop of horse hooves out front announced the arrival of two members of local law enforcement, one human and one equine. Charlotte came to a halt in front of my shop. The horse was a big, beautiful chestnut mare with a flaxen mane. Astride her was Officer Marlon Landers, dressed in a typical police uniform accompanied by black riding boots and a helmet rather than a hat. He slid down from the horse in one smooth action, tied her to one of the porch posts, and patted her flank. After giving her a kiss on the nose, he turned and came into the shop.

"Hey, Hattie." Marlon gave my grandfather a nod. "Ben." He reached up and unbuckled his helmet, pulling it off and running a hand through his buckskin curls to unflatten them. I was tempted to offer to take care of the task for him, but things were still new for us. We weren't quite there yet. "How'd things go at the train show this morning?"

I looked up at Marlon, who stood an entire foot taller than me. I was on the short side, and he was tall, well over six feet. "Things went well," I said. "There should be a good turnout for the mix and mingle tonight."

Nora came out of the storeroom with the sandwich board tucked under her arm. She lifted her chin to silently acknowledge Marlon without interrupting our conversation, then continued out front to set up the board. On it I'd written WELCOME MODEL TRAIN FANS! *CHUGGA-CHUGGA* SOME MOONSHINE! SHOW YOUR CONVENTION PASS FOR A 20 PERCENT DISCOUNT. The conventioneers could not only help my bottom line this week but could also help spread the word about my moonshine across the United States when they returned home after the event wrapped up on Saturday. Though my moonshine business was a small-batch operation for now, it was a dream of mine to expand across the country, just as the railroaders had dreamed of expanding across the nation, too. *Is it a pipe dream to think I could do it?* I supposed only time would tell.

I'd been about to fix lunch for myself and my grandfather. Might as well see if Marlon wanted to dine with us. "Want to join me and Granddaddy for lunch? I'm making peanut butter and jelly sandwiches."

"Classic," he said. "Sure. Will you cut mine into triangles?"

"Feeling fancy, are you?"

The two of us walked back to the storeroom. Marlon went to the sink and filled the bucket I kept on hand for watering Charlotte, then retrieved a carrot for her from the mini fridge. I kept both the bucket and horsey snacks on hand as a ploy to encourage Marlon to stop by my shop as often as possible. While he carried the bucket out front to his horse, I quickly fixed five sandwiches, three for Marlon and one each for me and Granddaddy. I cut my grandfather's sandwich and mine into two rectangular halves, the way God intended, and cut Marlon's on a diagonal, doing the Devil's work. I rounded up some cups, grabbed the jug of sweet tea from the fridge, and carried the lunch out front so we could eat it at the game table. Charlotte was loudly slurping up the cool water. When she'd drunk her fill, she raised her head, water dripping from her whiskery chin, and issued a soft whinny of thanks. Marlon patted her flank before wrangling a rocking chair over to the table so there'd be enough seating for all three of us.

Marlon and I had first met before my shop opened a few weeks ago. I'd been unloading cases from my van when he'd ridden up on his horse in the alley behind my shop and helped me move the heavy cases of moonshine into the storeroom. He'd saved my back that day and, a few weeks later, he'd saved my hide when that killer had come after me in the woods. But despite being a hero, the guy didn't get a big head about it. He just considered it doing his job. I liked that he kept his ego in check. I appreciated men with big muscles, but big heads I could do without.

As the three of us settled down to our sandwiches, I took a sip of my tea. "Anything exciting happening in the world of crime today?"

"No," he said. "It's been slow. That's a good thing, but it makes for a pretty boring shift."

"Is the convention center within your beat?"

"It is."

"You should check out the model train show. There's some really impressive displays." I told him about Patrick Jaffe's miniature version of Chattanooga circa 1880 and Bert Gebhardt's golden spike. "He had the tiny nail custom made. It's seventeen-point-six-karat gold, same as the actual gold spike."

"Sounds like the man's a stickler for detail."

"That's putting it lightly. Those train guys are fanatics." I was in no position to fault them for their obsession. I'd always taken my moonshine making just as seriously, even before I'd decided to start my own brand and open my shop.

Granddaddy said, "They're selling all kinds of trains there, too. Old ones. New ones. Electric. Wood. You name it, they've got it."

We made small talk as we ate our sandwiches and sipped our tea. When we finished our lunch, Marlon untied

Charlotte. "You two heading back to the convention center this afternoon?"

"Going back there right now," I said. "We weren't able to hit all the booths this morning. Some of the convention-eers were still setting up or hadn't arrived yet. Others were tied up with customers. I want to make sure everyone gets a flyer for tonight's moonshine mixer." In fact, I'd made notes to that effect, jotting down the numbers for the booths Granddaddy and I had bypassed for one reason or another.

Marlon angled his head to indicate his horse. "Hop on up behind me. Charlotte and I will give you a ride."

I scurried inside, rounded up my tote bag, and bid good-bye to Nora. "Kiki will be here by five. Feel free to use the petty cash fund to order yourselves some dinner."

When I went back out front, Marlon was already seated in his saddle. My grandfather had rolled his scooter into place in front of Charlotte, ready to lead our parade. Marlon reached down a hand, grabbed my arm, and lifted me up with impressive ease. I swung my leg over Charlotte's back, just behind his saddle.

Police used hornless English-style saddles rather than western. Marlon had told me the smaller saddles promoted ease of movement and lessened the weight on the horse's back. Fortunately, with my petite size and Charlotte's espe-cially large and strong build, our combined bulk wouldn't be too much for her to handle for a short distance. Even so, Marlon turned to eye me over his shoulder. "Scoot on up. It's easier on Charlotte if we keep our weight centered."

I scooted forward until the buckles on my overalls nearly touched the back of Marlon's uniform. I knew I'd have to hold on to Marlon for safety, but I felt self-conscious as I reached my arms around him. We'd shared some kisses, but this was the closest we'd ever been physically. *How tight should I hold on? Should I keep my arms up high or low?* I settled for wrapping my arms around the bottom of his rib cage, just above his six-pack abs, and holding on loosely.

Charlotte was not only beautiful, she was also as relaxed a horse as you'd ever find. Following my grandfather on his scooter, she clopped down the street, undisturbed by the cars easing past, customers going in and out of shops, even a door slamming loudly behind us that made me jump. Her docile demeanor made her perfect for police work, where a mounted team could find themselves in unpredictable, chaotic situations and a horse had to keep her head about her.

In too little time, we reached the front door of the convention center, where a group of the conventioneers' wives had gathered to chat away from the noise and their husbands inside. Granddaddy zipped up to them and stopped. While they hardly seemed to notice my grandfather, the women looked over as Marlon and I rode up, exchanging glances. Who could blame them? Marlon was much too young for them, but that didn't stop them from admiring his athletic physique.

Marlon crooked his arm so I could hold on to it as I slid down from the horse. "Thanks for the ride."

A naughty smile crossed the face of one of the women. "My turn!"

The group broke down in giggles.

Marlon was a good sport. He doffed his helmet and said, "Afternoon, ladies" in his sexy Southern drawl, giving them a smile. "You behave yourselves, hear?" With that, he gave Charlotte a gentle squeeze with his thighs, and off they went.

I took advantage of the women's being gathered to approach them about the mixer. "Come to the hotel bar tonight. We're having a moonshine special." Granddaddy and I handed out flyers left and right.

The woman who'd attempted to claim a turn on Charlotte's back with Marlon gestured after him. "Will Officer Hunky be there?"

It might be wrong of me to exploit Marlon's good looks for my own personal gain, but he'd want the event to be a success, wouldn't he? "I'll see what I can do."

Chapter Four

Back inside the convention center, my grandfather and I spotted a group of men standing around an exhibit. The ones at the front wore official-looking bright blue blazers and held clipboards. Gathered behind them were at least two dozen conventioneers, waiting in hushed reverence. Curious, we stopped to see what was going on.

The man whose exhibit was under evaluation addressed the judges, describing his diesel train display, why he had chosen this particular train, and what he hoped to convey with his exhibit. "My model depicts Grand Central Terminal in New York City, along with the adjacent New York Central Railroad headquarters. Although the New York Central Railroad operated some of the most modern steam locomotives, they found diesel engines to be more cost-effective. They switched to all diesel just over a hundred years later in 1957."

The group shifted our gazes as the exhibitor pointed to

a lone steam engine sitting idle on a side track. "Engine number 1977 was the last steam engine retired from service. My display is intended to show an important tipping point in the evolution of train travel, when local railroads merged to become part of a greater system and when diesel engines replaced steam."

I was standing near a judge with closely shorn once-ginger hair that now blended with white, as if his pink scalp were covered in apricot fuzz. When Bert stepped up to the edge of the crowd across from us, the judge glanced his way and his back stiffened. I didn't as much see the judge's jaw clench as notice his ear twitch with the pressure. *Hmm. Do the judge and Bert Gebhardt know each other? Share some unpleasant history?*

The judges were still questioning the man who'd created the display when Bert slowly ducked down and backed away. *Where's he going?* Maybe I was being nosy, but the way he'd snuck off was suspicious.

I leaned over and whispered in Granddaddy's ear. "Wait here. I'll be right back." Stepping lightly, I followed twenty feet or so behind Bert. Nearly all of the displays were unattended now, their creators gathered at the one being evaluated. While many of the models displayed Do Not Touch signs, none of the others was protected by plexiglass. Bert must be the only one who didn't trust people to obey the signs. *Could it be projection?* Seemed that the people least likely to trust others were sometimes the least trustworthy themselves.

When Bert cast a glance over his shoulder, I vectored off and pretended to be looking at a miniature version of the Durango & Silverton Narrow Gauge Railroad. He slowed and scanned the area before stopping at Patrick Jaffe's display of the freight train arriving in Chattanooga from

Cincinnati. When Bert looked my way again, I ducked behind a trifold board on which one of the participants had posted photographs and information about his display.

I peeked around the board to see Bert whip a tape measure from the pocket of his striped overalls, along with a notepad. He leaned over the display, measuring the length of the Missionary Ridge Tunnel, the buildings, the track. He stopped after each measurement to jot a note on the pad, apparently recording the measurements.

Applause came from two aisles over, where the judges must have finished evaluating the model of the New York Central Railroad. As if realizing his time to snoop was up, Bert stood and backed away from the table. But he wasn't quick enough. Patrick Jaffe rounded the corner at the end of the row and caught Bert slipping the measuring tape and notepad into his pocket.

Jaffe stormed up to him. "What the hell do you think you're doing, Gebhardt?"

Bert seemed to realize that it would only make him look worse if he denied what he'd been doing. After all, Jaffe had caught him red-handed. "I'm ensuring the integrity of this contest! That's what I'm doing."

Jaffe scoffed. "You just can't stand that I beat you in Toledo."

"You only won because you had the home field advantage."

Unlike sports, trains weren't played on a field. Was there such a thing as a home track advantage? Jaffe answered the question for me. "The judges weren't even from my region. You know that good and well. You're just a sore loser."

Bert leaned forward on the balls of his feet and clenched and unclenched his fists. "Your model wasn't true to scale! Stuart Speer gave you high scores you didn't deserve!"

Rather than respond with more words, Jaffe simply raised his right hand and formed an *L* for loser on his forehead. His eyes narrowed and his lips spread in an evil grin. The gesture was juvenile, but who could blame him? Bert Gebhardt was a spoilsport and seemed determined to be the least popular person in overalls and an engineer's hat at the convention.

Bert jabbed a finger in the air, called Jaffe a choice word, and stormed off. Jaffe laughed at Bert's retreating back. "If you can't stand the heat, get out of the steam engine!"

Wow. Who knew the world of model railroading could be so hostile?

I went back to the exhibit of Grand Central Terminal to collect my grandfather. We continued on our route and discovered Ronnie Wallingford sitting at an exhibit called "Making Tracks: American Cryptids." The board on which his train display sat was painted with a colorful map of the United States. Ronnie had added very detailed topography. Mountains. Lakes. Rivers. Real foliage from each region. The train running along the track was exceptionally long, filling half the track and seeming to contain a car from every railroad in the country. Burlington Northern Santa Fe. Kansas City Southern. Norfolk Southern. Union Pacific. CSX Transportation. Amtrak. Texas Central. Long Island Rail Road. The list went on and on, just like his train.

In every state, he'd featured a cryptozoological creature, with painted prints in its wake. Details about each monster were provided on small informational cards erected next to them. East Texas, a popular site for Sasquatch sightings, featured a furry bigfoot with huge footprints behind him. The Fouke Monster in Arkansas left very similar tracks in the state's western mountains. Arizona was home to a similar large humanoid type creature known as the Mogollon

Monster, though this creature had white hair rather than brown. The White Thang in Alabama could have been his cousin, but the Dark Watchers of California, fifteen-foot hairless humanlike creatures, appeared unrelated. Connecticut's cannibalistic Melon Heads bore a passing resemblance to the Golden State's monsters.

While many of the cryptids were humanlike, the others ran the gamut from winged creatures to beasts bearing scales and spines. In New Jersey, the Jersey Devil spread its wings, leaving a set of hoofprints as it prepared for takeoff. The red-eyed Mothman hovered on a mountainside in West Virginia, its birdlike feet leaving three-pronged prints with pointed talons. Wisconsin featured something called a Hodag with horns like a bull; curved spines down its back; and, as illustrated by its tracks, roundish feet with four claws. Iowa had the Van Meter Monster. Ohio had South Bay Bessie, the Lake Erie Monster. The Tizheruk sea serpent lurked in the waters off Alaska, its "tracks" left in the form of a telltale wake. So long as the passengers in the train didn't disembark and step onto a dock, they could be safe from the snatch of his strong jaws. Colorado featured the Slide-Rock Bolter, a whalelike creature with a hooked tail, sitting with his mouth open next to the train tracks, ready to devour the train as it passed.

I'd been terrified as a child by the legend of the Bell Witch, a disembodied female spirit that roamed my home state. Local lore was also replete with sightings of the Tennessee Wildman, a hulking hairy humanlike monster with a horrible stench and a terrifying war cry. But Wallingford had included neither of these nightmare-inducing cryptids in his model. Rather, he'd chosen another creepy critter.

Granddaddy pointed to the fanged, green-eyed creature representing our state. "I see you chose to go with Old

Green Eyes." He shook his head and inhaled through his teeth. "Saw that thing for myself in the woods one night. Scared the bejeezus out of me!"

I had a sneaky suspicioun my grandfather's alleged sighting of the beast with the glowing green eyes was nothing more than two fireflies lighting up in unison in close proximity. Moonshine probably also played a role in the event, though Granddaddy insisted he was stone-cold sober at the time.

After looking over Ronnie's entertaining display, I asked, "Are you competing?"

"Only in the humor category," he said. "I'm not the competitive type. To me, trains aren't about winning awards. They're about having fun." He smiled, flashing his dimples, looking like a boy who hadn't yet realized he'd grown up.

"Well, I've certainly had fun checking out your exhibit."

"Glad to hear it."

Granddaddy and I continued on and came across a makeshift classroom space in a quieter area behind the vendor booths, on the way to the concession stand and restrooms. Folding chairs were set up in rows facing a podium and white screen. A man stood at the lectern, holding up a small piece of lichen. On the screen behind him was a larger photo of the natural material, part of an educational slideshow.

While Granddaddy had been moving about on his scooter, I'd been on my feet most of the day. We decided to stop so I could take a load off. I cast a smile at the man in the adjacent chair as I took a seat in the back row. My grandfather pulled his scooter up next to me.

At the podium, the instructor said, "The methods for preserving natural materials in your model display are similar to those used by florists to preserve cut flowers. Glycerin is a cheap and easy method. The glycerin replaces the water in the flowers and keeps them looking bright and supple. If you go this route, use a mixture that is two parts water to one part glycerin. Of course, there are pluses and minuses to each preservation method. The upside of using glycerin is that it's inexpensive. It's also made from plant oils and is nontoxic. The downside is that glycerin can bleed from the foliage and might not get the job done as well as other methods."

He squeezed a button on the device in his hand and the image on the screen switched to one of lichen resting in a greenish-yellow liquid. "Antifreeze is another option for preserving natural foliage in your railroad scenery. Antifreeze contains propylene glycol, which is toxic, but it's also less likely to bleed from the preserved foliage. It has a lower viscosity that enables it to be more easily absorbed by the plant material."

Antifreeze preserves plants? I supposed it was true that you learn something new every day. Besides the earlier history lessons surrounding the railroad displays, I'd now had a lesson in science. Patrick Jaffe's display of Chattanooga contained a lot of foliage. I wondered if he'd used antifreeze to preserve his natural materials.

The instructor went on to say that, while antifreeze commonly had a yellow-green color, it actually came in a variety of hues. "Pink, blue, yellow, green. You can choose a variety that best matches the color of your scenery."

After a fifteen-minute break to rest my feet and learn about model railroad scenery, we spent another half hour completing our rounds. By then, we'd hit up everyone at the convention, other than whoever had rented the vendor booth that remained empty. They must've been delayed for some reason, maybe suffered a flat tire or run into unexpected traffic. In case the vendor showed up later that afternoon, we left a flyer at the empty booth before heading over to the hotel bar to get ready for the evening's event.

On our way, I texted Marlon. *Any chance you can come to the moonshine mixer tonight? I promised the wives I'd invite you.*

He texted back *I'm afraid of cougars* followed by a cat face emoji.

They're just bored and tired of being ignored by their husbands. Although the others hadn't said as much, my sense was their feelings were much like Dana Gebhardt's. While they supported their husbands' hobby, they wished their husbands would show as much interest in them as the trains. Of course, I wouldn't have asked Marlon to come if it was only the wives who wanted him there. I'd have to run the games at the mixer by myself. It would be nice to have someone there to assist me. *I could use your help with the games if you're willing.*

Marlon acquiesced: *All right. But it'll cost you a jar of candy apple 'shine.*

I replied with the kissy face emoji.

Marlon arrived at the hotel's bar at 5:45, dressed in jeans, boots, and an extra-large T-shirt I'd given him with my moonshine logo on it. The shirt stretched taut across his broad shoulders, chest, and well-developed biceps. If the wives thought Marlon looked good in his police uniform, they'd be even more impressed without a name badge and tool belt blocking their view of his pecs and abs.

I gave him a smile. "You make a very attractive spokesmodel."

"*Spokesmodel?* What am I supposed to say?"

"It doesn't matter," I teased. "Nobody's going to be listening to you anyway." I handed him a drink. "Try this. We're calling it a clown car. That's another name for a caboose."

Granddaddy and I raised our own glasses to clink them with Marlon's in a preemptive toast to a successful event.

Marlon plucked his cherry out by the stem and ate it before taking a sip. He raised his brows and nodded as he swallowed. "Not bad."

The clock had yet to strike six when conventioneers began to wander into the bar for the moonshine mix and mingle. While Granddaddy and I passed out small booklets I had printed with moonshine drink recipes, the bartenders fixed clown cars, brass collars, and derailments for the men and women. The ladies loved my fruity moonshine flavors, while the men went just as wild for Granddaddy's Ole-Timey Corn Liquor. While I'd feared Marlon would face an onslaught of flirtatious ladies, his presence made the men sit up and take notice as much as the women. Sensing a threat, they paid attention to their wives, draping an arm around their shoulders or wrapping one possessively around their waists. The women ate it up. After all, some attention from the men they loved was all they'd really wanted in the first place.

Dana and Bert Gebhardt came in. Bert sent Dana to the bar for drinks and grabbed a small table in the far back corner, away from the crowd. *It's clear who tonight's party pooper will be.* After taking a seat, he squeezed a dollop of hand sanitizer into his palm from a small plastic bottle and proceeded to rub his hands together vigorously, spreading the gel around. He even intertwined his fingers to make sure the sanitizing gel got between them, too. When Dana turned back from the bar, she had a derailment drink in one hand and a bottle of Miller Genuine Draft in the other. Miller beer was brewed in Milwaukee. No doubt it was for her husband, the self-proclaimed beer drinker. Her choice of one of my blackberry moonshine drinks said he'd been a little too quick to speak on his wife's behalf earlier. She had a broader palate. Dana carried the drinks to the table her husband had snagged.

Once everyone had a drink in hand and loosened up a little, I set up a whiteboard on an easel at one end of the room. I plugged in a small speaker and microphone to address the crowd. Mustering up my best game-show announcer voice, I called, "Whoo-whoo wants to play traaain trivia?" Okay, so it was corny. But appropriate for someone who made corn liquor, I supposed.

Hands went up amid calls of "I'll play!," "Me!," or "I do!" Marlon circled through the crowd, assigning numbers to everyone until they were divided into four teams. Dana had joined team two. Her husband had evidently opted out of the games and sat alone at his table. He nursed a derailment now, too. My guess was he'd taken a sip of his wife's drink and decided the wild blackberry moonshine concoction wasn't half bad. He might have a lousy disposition, but at least he had good taste.

He raised a hand to signal the server to bring him another. *Goodness, he's a guzzler!* But I supposed the train conventions were a fun time, a sort of vacation, and it's not like he'd be driving anywhere with his room just across the lobby and down the hall. Besides, he was a big guy. He could likely handle quite a bit of liquor before it fazed him much.

Now that the group was divided into teams, Marlon handed each of them a buzzer that I'd found online. Each one made a different sound so we'd be able to tell which team had hit their buzzer first. Each member of the winning team would receive a T-shirt with my moonshine logo on it as well as a certificate for a free jar of their choice redeemable at my shop. Of course, I hoped they'd buy an additional bottle or two when they came to claim their complimentary 'shine.

I launched into the first question. "Englishman and Baptist minister Thomas Cook organized an excursion by train for more than five hundred people with a set fare for travel and meals, thus starting the first travel agency. To what event were his first customers traveling?"

There were whispered conversations among the members of each team before Ronnie Wallingford slapped his team's buzzer. I pointed a finger at him. "Team two, what's your answer?"

Ronnie called out, "A temperance meeting!"

"That is correct!" I uncapped the dry-erase marker and added a hash mark for team two on the board. Team two cheered and hooted, while the other teams leaned in closer toward one another, readying themselves for the next question. From somewhere in the crowd came a distinctive giggle. *Hee-hee-HEE-hee!* The rhythm and intonation reminded me of the sound of train wheels. I rotated the index cards and handed the next one to Marlon to read.

He took the mic from me. "This is a tough one. Who was the first president to travel by train and on what railroad?"

Looked like the question wasn't so tough, after all. The words had barely left Marlon's lips when Patrick Jaffe slammed a hand down on team three's buzzer and shouted out the answer. "Andrew Jackson on the Baltimore and Ohio!"

"One point for team three!" I made a hash mark on their

score count. "Speaking of presidents," I said, launching into the next question, "which one was taken after his death to his burial site in a Pullman sleeping car, thus launching the success of the Pullman company?"

Team four got the right answer with, "Abraham Lincoln."

Team one knew that the miles of railroad track in place in the United States peaked in 1916, with more than 250,000 miles of track, enough to reach from the earth to the moon. Team three knew that the term *horsepower* had been devised by Scottish inventor James Watt as a marketing term to indicate how many horses an engine could replace. Team two answered the next question correctly, knowing that in October 1883 representatives of all major railroad companies met at what was called the General Time Convention to establish standard time zones. Prior to that meeting, localities could establish their own time, which made scheduling trains extremely difficult. Until I'd prepared these questions, I hadn't realized how widespread the influence of train travel was on other aspects of life.

When the game was over, team two emerged victorious. "Congratulations, team two!"

The team members, including Dana, exchanged high fives and generally whooped it up. It was nice to see her having a good time after witnessing her husband berate her that morning.

After I reminded the conventioneers that everyone was entitled to a twenty percent discount at my shop, Marlon and I passed out T-shirts and certificates for a free jar of 'shine to the winning team.

Dana held up her certificate. "Can I go down to your shop and redeem this now?"

"You sure can," I said. "In fact, now that we've wrapped

up the games, I'm heading there myself. We can walk down together."

"Let me round up the girls," she said. "They won't want to miss out."

I angled my head to indicate her husband, still nursing his drink alone at the back table. "Bert won't mind being left behind?"

"Not at all," she said. "He says we women sound like a bunch of cackling hens when we get together. He'd just as soon go back to the room and read a train magazine."

I eyed him again. "I'm glad to see he looks happier than he did earlier."

She leaned toward me and spoke softly. "He was upset to see Stuart Speer among the judges."

I thought back to the men with the blue blazers and clipboards who'd been judging the diesel competition earlier. Many of them were in the bar now, gathered at a table across the room, talking and laughing. I glanced their way before turning back to Dana. "Is Speer here now?" I whispered.

"Yes. That's him. The one who just got up." She surreptitiously angled her head to indicate the man with the apricot-colored hair as he walked to the bar for another round. "Bert believes the guy didn't give a fair shake to his entry last year. It was a great display of the Durango & Silverton Railroad in Colorado, but the others were good, too. Speer will be judging the steam engine displays Wednesday morning. Bert was all worked up about it earlier, but your moonshine has calmed him down."

"Glad I could help."

Marlon assisted me in packing up the buzzers, dry-erase board and marker, speaker, and microphone. I strapped everything to my dolly with bungee cords. By then, Dana had rounded up the other women and they'd congregated outside the doorway to the bar. Marlon rolled my dolly along behind me as I addressed the ladies. "Let's get you all some 'shine!"

Chapter Five

Granddaddy led the way, scootering down Market Street with the rest of us trailing behind. The women looked about, commenting on which stores they should visit this week. I made some restaurant recommendations and suggested some sights they might enjoy, including the riverfront park, the Southern Belle Riverboat cruise, and Rock City and Ruby Falls, a waterfall inside a cave formation.

"If you haven't had your fill of railroads," I added, "you could ride the Incline Railroad to the top of Lookout Mountain. There're beautiful views from up there."

We reached the Moonshine Shack. Smoky sprawled on his side on the checkout counter, as if trying to see just how much space he could take up. My friend Kiki sat on a stool behind him. During a semester abroad in London during college, she'd adopted a punk rock look, shaving one side of her head, piercing each ear multiple times, and wearing odd clothing combinations that clashed, such as the most feminine ruffled and lacy pieces with combat boots and spiked dog collars. Tonight was no different. She wore a pink polka-dot jumpsuit along with black lace-up boots and a studded bracelet. Nora sat next to Kiki and was working the computer keyboard. The woman was a whiz with social media and created engaging posts for the Moonshine Shack's accounts.

As we came in the door, Nora glanced up from the computer and Kiki glanced up from her sketch pad, where she was doodling Smoky in charcoal pencil. Smoky barely acknowledged our arrival, continuing to pose for his portrait session.

"Hi, Nora and Kiki." I held my hands palms up at my sides to indicate my entourage. "These ladies are with the train convention."

Nora gave them a smile. "Welcome to the Moonshine Shack."

"Ditto," Kiki said, circling her pencil in the air.

The women came inside and began to mill about, checking out my wares. Granddaddy parked his scooter near the jugs of his Ole-Timey Corn Liquor and pled his case for his pure, unflavored variety. "Y'all want a taste of the original stuff, this is it right here."

With me now back at the shop, Nora was free to go home to her family. I thanked her for staying late.

"No problem," she said. "Kiki and I had a great time chatting, and it was nice to eat a dinner that I didn't have to prepare myself." She gathered her things and went out the front door, calling back "See you tomorrow!" over her shoulder.

My assistant relieved of her duties, I now relieved Marlon of the dolly and handed him payment in the form of the candy apple moonshine he'd requested. "Thanks for your help tonight."

"Happy to do it," he said, taking the jar. "It was a lot of fun. If I ever retire from police work, maybe I'll look into becoming a game show emcee." As he turned to go, he gave me a light pat on the back, a small sign of affection that filled my heart with joy and my belly with butterflies. We hadn't yet been dating long enough to be at the kiss-goodbye-in-front-of-other-people stage, but the few private kisses we'd shared had been nearly enough to buckle my knees.

Once he'd left the shop, I quickly stashed my things in the stockroom. When I came back out, I circled around to the back of the tasting table and called, "Samples anyone?"

The ladies lined up at the table for shots of all my 'shine flavors, exclaiming when they found one in particular they especially liked.

One woman had short hair that stood up in pointy spikes, not unlike the hardware on Kiki's dog-collar style punk rock choker. But while Bert Gebhardt's Last Spike was gold, this woman's hair was platinum. The name tag attached to her lanyard read Kimberly Jaffe. She raised a shot glass in a toast. "Here's to not having to listen to another debate about scratch-built versus kit-built models!" She emitted the distinctive giggle I'd heard at the mixer, the one that had a train-like cadence. *Hee-hee-HEE-hee!*

The other ladies roared, a couple of them crying, "Hear! Hear!" before tossing back their shots.

As I poured the next flavor, I asked, "What do you mean by 'scratch-built' and 'kit-built'?"

Kimberly groaned. "We just escaped from that convention—are you really going to make us talk model trains?"

I grimaced. "Sorry!"

"I was just playing with you." She grinned and giggled again. *Hee-hee-HEE-hee!* "Kit-built means the buildings and such in the train display were manufactured scenery and bought already made. Scratch-built means that the scenery was made from scratch. It takes a lot of research and time to build scenery that doesn't look like it was made by a schoolkid. You have to take your time and really hone your craft."

Dana added, "Both of our husbands build most of their scenery. They'll buy the tiny people and cars and things like that already made, but most of the other stuff like the buildings and trees and bushes they make themselves."

Bert must have fashioned the desert grass and tumbleweeds in his Utah display himself, maybe out of hay. With all the greenery in Patrick Jaffe's model of Chattanooga, he must have spent days if not weeks putting it all together. "Building scenery must take a lot of time."

"It does," Kimberly agreed. "But on the bright side, it means our husbands spend a lot of time in the garage so we can curl up on the couch with a glass of wine and a good book."

"I'm on board with the books," I said, "but 'shine is sooooo much better than wine." I held up a jar, playfully tilting it back and forth.

She laughed once more and threw her hands up in surrender. "I stand corrected."

Once the women had a taste or two of everything the shop had to offer, I took a place behind the counter to ring them up.

Dana bought two jars of my wild blackberry moonshine. "One for me and one for Bert," she said. "Bert liked that derailment drink. I'll have to make it for him when we get back to Milwaukee."

As I recited the recipe, she typed it into her phone. "It's just two shots of blackberry 'shine, eight ounces of lemon-lime soda, and you garnish it with fresh blackberries and a mint leaf."

The spiky-haired woman in line behind Dana said, "I liked that drink, too."

I gestured to her name tag. "You must be Patrick's wife."

"I am," she replied. "You met my husband?"

"This morning," I said. "I stopped to check out his model. He did a great job capturing Chattanooga."

Dana concurred. "He certainly did. I recognized some of the landmarks we saw on our drive into town. The river. Lookout Mountain."

"Of course, he left out the most important place in town." I raised my palms. "My Moonshine Shack."

Kimberly cocked her head, her brows drawing inward. "This store didn't exist in 1880, did it?"

Kiki chimed in. "This store didn't exist four months ago."

"That's true," I conceded, "but the Hayes family was making moonshine in Chattanooga in 1880."

"For real?" Kimberly asked.

"For real," I said. "In fact, my ancestors brought their moonshine recipe with them when they immigrated from Ireland." Turning back to Dana, I asked, "How long was the drive from Milwaukee?"

"Mmm." Dana looked up in thought. "We left at seven yesterday morning and arrived at the hotel a little after ten last night, but we lost an hour when we crossed time zones somewhere along the way. Kentucky, I think?"

I did some quick math. "Fourteen hours. Wow. That's a long haul in one day."

"Tell me about it," she said. "My rear end fell asleep five hours in. I still can't feel my left hip."

"No stops along the way to see the sights?" A road trip seemed like a prime opportunity to visit tourist spots along the way.

"Oh, no," Dana said. "There's no time. Bert insists that we do these trips in one leg if at all possible. He's sure someone's going to try to steal the rental truck and he'll lose his models if we stay overnight anywhere or go inside. I can sometimes get him to stop at a diner with windows overlooking the parking lot so he can keep an eye on the truck, but that's about it. When we can't do a trip in a single day, he sleeps in the truck."

Kimberly cringed. "Guess I'm lucky it was only seven hours from Cincinnati to Chattanooga."

"You sure are," Dana agreed. "I'd much prefer to fly to the conventions and meet up with Bert after he arrives, but he won't hear of it."

"Because of the extra expense?" Kimberly asked.

"I'm sure that's part of it," Dana said, "but he claims it's because he likes having our time together on the road, just the two of us. He says it's romantic." She clasped her hands dreamily under her chin and batted her eyes for effect, making the rest of us laugh. It was nice to know that Bert had a soft side.

I finished ringing Dana up and put her moonshine in one of my heavy-duty fluorescent green bags. "Thanks, Dana."

Dana took her bag and Kimberly stepped up to the counter. She had only one jar of blackberry moonshine to Dana's two, but she was also purchasing one of the candy apple variety and a jug of Granddaddy's Ole-Timey Corn Liquor. I rang her up as well, and handed her the bag. "Enjoy!"

"Oh, I will!" she said with her trademark giggle. She

unzipped her backpack-style purse, crammed the moonshine into it, and forced the zipper closed before slinging it back over her shoulder. "Thanks so much!"

While Smoky oversaw operations from his place on the counter, Granddaddy and Kiki helped some of the other women make their selections. When the group left, we'd sold two dozen jars of 'shine and four of my grandfather's earthenware jugs. *Not bad at all.*

I watched through the window as Dana and Kimberly took up the rear of their group, heads turned toward each other, chatting amiably. Given that their husbands seemed to be at odds, it seemed surprising the two got along so well. Good thing they didn't let their husbands' petty squabble come between them.

Chapter Six

I stayed away from the convention center on Tuesday. I had deliveries to make to liquor stores in the area. I also had a big delivery on the way—my grandfather's new power chair. It was scheduled to arrive sometime this week, and I couldn't wait to surprise him with it. Besides, I'd already made the rounds of the convention booths on Monday. No sense making a nuisance of myself. But, since I'd spent a day away, I figured I could show my face again on Wednesday without seeming overly pushy, especially when I had another freebie to give to the conventioneers. Today's giveaway was a plastic jigger imprinted with my logo.

I pulled up to the Singing River Retirement Home at 9:30 Wednesday morning in my van. My grandfather was already out front, sitting on his red scooter, ready to get going. His face was lit with excitement. To get him moving along at the convention center on Monday, I'd promised that when we returned he could spend more time at the vendor booths, looking at the trains and accessories they had for sale. No doubt he planned to hold me to that promise.

I rolled down the passenger window. "Good mornin', Granddaddy!"

"Right back at ya', Hattie."

I parked my van, helped him into the passenger seat, and then lowered the ramp in back so I could drive his scooter up into the cargo bay. Once everything and everyone was in place, we motored down to the convention center and turned into the parking lot.

The doors had yet to open, and a long line of contestants and train enthusiasts were lined up along the walkway, waiting to be allowed inside. Dana and Bert Gebhardt stood among them, Bert's size making him easy to spot. He carried his toolbox in his hand. As a sign of support for her husband's hobby, Dana wore her bonnet again today. Kimberly and Patrick Jaffe stood thirty feet or so farther back. I recognized her by her platinum blond spikes. Not far behind them stood a woman who resembled Martha, the hotel housekeeper I'd come upon Bert berating on Monday morning. Given that the woman wasn't wearing a hotel housekeeper's uniform, I couldn't be certain whether it was her. After all, I'd only seen her the one time and our conversation had been brief. But this woman had the same maple syrup–colored hair coiffed into a soft poof. I parked my van, helped my grandfather onto his scooter, and we rolled our way over to take places at the end of the line.

Conversation from behind caught my ear and I glanced over my shoulder to see a group of men in blue blazers approaching. Stuart Speer was among them. The apricot fuzz on his head reflected the morning sunshine as he passed by us. He carried a cardboard coffee cup from the coffeehouse down the block, along with a stir stick and several small brown packets I recognized as containing raw sugar. As the convention's VIPs, the judges bypassed the line and walked right up to the doors. The security guard working the entrance allowed them inside.

A few minutes later, at precisely 10:00, the doors opened for all. Most of the people in line already had their tickets and the line moved much faster today.

As my grandfather and I headed down the line of vendor booths, Stuart Speer emerged from one of the perpendicular rows that housed the model train displays for the contest. He held his coffee cup aloft in his left hand, his clipboard cradled in the crook of the same arm. He paused for a moment, his posture rigid and his expression pensive. While his head barely moved, his eyes darted left and right, as if he were attempting to survey the area without being obvious. *What's he looking for? And why does he seem to be hiding the fact that he's looking around?* His gaze rolled right over Granddaddy and me. He began moving again, walking past an open-topped trash can. In a split second, he dipped his right hand into the hip pocket of his blazer, pulled out his stir stick and torn sugar packets, and dropped them into the garbage can without looking down or breaking stride, like a magician performing a sleight of hand. He headed off again with his clipboard and coffee cup.

"What do they have here?" My grandfather braked his scooter to a stop at a booth selling basic, inexpensive train sets and climbed off to take a look. I stood next to him, running my gaze over the options. Many of the train sets were based on movies or television shows. The train Harry Potter took to Hogwarts. Thomas the Tank Engine. The Polar Express. Rather than having electrified tracks, most of these trains ran on plastic tracks and were powered by batteries inserted into the engine.

"Look!" Granddaddy pointed to one of the packages. "That one even blows smoke!"

Funny how these model trains turned grown men back into exuberant little boys.

Behind my grandfather, Patrick Jaffe eased up to the trash can Stuart Speer had used a moment before. Jaffe glanced around, too, before bending over and reaching an arm way down into the bottom of the trash can. When he pulled his hand out, he held the stir stick and sugar packets Speer had just discarded. *What in the world would Jaffe want with the sugar and stir stick?* I'd heard that one man's trash is another man's treasure, but in this case, wasn't one man's trash just that—trash?

Before I could finish my thought, a voice came from behind me. "There you are."

I turned around to see Marlon walking our way. He was dressed in his Chattanooga PD uniform and riding boots, looking as swoon-worthy as ever.

He came over and greeted my grandfather. "How you doin' today, Ben?"

My grandfather pointed at a cheap but cute plastic train set. The price was only $49.99. "I'm thinking of buying that train. It's got a horn and a place where you can add water so it'll make steam, too. We could set it up in the 'Shine Shack. It'd be something fun for the customers to look at."

I was pretty sure Granddaddy thought the train would be something fun for him to play with, but I wasn't going to embarrass him by pointing it out. Besides, I felt the same. A train could be a cute, kitschy addition to the décor of the Moonshine Shack. The conventioneers who visited the shop this week would appreciate the nod to their hobby.

"If we're going to put it in the Shack," I said, "I'll pay for it." After all, my grandfather lived on a fixed income.

He scowled. "I can afford my own toys."

He'd just admitted it was a toy for himself, as I'd expected. "I know you can afford it yourself, Granddaddy," I said, "but if I pay for it, it's a tax write-off for the shop."

He shrugged. "I suppose I can't argue with that."

Marlon raised a finger and circled it in the air. "I've seen places with a shelf-type platform around the top of their walls for model trains. They mount the shelving over the doors so the train can make a complete loop around the room. The train would be less likely to get broken up high like that than it would be down lower where customers might be tempted to put their hands on it."

"That's a great idea, Marlon. If we put the train on a shelf, it won't take up space in my shop, either." I turned to my grandfather. "What do you think?"

He answered my question by addressing the vendor. "Looks like we're going to need some extra track."

We bought the train, along with a hundred additional feet of plastic track. The contractor who'd built the façade of the Shack had left the extra wooden planks in my storeroom. I felt confident there were enough boards remaining to build a narrow train platform around the perimeter of the room. We'd just need some shelf brackets to support them.

I stashed the purchase in the basket on Granddaddy's scooter and we continued along, making stops at other vendor booths where we purchased scenery pieces to add to the display we planned to build.

Granddaddy pointed to the assorted foliage. "Let's get some of those pine trees," he said. "Some with snow on them, too. That way, we can change them out when winter comes."

The plastic trees weren't as pretty as the natural foliage

in Patrick Jaffe's model of Chattanooga, but they'd none-theless add a nice touch to the store's display. Besides, with the track being mounted high on the wall, nobody would see the trees up close. We also bought a train station build-ing, an old-fashioned schoolhouse, a covered bridge, a cabin that looked much like the one my grandparents had owned and in which I lived now, and an assortment of minia-ture people. To round things out, we added some yellow and black railroad crossing signs and a red-and-white striped arm.

"Lookie there!" my grandfather cried as we approached another booth. "It's a still!"

Sure enough, one of the vendors had a little copper moon-shine still for sale, complete with the coils and barrel. We had to buy that piece, of course. I whipped out my credit card again. "We'll take the still."

By then, I'd spent far more than I'd expected, though it was worth every cent to see my grandfather so excited. As we made our way along, we passed Stuart Speer. He'd set his paper coffee cup down on the table at the empty vendor space, placing it next to the flyer I'd left at the booth on Monday. His first name was written on the side of the cup in black Sharpie. Speer was speaking to the woman I'd seen in line outside earlier. Seeing the woman up close like this, I felt even more certain it was Martha the housekeeper. Looked like she had the day off and had decided to spend it here at the model train show.

The two finished speaking and Speer walked off, leav-ing his coffee cup behind. Martha picked up the cup and carried it off with her. *Weird.* Why did she, like Patrick Jaffe, seem interested in Stuart Speer's trash?

After nearly half an hour in our company, Marlon said, "I've stayed as long as I should. I better get out on my beat."

He said he'd come by the Shack that evening to see about hanging the shelves for me.

"That's going well beyond the call of duty," I said.

"It is," he agreed. "But there's this little filly I'm trying to impress." He shot me a wink, and with that he walked off, leaving this little filly wanting to kick up her heels.

Once my grandfather and I had made the rounds of all the vendors, we turned down the rows of train displays. Bert Gebhardt's Last Spike model sat up ahead. Granddaddy rolled along beside me as I walked up to the exhibit. Bert stood behind the plexiglass. Once again, he squeezed a liberal squirt of hand sanitizer into his palm and rubbed it over his hands before returning the bottle to his toolbox. As much as the guy used, he should buy the gel by the gallon. I turned to greet Dana. "Good mornin'."

She gave me a broad smile and stood from her chair. "Nice to see you again, Hattie."

I introduced her to my grandfather and showed her some of the things we'd bought. "We're going to put in a track around the walls of my shop, near the ceiling."

"Uh-oh," she said with a wide smile, "don't tell me you're getting hooked on model trains, too."

I raised my hand and extended my thumb and forefinger, leaving only a thin space between them in the universal sign for itty-bitty. "Maybe just a little."

Dana angled her head to indicate her husband. "Bert's pretty keyed up. The judges will be starting on the steam train displays soon."

As my gaze ran over the display, I noticed that the sand seemed to have a little more sparkle today. Maybe Bert had used some of his glass cleaner on the plexiglass and I could simply see better. Or maybe the overhead lighting was brighter today. Or maybe I'd been too preoccupied with Bert's tiny vacuum and the details of the golden spike, the champagne-wielding miniature man, and the period American flag to get a good look at the sand when I'd been here before.

My eyes were drawn down to Bert's toolbox, which sat open on the floor a few feet behind the table. A half-empty jar of my wild blackberry moonshine sat in the top of the toolbox. Unlike the jar of moonshine, both bottles of blue glass cleaners that sat next to it were full up to their necks.

Ronnie Wallingford wandered up to speak to Bert again. "You change your mind about selling me that caboose?"

Bert stared vacantly at the man, as if he had no idea what Wallingford was talking about. Bert blinked several times forcefully, as if trying to clear his vision. *Is it my imagination, or is he swaying?*

Wallingford took Bert's silence as a negotiation tactic. "Not even gonna respond, huh? All right. What do you say to two fifty? No one will ever offer you that much again, I guarantee it."

Bert shook his head.

Dana stepped over. "Two hundred and fifty dollars is a generous offer, Bert. I think you should take it."

Bert shook his head again, but just as he'd blinked in what looked like an attempt to clear his eyes, the headshaking appeared to be a possible attempt to clear his mind.

Once again, Ronnie Wallingford spat a curse and stalked off without his prized caboose. As he went, he turned and sent a glare back over his shoulder, calling, "If you come to your senses, let me know!"

Dana sighed, casting her husband a doleful expression before returning her attention to me and our conversation about his anxiety. "I'll have to make another trip to your shop. Bert drank half a jar of your blackberry moonshine last night. He even did a couple of shots this morning to settle his nerves for the competition."

"Big mistake," he muttered, putting a hand on his sale cabinet to steady himself. "That stuff packs a wallop. You got any aspirin on you?"

"Sure, hon. I took one this morning myself. My head was pounding when I woke up." Dana reached under the back of the display table and retrieved her purse. She dug around inside and pulled out a small bottle of aspirin. She handed it to her husband.

Bert gave her a grateful smile, the pain of the effort making it appear more of a grimace. "I can always count on you to take care of me. I don't say it enough, but I do appreciate you."

Dana exhaled a light laugh that was mostly air and patted her husband's shoulder. "Don't worry, Bert."

Bert shook two of the aspirin into his hand, dropping another two to the floor. As Dana picked up the errant pills, he washed down the ones he'd managed to hang on to with water from a bottle he'd stashed in the cup holder on his chair.

He pulled a watch on a chain from the hip pocket of his overalls and checked the time, blinking several times as he stared at its face. "They'll be . . . they'll be starting the judging soon. We better . . . better get a move on."

His stammering told me that he just might have drunk too much moonshine. His nerves might be settled, but his speech was a little slurred.

Dana looked from her husband back to me and my grandfather. "Bert likes to watch while the judges evaluate the displays, and gauge their reactions. Some of them have poker faces, but others give themselves away when they really like a model."

Dana, Granddaddy, and I trailed along in Bert's wake, following him to Jaffe's model of the historic Chattanooga station. Fortunately, we arrived early enough that we were able to get up close so Granddaddy would have a good vantage point from his scooter and wouldn't have to try to stand up to see what was going on. Soon thereafter, other exhibitors joined us. Bert was not the only one who wanted to observe the judges as they scored the model.

While Patrick Jaffe ignored Bert, who stood with his arms crossed over his chest, Kimberly Jaffe stepped my way. "Hi, there, Hattie."

After returning the greeting, I introduced her to my grandfather. "He's the one who taught me how to make moonshine."

"Is that right?" Kimberly said. "That's wonderful. My grandpa taught me how to play gin rummy and my grandma taught me how to make pineapple upside-down cake. I've passed both of those skills on to my grandkids."

If I had children someday, I'd pass down the secrets of moonshining to them, too. Funny how things like recipes and games could tie people together across decades or even centuries.

Other contestants walked up and joined the group of spectators. Soon thereafter the judges arrived together, having met up elsewhere. Maybe in a secret judge's station? Stuart Speer was among them, of course, along with a handsome white-haired man whose silver badge identified him as the chief judge.

The judges took several minutes to look over the display, leaning over it, bending down to examine parts of it straight on, circling around it to ensure they got a full 360-degree view. After they examined the display, the chief judge instructed Jaffe to start his train. They watched for a minute or so as the train completed several cycles around the display. The chief judge exchanged glances with the others, who nodded in return. He instructed Jaffe to turn the engine off.

In response to a set of prepared questions from the judges' panel, Patrick Jaffe filled them in on the materials he'd used and why he'd chosen this particular scene to depict. "In 1880, our country was still feeling the effects of the Civil War and had yet to truly come together. The joining of the North and South by railroad was symbolic. It provided hope for a reunification of the country. The fact that freight cars were the first to go down the tracks showed that the economies and fortunes of the North and South were interconnected, and that Northerners and Southerners were reliant on one another. The journey was so much more than simply a delivery of goods."

The judges nodded thoughtfully, making notes on their clipboards. Speer cast Bert a narrow-eyed look that was equal parts disgust and distrust before pulling a ruler from the inside pocket of his blazer. He proceeded to measure various pieces of scenery in the display, including the Missionary Ridge Tunnel.

Jaffe's brow folded in deep furrows, making him look like a Klingon. "What's going on?"

Speer cut another look at Bert before turning back to Jaffe. "We received an anonymous report from an unknown e-mail address that some of your structures were not to scale, particularly the Missionary Ridge Tunnel."

Jaffe raised his palms. "I admit it's not exact. The actual tunnel is more than nine hundred and eighty-six feet. At HO scale, that would be more than eleven feet long. But I wasn't about to leave it out. The tunnel is a critical historic detail." He noted that the U-shaped tunnel had been built by slaves using shovels, picks, and black powder to dig and blow their way through the mountain. "My measurements might not be right on the nose, but including the tunnel furthers my message. A dark era in American history had ended, and a new one was beginning. Things were starting to turn around, just like the tunnel does. It's symbolic."

The judges turned to each other, gauging each other's reactions. From their expressions, it seemed most of them believed Jaffe had made a valid point, as well as a difficult decision when it came to rendering the landmarks. My guess was they'd count off a point or two for the imprecise scale, but that they'd give him high marks in other areas. But Jaffe hadn't seen their silent interactions. He was too busy staring down Bert Gebhardt.

His chest heaving with fury, Jaffe walked over to Bert and jabbed a finger at him, not quite poking the large man in the chest but coming darn near close. "It was you who sent that e-mail to the judges, wasn't it? You couldn't stand the fact that you might lose to me again. You think I don't know about all the appeals you've filed?"

Chapter Seven

Bert's face turned as purple as my blackberry moonshine. He bent down slightly and spread his legs farther apart, as if steadying himself in preparation for a brawl. "You calling me . . . calling me a bad sport?" he bellowed. "All I've ever done is try to . . . try to ensure the integrity of these contests!"

The judges again exchanged looks that said Bert had done more than attempt to protect the competitions. He'd accused them of favoritism, which was an attack on their personal ethics. *I wish Marlon hadn't gone.* If things continued to escalate, these two blowhards might come to blows. *Clang-clang-clang!* The sound of a warning bell came from somewhere in the convention center, as if cautioning the crowd of an approaching danger. Too bad there wasn't a railroad arm that could be brought down between these two.

The chief judge raised his palms. "Enough! If you two don't stop arguing right now, you'll both be disqualified!"

Bert and Patrick shut their mouths, but they continued to stare each other down, locked in a death glare, their chests heaving as they fumed. Neither man wanted to be the first to back down. *Cheese and grits.*

Dana and Kimberly scurried over, pleading with their husbands. When words didn't work, both tried to pull their husbands back, but to no avail. Their husbands shrugged off their hands. Fortunately, Granddaddy stepped in . . . or rather, rolled in. Beep-beep-beeping his horn, he barreled down on the men on his scooter. Not quite an oncoming train, but close enough. Lest he run over their toes, the two men were forced to step away from each other.

The impasse thus ended, Bert turned and stormed off. Or perhaps staggered off would be a more precise description. He weaved a wonky route, looking as if he were performing a grapevine. He bumped the edge of another display, shaking the exhibit. The man behind the table was none too happy to see the lumbering man collide with his carefully crafted model. "Hey! Watch it, buddy!"

Martha stood at a nearby vendor table. She looked back over her shoulder at Bert, a smirk on her face. She seemed glad to see the bully get a taste of his own medicine.

Dana hurried after her husband as he continued on his way, careening down the row. *Could he be drunk?* I'd wondered earlier, but now I was pretty sure. Still, he was a big guy. He should have been able to handle two shots of moonshine this morning without it affecting him this much. *Is something else going on?*

Now that his nemesis was gone, Jaffe turned to the judges and apologized. "I'm sorry. I shouldn't have lost my temper. But that man's been a thorn in my side for years now. These competitions are supposed to be good clean fun, not some type of dirty *Game of Thrones* battle."

Jaffe might have gone a little overboard with his comparison, but he had a point. Bert Gebhardt was turning what should be a friendly competition into an ugly rivalry.

When Granddaddy motored back around to my side, I leaned over. "Quick thinking. You saved the day. Maybe Marlon can get you a job with the Chattanooga PD."

"It was nothing." Granddaddy waved an arthritic hand dismissively, but his grin gave him away. He was proud to be a hero, even if only for a moment.

When the judges finished evaluating Patrick Jaffe's display, they continued on to assess two more models, the crowd moving along with them to observe. These examinations complete, the chief judge looked down at his roster. "Next up is Bert Gebhardt's Last Spike model."

The judges moved en masse with the group of onlookers trailing behind. We made our way to Bert's display. To my surprise, the man lay reclined in his chair, his eyes closed and his jaw slack. How he'd fallen asleep so soon after his heated confrontation with Patrick Jaffe was beyond me.

Dana stood from her chair and glanced from the blue-jacketed band of judges to her husband. She bent over and put a hand on his shoulder. "Bert? The judges are here." When he failed to respond, she gently shook him. "Bert? Wake up now. It's your turn." When he still didn't react, her eyes went wide. "Bert?" she cried, putting both hands on his shoulders now, desperately trying to rouse him. "Bert?" She shook him so hard his folding chair collapsed under him. She shrieked as he fell to the floor and keeled over onto his side. I sucked in air. *Oh my gosh!* The crowd gasped and exclaimed around us.

As her husband lay motionless at her feet, Dana dropped to her knees beside him, putting her hand to his cheek in one last, desperate attempt to get a response from him.

When he again failed to react, she looked around, her eyes bright and bulging in panic. "Help!" she cried. "Someone help him!"

The chief judge yanked a radio from his pocket and called security. "We need medical attention at Booth B5 right away." Help having been summoned, the judge turned to the crowd and shooed everyone back. "Make way! Make way!"

In seconds, an EMT rushed up with a medical bag. Dana stood and stepped back to give the medic room to work. He whipped out a stethoscope and listened to Bert's heart and lungs.

Dana swallowed hard, and her voice quavered. "Do you hear anything?"

"He's got a pulse, but it's weak." The EMT lifted Bert's eyelids and shone a penlight in them. His initial assessment complete, he radioed for an ambulance, then looked up at Dana, stood, and engaged in a quick, quiet conversation with her, probably asking whether Bert had any preexisting health issues.

While I couldn't hear the EMT's questions, I heard Dana's response. "No, he didn't take any medications. He hasn't been to a doctor in years. He says they're all quacks. He doesn't drink much usually, but he drank a lot of moonshine last night. A little this morning, too."

Both my heart and stomach performed a backflip. She wasn't blaming Bert's current condition on my moonshine, was she? My 'shine was intended for refreshment and relaxation, not to get rip-roaring drunk. If Bert drank half of one of the jars Dana bought at my shop after the mixer, that was on him. He'd ignored the warning on the label that directed users to "Shine Smart." Even so, he'd had the entire night to sober up and sleep off the effects of overindulging in the

moonshine. He might have a hangover, but if he'd over-
dosed on alcohol it would have been evident long before
now. A couple more shots this morning shouldn't have sent
him over the edge. Maybe Dana had only mentioned the
moonshine so that the medics would know Bert had alcohol
in his system. It might affect the treatment they'd provide.
I was no medical professional, but judging from Bert's size,
his broken capillaries, and normally tense demeanor, it
seemed most likely he was suffering a stroke or heart
attack.

Dana must have come to the same conclusion. "Is it his
heart? He eats a lot of red meat. His cholesterol must be
through the roof."

The medic declined to make a diagnosis. "I can't be sure,
ma'am." In minutes, paramedics were loading Bert onto a
gurney.

Dana turned to the judges as they prepared to take her
husband away. "Please judge Bert's model! He spent months
building it. When he comes around, he'll be upset if he
finds out it didn't get judged."

When he comes around. While the woman remained
hopeful about her husband's condition, I feared she was
being overly optimistic. Bert looked like he was halfway to
meet his maker already. Unless Saint Peter put Bert on a
turntable and reversed his track, we might have seen the
last of the man.

The chief judge assured Dana they'd evaluate Bert's display. "Your husband's a mainstay at these conventions.
They wouldn't be the same without him. Let him know we
all wish him well."

The expressions on Stuart Speer and Patrick Jaffe's
faces told me that the chief was incorrect and, in fact, not
all wished Bert Gebhardt well. Patrick Jaffe had already

explicitly said that Bert had been a thorn in his side for years. Now, Jaffe ran his fingers over his walrus mustache in what seemed more an attempt to hide a vengeful grin than a self-calming gesture. He'd probably just as soon the conventions went on without Bert. By contrast, Speer's lips formed a somber line, his eyes hard and cold. Ronnie Wallingford was more of a blank slate, his face void of emotion as he watched Bert and Dana depart. Once they'd rounded the end of the row and out of sight, his gaze shifted to the caboose in Bert's sales case. His expressionless face changed, his mouth widening into an almost smile and his eyes brightening in hope.

The judges proceeded to evaluate Bert's display. While he wasn't there to describe his model in person, the chief read aloud the statement Bert had provided on his entry form about the importance of joining the East and West at Promontory Point, how the connection of the railroads led to western expansion. They read the information on his display board, and compared his model to the image in the picture.

Stuart Speer looked from the photo to the model several times. When he finished, he crossed his arms over his chest, as if wishing he could contain the words he felt obligated to impart. "Gotta say, this might be the best photo match I've seen in all my years of judging model railroads."

The other judges concurred, commenting on the meticulous attention to detail. From their discussion, it looked like Bert had the Photo Match category locked down. Bert was competing in both the Photo Match and Steam Train categories, though. From what I could gather, the latter contest required that the train make a complete circuit of its track. To that end, the chief judge circled around the back of

Bert's plexiglass dividers. He stopped at the control switch and flipped the lever so they could see the trains in action. The model sprang to life. The Jupiter and Union Pacific 119 steam trains rolled out from their starting points at the back corners of the display, their movements accompanied by a soft *chugga-chugga* sound, soft billows of gray rising from their smokestacks. The two cars slowly approached the center, where they were to meet up on either side of the golden spike. But while the Union Pacific 119 rolled gently to a precise stop, the Jupiter train jerked and stalled. An odd burning smell arose from the display, along with a grinding sound. The engine rocked forward, the back end lifting from the track like a bucking bronco. A second later, the engine keeled over sideways, much like Bert had done only moments before, landing with a soft thud on the sand. The spectators broke into murmurs of surprise and dismay.

Jaffe squeezed closer, stepping up to the plexiglass. He squinted as his gaze assessed the scene. "Is there something on the tracks?"

The chief judge leaned in to take a closer look, too. "Yes. It looks like some of the sand came loose."

Ronnie Wallingford harrumphed. "You'd think the man would've known to use spray tack to keep the sand in place."

Wallingford made a good point. In light of Bert's meticulous maintenance of his model, this turn of events was certainly unexpected. Then again, Bert hadn't seemed to be fully lucid this morning. Maybe he had forgotten to inspect his tracks again. But how could anything new have ended up on his tracks? He'd carefully cleaned the tracks Monday, and his entire display was enclosed in plexiglass that he'd wiped down just as carefully. *Hmm.*

I looked around, seeing nothing of note between the back of his display and the portable wall that separated this row from the one behind it. Moving my gaze upward, I spotted a vent for the HVAC system hanging a dozen feet overhead. Though I couldn't feel any airflow at the moment, maybe the air-conditioning vent had blown some of the sand loose earlier, or had blown dust or lint out of the duct and down onto the tracks. It was also possible that Bert might have inadvertently jostled his model, knocking some of the sand loose. After all, he'd bumped into the other conventioneer's display on his walk from Jaffe's model to here.

Whatever the cause of the derailment, it was apparently irrelevant to the judging process. The judges wrapped up their evaluation and headed on to the next entrant, who had built a model of the White Pass and Yukon Route steam train line complete with craggy peaks, pine trees, and imitation snow. For fun, the model railroader had included snowmen, reindeer, and grizzlies among the peaks and pines.

When the judges finished with the exhibit, my grandfather and I decided to leave the convention hall. The mood had become subdued, and I didn't feel right pushing my products when a man's life was on the line in a nearby hospital. Instead, my grandfather and I drove to a hardware store and purchased brackets, wall anchors, and screws to support the platform for the train display to go in my shop. Afterward, we picked up Smoky from the cabin and drove to the Moonshine Shack.

Although it was a busy afternoon in the store, I found myself unable to shake the image of Bert keeling over in his chair. *Poor Dana.* She was miles from home without the support of friends and family, and could lose her husband.

For her sake, as well as Bert's, I hoped he would make a quick and complete recovery.

At 8:30 Wednesday evening, Marlon was using a screwdriver to attach one of the last brackets to the wall of my Moonshine Shack, while I stood on my step stool, putting a narrow board into place atop the brackets he'd already installed. Granddaddy stood leaning on his cane, supervising. "Make sure the ends of the boards fit together tight," he said for the umpteenth time. "Don't want the track to break because it's not supported."

As Marlon and I had built the model train platform, I'd filled him in on the events that occurred after he'd left the convention center, how an ambulance had been called to take away an unresponsive Bert Gebhardt. Smoky lay atop the checkout counter, eyeing what to him must look like a fun catwalk along the upper wall. I should probably let him make a round or two on the shelves before we installed the train. The chunky cat didn't get much exercise. It would be good for him.

I'd just handed Smoky to Marlon when the door of my shop opened and in walked Detective Candace "Ace" Pearce. *Uh-oh.* Her presence at my store couldn't be good.

Marlon must've had the same thought. He froze for a moment before lifting Smoky up to the platform, then turned to greet the detective. "Evening, Ace."

Ace was a full-figured, dark-skinned detective with impeccable fashion sense. She wore her hair in a copper-colored pixie cut, complemented by metallic-tone makeup and copper jewelry. Her enormous, ever-present gray tote bag was slung over the shoulder of her jade-green blazer.

We'd met on an earlier investigation involving an attack that had taken place just outside the front door of my shop. While Ace had initially thought I could have been the perpetrator of the heinous crime, she'd completely changed her mind about me once I'd put the clues together and helped solve the crime.

I climbed down from the step stool and greeted her as well. "What brings you by?"

She wasted no time filling us in. "Bert Gebhardt passed away this afternoon."

Granddaddy tsked and shook his head. "Ain't that a shame."

While I'd anticipated that Bert might not make it, the news was still hard to hear. My heart broke for Dana. At least her husband had told her he'd appreciated her before he passed. She'd have that to hang on to. Feeling the squeeze in my heart made me wonder if Bert's heart had been the problem, too. "Did he have a heart attack?" But even as I asked the question, I realized Ace would not likely be here to talk to me if Bert had died of cardiac complications.

"No," Ace said. "It wasn't a heart attack that killed Mr. Gebhardt. He was poisoned."

"Poisoned?" Granddaddy said. "How?"

"We don't yet know how," she said, turning from my grandfather back to me, "we only know what type of poison it was."

I gulped, terror sending adrenaline shooting through my veins. My voice squeaked when I asked, "What type of poison was it?"

"Methanol."

A sick feeling flooded my gut. Methanol was a toxic

byproduct of the fermentation process, which was one of the steps in making moonshine. It was a type of alcohol, one not intended for consumption. "Are the doctors certain it couldn't be something else?"

"Yes, they're certain. His blood work showed a lethal level of methanol in his system. No other toxins."

I found myself taking an involuntary step back, as if to distance myself from the situation. My head spun just like the apparatus on the bottling machine when it screwed the shiny aluminum lids on my mason jars of moonshine. Unable to form a coherent thought, I stammered, "How would . . . where did . . . ?"

Fortunately, Ace seemed to know where my questions were heading. "Dana Gebhardt says that, other than breakfast in the hotel restaurant, the only thing Bert ate or drank since they went to happy hour in the concierge lounge last night was your wild blackberry moonshine. No one else who has eaten at the hotel has become ill." She retrieved an electronic tablet from her tote bag, turned it on, and held it out so I could see the screen. The image showed the jar of my wild blackberry moonshine sitting in Bert's toolbox, nestled between the two bottles of blue glass cleaner. She pointed to the jar. "That's your brand of moonshine, isn't it?"

Though only part of the label was visible, there was no mistaking the signature firefly in the logo. "Yes, it's mine." I swallowed hard. "You think *my moonshine* killed Bert Gebhardt?"

Granddaddy scoffed and waved a gnarled, dismissive hand. "Ain't no way that can be true."

He had a point. My grandfather had taught me how to make moonshine, and he'd instilled in me everything he

knew about distilling it safely. My procedures were meticu-
lously designed to ensure none of the toxic liquid made it
into my products. I took a long breath in an attempt to calm
myself. Though I knew I'd followed safe and proper procedures, the fact that my moonshine was under suspicion was
understandable. After all, how else would Bert have ingested methanol?

Ace raised a shoulder in a half shrug. "People get sick or
die from bad homebrew on occasion."

"Yes," I agreed, "when it's made by amateurs. I'm a professional moonshiner. I know what I'm doing."

Insulted, Granddaddy lifted his cane from the floor and
waved it. "She sure does! Hattie learned moonshining from
the best." He thumped his chest. "Me!" He began to wobble
and returned his cane to the floor to steady himself.

To prove I knew my stuff, I explained my meticulous
process. "I carefully monitor the wash temperature." Methanol had a lower boiling point than ethanol and would boil
off during production, leaving only the ethanol behind. Even
so, for safety's sake, it was standard process to throw out
the first few ounces of each batch, what was known as the
"foreshot." The foreshot was discarded not only because it
could potentially contain methanol, which was extremely
toxic even in small amounts, but also because the foreshot
was very concentrated and could ruin the flavor of the batch.
"I discard the first full pint of product every time I make a
batch." Not to mention that I carefully inspected my equipment before making each batch. Alcohol vapor could be
highly explosive. I wasn't about to risk getting burned to a
crisp. "My manufacturing and bottling facility is in good
working order."

Ace sighed. "I know from before that you're a smart
cookie with an eye for details, so I'm tempted to believe

you. But I've got a suspicious death on my hands, and the most obvious source of the methanol is the moonshine. Dana told us she woke with a headache this morning. The doctors tested her blood and found a small amount of methanol in her system, too. They've treated her for it. Until the lab verifies that it wasn't your moonshine that killed Bert Gebhardt and made his wife ill, you're going to have to shut down sales."

My jaw dropped. I was sorry Bert had died but, if my moonshine was associated with a fatality, it could also mean the death of the business I'd worked so hard to build. Granddaddy seemed to realize the potential enormity of the situation, too. He muttered under his breath and ground his jaw so hard I was afraid he'd shatter his shiny new dentures.

I gestured to her tablet. "Can you send me that photo?"

"All right." Ace tapped her screen and sent the pic to my phone, which pinged when it arrived. She slid the tablet back into her tote bag and went on to repeat more of what she'd learned from the doctors at the hospital, that methanol was acutely toxic and could be introduced to the body via an oral or dermal means, or through inhalation. Methanol was metabolized into formic acid that depressed the central nervous system. The process was slow but horrific, with the initial symptoms showing up within twelve to twenty-four hours. Effects started with a headache, dizziness, and nausea, developing later into confusion, lack of coordination, and finally loss of consciousness. A person could feel fine for hours before reacting, and could be rendered blind before losing consciousness. The information explained why Bert had been blinking and wobbling this morning, why he'd failed to respond to Ronnie Wallingford, why he'd seemed to have had a delayed reaction to moonshine he'd drunk the night before.

"The docs said it takes as little as ten milliliters of pure methanol to destroy a person's optic nerve and cause permanent blindness."

"Ten milliliters? That's not much at all." A typical mason jar, like those I used to bottle my moonshine, held 750 milliliters.

"It's about a third of an ounce." Ace went on to say that a mere fifteen milliliters, around a tablespoon, was potentially fatal, though a lethal dose was generally around 3.4 ounces. "I've notified the model railroad folks. They're going to send out an e-mail and a text suggesting anyone who bought moonshine from your shop hold off on enjoying it until we've tested your inventory. Mrs. Gebhardt mentioned that there'd been a moonshine event in the hotel bar. We've told them not to serve your 'shine for the time being, either."

Knowing the effect Ace's plan could have on my livelihood, Marlon exhaled sharply and gave Ace a pointed look. "The stuff at the bar can't be tainted, can it? Nobody got sick the night of the mixer. We would've noticed."

"Methanol poisoning isn't instantaneous," Ace reiterated. "It takes several hours for the poison to process and the effects to be felt."

"Was anybody sick yesterday?" I asked. "If any of the 'shine served at the mixer had been bad, seems they would have been."

"Not that I know of," Ace said, "but I haven't had a chance to talk to all of the conventioneers yet."

"A bunch of the women came down to the shop after the mixer and bought jars of 'shine," I said. "They probably drank some of it since. Nobody's complained to me about it making them ill."

"That was my initial thought, too," Ace said. "That if the moonshine had been adulterated on a broad scale, more people would've gotten sick. But the doctors told me something that made me change my mind. Just because other people didn't get sick doesn't mean your moonshine didn't have methanol in it. The ER doctor told me that a higher amount of methanol is needed to kill someone when the person simultaneously ingests ethanol."

Marlon cocked his head, incredulous. "What are you saying? That one alcohol cancels the other out?"

"In a sense," Ace said. "The doctor said that ethanol counteracts the acidosis effect of the methanol. In fact, ethanol is used to treat methanol poisoning."

I sussed things out. "So, if someone was drinking bad moonshine but also good moonshine or another alcoholic drink, they'd be less likely to get sick?"

"Exactly," she said.

I remembered Bert drinking a beer at the mixer, before later enjoying a couple derailments made with my moonshine. If he'd been exposed to methanol that night, either at the mixer or from a jar Dana had purchased here at my shop, the ethanol from the beer might have kept him from getting sick then. Too bad he didn't have beer in his system later, when he was exposed to the methanol.

Ace went on. "Another option for treating methanol poisoning is via an injection of a drug called"—she consulted her notes—"fomepizole." She slid her tablet back into her tote bag and gave me a pointed look. "That foreshot you mentioned. If it was the source of the methanol, all of it would have ended up in a single jar, wouldn't it?"

"In theory," I said. "The bottling machine fills each jar successively."

Her pointed look became even sharper, her eyes narrowing. "Any chance you might have forgotten to get rid of the foreshot with one of your batches?"

The mere thought made me numb with shock. *Had something gone wrong in my processing? Had I forgotten to toss out the foreshot on a recent batch of wild blackberry moonshine? Had I killed Bert Gebhardt?*

Chapter Eight

"A in't no way!" Granddaddy hollered. "Hattie would never forget to toss out the foreshot!"

While I appreciated my grandfather coming to my defense, Ace couldn't take his word for it. Mine, either. Smoky watched from his high perch on the train platform as Ace rounded up multiple jars of my moonshine for testing at the police lab. She consulted the labels and selected one jar from each batch still in stock. She slipped them into her tote bag, said "I'll be in touch ASAP," and headed out the door.

As Ace left, a couple attempted to enter my shop.

"Sorry," I told them. "We're closing up for the night." *Or maybe forever.*

"But we've heard such good things about your moonshine." The woman pointed to my sign. "And your posted hours are noon to nine on weekdays." She consulted her phone. "It's only eight fifty."

I bit my lip, unsure what to say.

Luckily, Marlon came to my rescue. "There's been an unfortunate situation. Until it's taken care of, it might not be safe to come inside the shop."

His phrasing was perfect. It wasn't a lie, yet it didn't directly implicate my products. Maybe they'd assume a gas line had broken or a water main, or that a portal to hell had surfaced in my stockroom.

To save what little goodwill I could, I grabbed a couple of my promotional T-shirts, coasters, and jiggers, and handed them over. "I'm so sorry. Please take these things for now and, when you come back, I'll give you a free jar on the house."

The couple walked off, disappointed. I could only hope they'd return someday to claim that free jar, and that my shop would still be here when they did.

Seeing me lose a sale, Granddaddy huffed in indignation, shaking both his head and his cane. "This is outrageous! That detective's got no right to shut you down!"

Smoky circled around on the platform until he could jump down to the checkout counter. He stood next to the register and swished his tail, also indignant, though he probably didn't know why. Even so, I appreciated his support. "It'll only be for a short time, Granddaddy," I said, hoping my words were true. "Once they clear my 'shine, we'll open right back up."

Lest we have to make excuses to more customers, I locked the door, turned the sign in the window to closed, and extinguished the interior lights.

I pulled my cell phone from my pocket. "I suppose I better tell Nora what's going on." I only hoped she wouldn't jump ship. She was a good worker. I'd hate to lose her.

After I explained the situation, she said, "This is all so unbelievable!"

I'd have felt the same way if I wasn't smack-dab in the middle of it. "I don't know when the shop will open again," I said, "but for the time being I will continue to pay you even for the days the shop is closed. I don't want to lose you."

"Thanks, Hattie," she said. "I appreciate that."

When we completed the call, I counted out the cash in the till in only the dim light coming through the cracked stockroom door and prepared a deposit slip for the bank.

As I performed my end-of-workday duties, Granddaddy shared some horrifying stories with us. "Back during the Great Depression, men in hobo camps would use canned heat to make what they called jungle juice or sock wine because they'd strain it through their socks. Bunch of 'em got sick from it. In the early sixties, right around Christmas, a bunch of fellers died from methanol poisoning on Philadelphia's old skid row, too. They used Sterno to make what was called a pink lady or a squeeze."

He explained that the homemade beverage was made by straining Sterno heating gel through a cloth to separate the pink liquid methanol from the other ingredients. Water or soda was then added to the methanol to make a cheap and potent cocktail. The percentage of methanol in the Sterno was not normally high enough to cause death, just intoxication. A guy who ran a cigar store nearby knew the men bought Sterno from him to make the drinks. Unfortunately, over a brief period of time, he inadvertently sold those customers an industrial-strength product containing a much higher percentage of deadly methanol rather than the usual cans, which contained only a small amount.

"Some of the men were found dead in a boardinghouse," Granddaddy said. "Others were found in various locations nearby." He shook his head sadly. "With my father running moonshine and teaching me the business, those stories stuck with me. It's important to know what you're doing when you're making liquor."

Once I'd stashed the money in the safe, I wrangled Smoky into his carrier and set the alarm. Marlon walked us out to my van, which was parked behind my shop. After I slid Smoky into the vehicle and got my granddaddy and his scooter loaded, I turned to Marlon and whispered, "What if something went wrong when I made my moonshine? What if I killed Bert Gebhardt? What if someone else dies or gets sick before we figure this out?"

"*We?*" Marlon's face darkened. "It's best you stay out of this, Hattie. Anything you do could backfire on you, look like you're trying to cover something up or interfere. Leave the investigating to Ace. Hear me?"

"I hear you." Just because I heard him didn't mean I was going to follow his advice, though. I needed to clear my name, if possible, or at least try to figure out the truth, whatever it might be. I had to know what happened. I was careful when manufacturing my 'shine, sure, but as things had become more routine might I have slacked off inadvertently? I tried to recall the last time I'd been at the bottling company. The floor supervisor had come over to say hello, as usual. Could the interruption have thrown me off my game, made me forget to throw out the foreshot? I prayed that wasn't the case.

Marlon seemed to sense my insecurity. He reached out and put a comforting hand on my shoulder, giving it a little rub. "If something went wrong with your moonshine, Hattie, it would be an accident."

Knowing that I hadn't intended to kill anyone was little consolation if something I'd done—or didn't do—had nonetheless cost someone their life. I'd never be able to forgive myself. But what else could Marlon say? There really were no words for a situation like this. I'd just have to wait and see what the police lab results showed and take things from there.

"Oh, my gosh!" I cried, when a horrible realization hit me. "What if you end up having to arrest me?"

Marlon's great-grandfather had been the Hamilton County sheriff during the days of Prohibition a century before. He'd arrested my great-grandfather, who'd made a good living running bootleg hooch manufactured at the still that sat behind my cabin to this day. *How ironic would it be if a Landers arrested a Hayes once again for an alcohol-related offense?*

"I'm not going to arrest you, Hattie," Marlon assured me. "Nobody is."

I wished I could feel as certain as he sounded. I bade him goodbye, climbed into my van, and drove my grandfather back to his home.

As Granddaddy climbed onto his scooter to go inside, he wagged a finger at me and narrowed his eyes. "Don't you dare set up that train without me."

"I wouldn't dream of it, Granddaddy."

He wagged the finger a second time. "Don't you fret about what that detective said, neither. There's no chance your liquor was tainted." He snorted. "If your moonshine killed that man, I'll eat my hat."

I forced a smile. "Your Stetson would make a sorry supper, even with a side of cornbread and beans."

He beeped his horn in goodbye and drove through the automatic doors of the retirement home.

I continued on, driving up the winding mountain road to the cabin. Fireflies flitted about outside, lighting up for a second or two before going dark again, as if trying to hide their secrets. Maybe Marlon was right. If I insinuated myself in the investigation, maybe I'd look like I was trying to hide secrets, too, to divert suspicion away from myself. Then again, maybe I'd find evidence to exonerate me and my moonshine.

Inside, I released Smoky from his carrier. He aimed directly for his food bowl, casting me an irritated look on finding it empty. He promptly placed his dinner order. *Meow.* I filled his bowl with dry kibble and added a heaping spoonful of wet food on the side. My pet dealt with, I poured myself a shot of my wild blackberry moonshine. I'd fixed drinks from this jar many times before, so I knew the batch I had at the cabin was unadulterated. I tossed back the shot and gave it a minute or two to settle my nerves and my mind.

I plopped down in one of the wooden chairs at the kitchen table to try to think things through. The big question was, if methanol ended up in my moonshine, how did it get there? Though methanol contamination was all too common with homemade stills operated by folks with little to no training, I used professionally manufactured equipment and had faithfully followed all of the maintenance instructions. Even so, no piece of machinery was infallible. Had the thermometer or heating element malfunctioned so that the methanol didn't boil off as it should? If the police found methanol in one of the jars from my shop, I'd have to have my equipment thoroughly inspected and repaired or replaced. I'd likely face a wrongful death lawsuit, too. The thought made it feel as if someone had wrapped invisible hands around my throat and was slowly choking me.

The sensation of being choked made another thought occur to me. Although Bert's death was suspicious, we'd assumed that it was accidental. But what if it wasn't? What if someone had intentionally killed the man by adding methanol to my 'shine after Dana bought the jar at my shop?

I grabbed my phone and pulled up the pic Ace had sent me, enlarging it on the screen to take a close look at the suspected jar of 'shine. As I stared at the photo, I realized the color of the moonshine appeared violet rather than its usual plum purple. *It's off, isn't it?* Just to be sure, I grabbed the bottle of blackberry 'shine I had on hand and held it up next to the phone's screen. *Yep, definitely off.*

The discovery was good news for me. It meant that if the jar had methanol in it, the poison wasn't there when it was bottled. Of course, Ace wouldn't be convinced until the other jars had been tested, but the finding brought me some relief. Though I'd pondered the possibility I'd messed up, I'd known in my core that I hadn't. I could make moonshine in my sleep. I'd gone through the process hundreds of times and it was second nature to me. On the other hand, Bert seemed to have no end of people he'd upset or angered who might want to get even, to hurt him, or worse.

Patrick Jaffe was the first person who came to mind. Heck, he and Bert had been at each other's throats only moments before Bert lost consciousness. There seemed to be no love lost between Bert and Stuart Speer, either. He clearly hadn't appreciated Bert questioning his judging capabilities or his authority. Ronnie Wallingford had a beef with Bert, too. Bert had tried to gouge him with the exorbitant price for the caboose Ronnie had longed for over several decades. Martha, the hotel housekeeper, surely wasn't fond of the Bert, either. He'd been a royal jerk to her. Of course, a victim's spouse was always a likely suspect, too.

Often, when a person was murdered, the killer was some-one close to them. Though he'd expressed some apprecia-tion for his wife when she'd given him the aspirin, Bert didn't treat Dana well overall. She couldn't be ruled out. Even so, she'd seemed to have found a way to tolerate him, as if she'd learned not to take his bad temper too seriously. The fact that she'd become sick herself also pointed away from her. Even if she wanted to get rid of her husband, would she risk poisoning herself, too?

It seemed whoever had killed Bert would know that Dana might drink the 'shine, too. Maybe they figured Dana was more likely to drink in moderation so that she wouldn't be severely or fatally harmed. I'd hate to think someone could have been so callous as to have had no regard for Dana at all if Bert was their real target.

I went to bed, mentally exhausted and weighted with worry, my only consolation the warm body of my cat as he curled up against me. I scratched his cheek. "What would I do without you, boy?"

Smoky lifted his head and looked at me as if to say *You'd be a train wreck.*

I slept horribly and woke feeling groggy Thursday morn-ing. It didn't help that it was gray outside, a cloudy, omi-nous day, the sunshine at bay. In a rare act of solidarity, Smoky had lain next to me all night, seeming to sense I needed his comfort. But now I needed something else—human sounding boards.

I texted Kiki. As a freelance artist, she set her own schedule and had quite a bit of flexibility. I could really use my friend right now. I could also really use some good cof-fee to clear the fog from my brain. She looped our other

BFF Kate Pardue into the text. Kate had recently given birth to an adorable baby boy and, far as I knew, hadn't left her house since. With a newborn at home, she wasn't getting much sleep and could surely use some good coffee, too, as well as a reason to get out and see her friends. We arranged to meet up at a coffeehouse in the riverfront area, which was centrally located for all of us. It also just happened to be the shop where Stuart Speer had bought his coffee yesterday. I'd recognized the shop's logo on his cup.

I gave Smoky a kiss on the head and headed to the door. He trotted along with me, probably expecting me to put him in his carrier and take him to work with me. When I didn't put him in the plastic crate, he looked up at me and asked *Mew-mew?* I was fairly certain it was cat talk for *Why aren't you taking me with you?* "Sorry, boy," I said. "The police closed the shop. You and I are unemployed for the time being." Maybe he'd find a spider to chase to occupy his time. There were plenty of them out here in the woods.

I locked the door and walked out to my van. Dark clouds hung over Chattanooga as I drove down the foothills and into the city, an errant drop or two of rain splatting on my windshield, the blustery wind pushing on the side of my van as if wanting to sweep me off the road. *Mother Nature is in a foul mood today.* Good thing I kept an umbrella tucked under my seat.

Street parking could be difficult to come by on Market Street, so I parked in the small lot behind my shop. Kiki had evidently had the same idea, as her bright red Mini Cooper sat behind the Moonshine Shack, too. I cut through my closed store and came out the front, walking down to the coffee place. I arrived at 9:30 to find Kiki and Kate already seated, with mugs of steaming coffee sitting on the table in front of them. Kiki wore a newsboy cap along with knee pants and a vest over a loose white blouse. She'd recently painted scenery for a local theater production of *Newsies*, and my guess was she'd adopted the look after seeing the show. Kate's rail-straight blond hair was pulled back in a messy ponytail. She wore yoga pants, a wrinkled T-shirt, and no makeup, which was unusual for her. With a new baby to care for, she probably didn't have the time or energy to fix herself up. It appeared new parenthood was simply about survival. Kate's son, Dalton, reclined in his stroller next to the table, shadow-boxing the air in that uncoordinated way babies do when they haven't quite figured out yet how their limbs and digits work. Unlike his mother, he'd clearly been well cleaned up and groomed. He smelled baby fresh, and what little hair he had was neatly combed back against his scalp.

I bent over him. "Hey, Dalton," I cooed. "How's my precious little puddin' today?"

He hadn't quite learned how to smile, but he looked up at me and burped, which made his lips curl up. *Close enough. I'll take it.*

After I greeted my friends, I went over to the counter to get in line. Ahead of me was a man with apricot hair and a bright blue blazer. Though I couldn't see his face, I felt certain it must be Stuart Speer.

After he placed his order with the barista, I watched her fix his drink. He'd ordered a simple black coffee, so it took little effort on her part. He paid for his drink and turned around with the cup in his hand, giving me a good look at him. Yep, as I'd suspected, it was Stuart Speer. To my surprise, he didn't go to the condiment counter to get a stir stick and raw sugar like he'd been carrying along with his cup yesterday. *Don't people usually drink their coffee the same way most days?* Seemed like everyone had their "usual." I tended to get the same drink over and over, switching things up only when a seasonal variety was available. I was a sucker for the pumpkin spice and gingerbread lattes that were offered for a limited time only each winter.

As he left, the line moved forward. I ordered a coffee and a blueberry muffin at the counter, carried them back to the table, and plopped down in a chair.

"So," Kiki said, reaching out to pinch off a bite of my muffin, "what's this big problem you texted about?"

"Oh, nothing much," I said. "Just a matter of life and death."

Chapter Nine

Without further preamble, I said, "The Chattanooga Police Department shut down my shop."

"Shut you down?" Kate said. "Why?"

"One of the men from the model train convention died yesterday from methanol poisoning. A guy named Bert Gebhardt."

"I don't understand." Kiki cocked her head, nearly losing her jaunty newsboy hat in the process. "What does that have to do with you?"

"Methanol is a byproduct of the distillation process," I explained. "The guy had drunk half a jar of my 'shine."

"Oooooh." Kate grimaced. "That's bad."

I nodded as I tore a bite from my muffin and popped it into my mouth. *Yum.*

Kiki's face turned thoughtful. "But you're so scrupulous with your process. How could your moonshine have been contaminated?"

I chewed and swallowed as I raised my palms. "I have no idea. I know how careful I am. I just can't believe any of my products were contaminated." I took a sip of my coffee. "I think someone might have slipped the methanol into the jar of 'shine." I told my friends about the photo, how the color of the 'shine looked off to me. "With any luck, the detective will catch someone with a bottle of methanol and solve the case quickly."

From his seat in his stroller, Dalton emitted a wet *urp* sound. Kate whipped out a package of organic baby wipes to clean the goo from Dalton's chin.

"Ick." Kiki cringed. "Babies are disgusting."

"Maybe," Kate said, taking Kiki's comment in stride. "But those are pretty strong words coming from someone who cleans up hairballs on a regular basis."

It was true. Kiki's cats, Kahlo and van Gogh, coughed up a constant supply of wet, half-digested fur. Kiki doffed her cap. "Touché."

Returning to the topic of poison, Kate said, "We baby-proofed the house before Dalton was born. I went through all of our cleaning products to make sure we only had non-toxic ones on hand. It's shocking how many cleaning products and household items contain petroleum, formaldehyde, and other toxins. I got rid of my nail polish remover and the plug-in air fresheners. We replaced our polyblend bedding with one hundred percent cotton sheets. I got rid of the fuel for our camping lantern and our windshield wiper fluid and antifreeze, too. They contained methanol."

"Antifreeze contains methanol?" My mind went back to the presentation Granddaddy and I had listened in on, the one about preserving natural foliage in model railroads. The instructor had noted that antifreeze could be used to keep the foliage looking fresh.

Kate nodded. "Antifreeze is often a bright color, yellow or blue or pink like juice or punch, and it's got some other chemical in it that makes it taste sweet, too. That's why it's such a hazard for kids and pets."

I remembered the lecturer on Monday also mentioning that antifreeze came in a variety of colors. To supplement what the lecturer and Kate had noted, I used my cell phone to run a quick Internet search while taking more bites of my muffin. I learned that methanol was used both to thin paint and to clean painting equipment, and was a common primer fuel for certain types of lamps and heaters. During winter months, it was used to prevent gas lines from freezing in vehicles and heavy equipment, and it was a common additive in fuel treatment products. While methanol had myriad industrial uses, the links indicated that various common household products contained methanol, too. At the top of the list was antifreeze, as Kate had mentioned. Carburetor cleaner. Fuels used to warm food. Windshield washer fluid contained an extremely high percentage of methanol, generally ranging from thirty to fifty percent.

If something had been mixed with the blackberry moonshine, it would explain the off-color appearance of the 'shine in the jar in Bert's toolbox. He'd had the jar sitting right next to his display. Could he have accidentally poisoned himself? Maybe spilled some cleaner into the jar of 'shine while the lid was off?

I remembered his bottles of glass cleaners had been full, Bert having used only a small amount of the fluid from one bottle to clean the plexiglass and a small amount from the other to clean his tracks. That meant that neither he nor Dana had poured cleaner from the bottles into the jar, whether intentionally or accidentally, didn't it? The realization brought me worry, in that it looked more likely that my moonshine was adulterated, but it also brought me some relief. Dana had been kind to me, said nice things about my moonshine. I was glad she seemed to be an unlikely suspect. Besides, I didn't even know if Bert's glass cleaners contained methanol. I hadn't paid attention to the brand names on the bottles. I hadn't realized the information would be important at the time.

Unfortunately, if the source of the methanol was, in fact, glass cleaner, all of the other contestants and exhibitors could be suspects. After all, they were likely to have glass cleaner in their possession, too. That included Patrick Jaffe and Ronnie Wallingford. Jaffe had already said that Bert had been a thorn in his side for years. Bert would continue to be a thorn for years to come—*unless Jaffe did something about him.* Maybe he'd finally had enough of Bert trying to sabotage his chances of winning the contests with his measuring tape and anonymous e-mails. Even though Ronnie Wallingford wasn't competing against Bert, he'd put up a display, too. Surely, he'd have glass cleaner. Maybe he'd realized that if he killed Bert, he'd have a better chance of negotiating with Dana regarding his proposed purchase of the collector's caboose. He sure had seemed intent on taking it home with him. He'd even muttered that he'd get the caboose *one way or another.*

As a hotel housekeeper, Martha had easy access to glass cleaner, as well. In fact, she'd pretended to shoot Bert with the spray bottle of cleaner Monday morning when I'd come across the two of them in the hotel hallway. Maybe she'd noticed that the model railroaders used glass cleaner, too, and she figured she could get away with poisoning Bert with a common substance. She'd had access to the Gebhardts' hotel room. She could have easily added glass cleaner to his moonshine while cleaning their room. But would Martha murder a man simply because he'd berated her and complained to her boss? It seemed like overkill, especially when he'd be leaving by the end of the week and she wouldn't have to see him again. I'd seen her at the train convention, though. She'd had to pay the entry fee to come inside. Had she come to the convention to spy on Bert, make a plan to do away with him? Given that the hobby seemed to appeal primarily to men, it seemed doubtful she was a model railroad fan, but I could be wrong about that. After all, I'd enjoyed looking over the displays, and I was a woman.

Stuart Speer couldn't be ruled out, either. He clearly hadn't appreciated Bert questioning his expertise in model railroading and his authority as a judge. He could have borrowed or stolen someone's bottle of glass cleaner and used it to poison Bert.

There was also the possibility that I was getting way ahead of myself here. My moonshine hadn't yet been ruled out as the source of the contamination, and it was only supposition on my part that something added to my 'shine was to blame. Even so, I trusted myself and my products. I knew the dangers of bad 'shine. My grandfather had drilled it into me when he'd taught me how to make 'shine at the old still behind the cabin. He'd warned that bad moonshine had killed people or turned them blind. I remembered Bert blinking, as if he couldn't see straight. Had he been suffering vision problems at the time but been too influenced by the methanol to realize what was happening?

After I shared my thoughts about the glass cleaner with my friends, Kate sighed, weary. "I swear, it feels like the whole world is a danger. It's exhausting trying to deal with it all."

I reached across the table and gave her hand a squeeze.

"The fact that you're worrying so much means you're a good mother."

She smiled. "That's the best compliment I've ever received."

Kiki said, "It's the only compliment we can offer you right now. Your hair's a mess and your clothes look like you slept in them." She gestured at Kate's wrinkled outfit and sloppy hair. "Of course, those are also signs of a good mom. You've clearly put Dalton's needs ahead of your own."

"I did sleep in these clothes," Kate said. "Is it that obvious?"

"Oh, honey," Kiki said, reaching over to pat Kate's shoulder. "Yes. Let's book a spa day soon. My treat. You need some *you* time. That way, you'll look refreshed and beautiful when you win mother of the year." Returning to the previous topic, Kiki said, "But Kate's not wrong about poisonous products being common. Some of my art supplies are toxic. There's methanol in lacquers and varnish. If I'm not mistaken, it's used in products to remove paint and shellac, too. I have to make sure to use them only in well-ventilated areas. I think there's also methanol in the fuel Max puts in his welding torch." Kiki's boyfriend, Max, was a successful metal sculptor who could turn scraps of steel into intriguing works of art.

"Sheesh," I said. "Seems like methanol is everywhere." Kate was right. The world was a dangerous place. I mulled over her statement about antifreeze, how it tasted sweet. "I wonder if someone put antifreeze in the moonshine Bert Gebhardt drank. If antifreeze tastes sweet, Bert might not have noticed. The taste would have been masked by the flavor of the 'shine." It seemed that most of the other sources of methanol would have caused the moonshine to have an obvious foul taste.

Kiki's brows rose. "You think his death might not be an accident? You think someone would want to kill the guy on purpose?"

I hated to speak ill of the dead, *but* . . . "Bert was a jerk. I spent maybe three hours total with the guy, and in that time I saw him berate a hotel housekeeper, insult his wife, try to price gouge another model railroader who wanted to buy a caboose from him, and get into a shouting match with one of his competitors." I told them how he'd also questioned one of the judge's scores in earlier contests. "Sounded like he made a habit of appealing when he lost."

"He was a bad sport," Kiki said.

"The worst," I agreed. "Who would've thought model train buffs would be so hostile?"

Kiki raised her coffee cup. "If he was killed intentionally, it's probably the wife who did it."

"I'd wondered about Dana, too," I said. "You think she should be the prime suspect?"

Kate looked from Kiki to me and bobbed her head in agreement. "When a married person is murdered, it's often the spouse."

Kiki elaborated. "The news is always running some story or another about a man who killed his wife, usually so he can run off into the sunset with a girlfriend. It's, like, just get a divorce, dude. No need to end anyone's life."

It wasn't unheard of for a wife to become violent, especially if her husband had done her wrong. "But Dana drank some of the moonshine, too," I pointed out. "She even had a reaction. A headache. Once the doctors realized it was methanol that killed Bert, they tested her and gave her treatment."

"None of that proves she's innocent," Kiki said. "She

could have drunk a small amount herself to throw law enforcement off her trail."

Kiki's hypothesis was certainly possible, but it would have required some forethought. Could the woman knitting in her old-fashioned bonnet be a criminal mastermind? "Dana was kind to me and, even though her husband was obnoxious, I got the impression she'd long since resigned herself to putting up with him. She seemed to just ignore the rude things he said."

Kiki fingered her napkin. "Even with a coping strategy, that stuff has to get old."

"Yeah," Kate concurred. "Marriage isn't always a happily-ever-after fairy tale, but it's not supposed to be miserable. Your spouse is supposed to be your partner and supporter, not a cross to bear."

"True." I finished my muffin and pointed out that we'd come full circle in our discussion. "But then we're back to what Kiki said. If Dana decided that, after all these years, she'd finally had enough, why not just file for divorce?"

Kiki said, "Maybe her religion frowns on divorce?"

"Religions frown on killing, too," Kate said. "*Thou shalt not kill*, remember?"

Kiki raised a finger to emphasize her point. "But if she made it look like an accident, or like someone else was to blame, she wouldn't have to worry about becoming a pariah."

I slugged back a big gulp of coffee in the hopes the caffeine would give me clarity. It didn't, at least not instantly. "What am I going to do if I have to close my shop? I've dreamed of running a moonshine store for years." Not only would Bert Gebhardt be dead but my dreams would be, too.

Kate reached over and took one of my hands in hers. "If

you can't do moonshine," she said, "maybe you can pursue a new dream."

"Like what?" I asked. Moonshine was all I knew. I was a one-trick pony.

"What about opening a cat café?" she said. "They're really popular right now."

As much as I'd love to rescue cats, I knew nothing about running a commercial kitchen. I'd have to hire a cook and a staff, order ingredients, develop a menu. It sounded overwhelming. Expensive, too. "I'm not sure that's a feasible option. All of my capital is tied up in the Moonshine Shack. The only thing I'd have to offer for collateral is the cabin and it's not worth much. I wouldn't qualify for a loan."

Kate angled her head to indicate her baby. "A little one like this makes everything else seem unimportant."

"Whoa." I raised my palms. "I'm nowhere ready for a baby. I'm not even ready to think about marriage. Marlon and I haven't even put a label on our relationship yet."

Kiki took a different tack, coming up with concrete options that could help in the near term. "If your shop and 'shine get tainted by scandal, you can reinvent yourself under a new name. Brands do it all the time."

"You've got a point." In fact, rebranding had been covered in one of my marketing classes in college. I recalled the professor giving several examples. When cigarettes became synonymous with lung cancer, a well-known tobacco company changed its name. An airline rebranded after a horrific plane crash. Cable television and telecommunications companies were constantly changing their names, too. I supposed I could do the same.

Kiki said, "If your Firefly brand gets bad press, reinvent yourself as Lightning Bug. Better yet, Bumble Bee." She raised her hands as if reading words on a marquee. "Drink Bumble Bee Moonshine for the best buzz around."

I frowned. Although I knew intoxication was a side effect of my products, I certainly didn't advocate using alcohol excessively. Still, Kiki had a point. "Maybe I could rename the Moonshine Shack the Hooch Hut or the 'Shine Shanty." I sighed. "But I've already spent a fortune on a domain name, T-shirts, labels, and my van. Let's all hope it doesn't come to that." I took another sip of my coffee, and the caffeine and my determination finally kicked in. "Of course, there is another option we haven't discussed."

"What's this other option?" Kate asked.

I leaned forward over the table. "I don't wait for the lab and the police to sort things out. I figure out for myself who killed Bert Gebhardt."

Chapter Ten

Investigate the mystery yourself?" Kiki raised her coffee cup in salute. "Now you're talking."

Kate bit her lip. "What would Marlon think of you snooping around?"

"He wouldn't like it," I said. "He's already warned me off."

Kiki snickered. "If any man thinks he can tell Hattie Hayes what to do, he's sorely mistaken."

"Exactly," I said. I only hoped my stubbornness wouldn't make Marlon rethink whether he wanted to continue dating me. I'd been having fun with him and was hoping to see where our relationship would take us, but I couldn't change who I was, for him or anyone. "Finish your drinks, ladies. We've got a murder to solve." I hoped we could do it quickly. Most of the suspects were from out of town and would be leaving once the convention wrapped up. The final event would be the awards ceremony at 4:00 p.m. Saturday afternoon.

Kate stuck out her tongue and raised her cup. "I'm not sure I can finish this coffee. It's decaf with no sugar."

"Ew," Kiki said. "Why didn't you get your usual caramel macchiato?"

She angled her head to indicate her baby again. "I'm breastfeeding. I didn't want to fill my little boy with all that caffeine and sugar." She glanced longingly over at the condiment station. "You think half a packet of sugar would be okay?"

"He'll be fine," Kiki said. "The American diet is eighty-three percent sugar. He might as well get used to it."

While I doubted Kiki's statistics, I agreed that a little sugar on occasion wasn't likely to harm the baby. I stood and addressed Kate. "I'll get the sugar for you while you round up your things." Besides the stroller, Kate had her purse, a diaper bag, and some kind of harness contraption, not to mention bottles, blankets, burp cloths, and toys. Amazing how someone so little required so much equipment.

I walked over to the condiment stand to snatch a sugar packet. With it being a fairly busy morning, the counter hadn't been wiped in a while. A couple of crumpled sugar packets lay next to the trash hole, left there by someone who either had bad aim or was too lazy to ensure the used packets fell into the bin below. The divided plastic sugar bin had white packets of refined sugar, pink packets of alternative sweetener, and brown packets of the raw sugar Stuart Speer seemed to prefer. As I grabbed one of the white packets for Kate, along with a wooden stir stick, my eyes spotted a few granules of the raw sugar on the countertop. The grains were coarse and a cloudy brownish-yellow in color, like minuscule diamonds of questionable clarity, yet they sparkled when the light hit them just right.

Cheese and grits! Could the sparkling sand I'd seen on Bert Gebhardt's track yesterday not have been sand at all? Could it have been raw sugar? And if it was, who had put it there and why?

My mind immediately went to the man I'd just seen here. Stuart Speer. After all, I'd seen him carry packets of raw sugar into the convention center. But might he have picked them up for another judge, much as I was retrieving sugar for my friend now?

I recalled Patrick Jaffe fishing the packets of raw sugar and the stir stick from the trash can in the convention center shortly after Speer had tossed them out. Could Jaffe have spotted Speer with the packets and realized the sugar would be an easy and discreet way to sabotage Bert's display?

What about Martha, the housekeeper? She'd have reason to want to get back at Bert, and she'd walked off with Speer's coffee cup after he'd left it on the table at the empty vendor booth. Had she seen some sugar crystals on the plastic lid and realized she could get revenge on Bert by flinging them onto his display? This scenario seemed far less likely, but not entirely impossible. Would a few granules of sugar even be enough to derail a model train? It could be possible. After all, a small pebble could jam the wheels of a roller skate and send the skater skidding palms down across the asphalt. I'd learned that fact the hard way back in junior high.

I grabbed three packets of raw sugar and stuck them in my pocket. When I returned to the table, I handed Kate the white refined sugar packet and shared my thoughts with her and Kiki. "I'm thinking one of them might have thrown sugar on Bert's tracks to get revenge on him."

The question then was, did they stop there or did they

take things further and slip poison into his moonshine? Because Stuart Speer was allowed into the convention center before the conventioneers each morning, he would have had the easiest access to Bert's booth. But would he have had access to Bert's jar of moonshine? And would someone who simply wanted to ruin Bert's chances of winning the competition feel the need to take his life, too?

I'd seen the jar in Bert's toolbox yesterday morning, and I knew Bert carried his toolbox with him to and from the convention center rather than leaving it at his booth. That meant Speer would have had to slip the methanol into Bert's jar of moonshine either right under Bert's and Dana's noses, which seemed unlikely, or that he'd done it when they'd been away from their booth. Same for Patrick Jaffe and Ronnie Wallingford. The jar of blackberry 'shine would have been in Bert's hotel room outside of convention hours. As a hotel housekeeper, Martha would have had access to his room and could have poured something into his jar without fear of being spotted.

Ready to find some answers, Kate, Kiki, and I tossed back what remained of our coffee and stepped outside.

"Let's take my minivan," Kate said. "Otherwise, I'll have to move Dalton's car seat."

Kiki leaped off the curb. "I call shotgun!"

We loaded into Kate's car, which she and Parker had bought only a month before she'd given birth. It still had the new-car smell.

Kiki buckled herself into the passenger seat and bounced a little before settling in. "This minivan has zero sex appeal, but at least it's really comfortable."

Kate said, "Sex appeal is the least of my concerns right now."

I sat next to Dalton, who faced backward in his seat. I

put my hands over my face to cover it, then removed them and called, "Peekaboo!" He just stared at me like I was nuts.

Kate caught my eye in the rearview mirror. "He's too young to have a concept of object permanence yet."

"Object permanence?" I repeated. "Someone's been reading their mommy manuals." I settled for putting my index finger in Dalton's tiny fist, letting him wrap his itty-bitty fingers around it, and bouncing our hands up and down.

We parked in the convention center lot, where Kate returned Dalton to his stroller. We made our way past the cars and rental trucks, aiming for the entrance. When a single drop of rain came down on the hood of the stroller, Kate stopped, pulled a clear nylon cover from the basket underneath, and situated it over the top to keep her baby protected from the elements.

Kiki bent over and tapped on the plastic. "You okay in there, bubble boy?"

Kate pointed to the sides. "It's got air vents. See?"

"In that case," Kiki said, "can I climb in there and ride with him? I want to stay comfy and dry, too."

"No," Kate said. "But you can borrow this." She whipped a collapsing umbrella from her diaper bag and held it out to our friend.

"Wow," Kiki said. "You really have become a mom. I bet you've got tissues and gum and a little coin purse full of change, too."

"Of course," Kate said. "I'm prepared for every emergency."

I glanced up at the sky. "I didn't realize we were in for rain until I left the cabin this morning." With no outdoor activities planned for days, I hadn't had a need to consult the weather app on my phone or watch the weather report on the television news.

Kate, who'd been home with her son and probably had the TV on all day for company said, "There was a small hurricane earlier in the week, a category one. There was some talk on the news about it having the potential to escalate into a bigger storm, but it never did. It skirted the East Coast and fizzled out."

Even when large hurricanes hit the East Coast, which was becoming more and more common, by the time the effects traveled across the coastal states and over the Appalachian Mountains, all that was normally left by the time the storm reached Chattanooga was a little wind and some rain. But I'd seen reports in the past and knew how devastating the storms could be closer to the coast. I remembered when Hurricanes Fran and Floyd had hit in the mid and late 1990s. I'd been just a kid, and the reports of the flooding and fatalities had given me nightmares. While we felt only minor effects here in Chattanooga weatherwise, the hurricanes tended to have a greater impact on vacation plans, as many Tennesseans ventured to the beaches for summer vacations. I opened my umbrella, too, and we continued on our way.

The convention center doors had just been opened when we stepped up to them. We stashed our umbrellas underneath Dalton's stroller, and I bought entry tickets for Kiki and Kate. In light of the fact that they were here to help me protect my business, I figured I could claim the cost as a business deduction. Being under the age of ten, Dalton was allowed in free of charge.

Kiki glanced around. "Where to first?"

"I need something to collect the granules from Bert's tracks." *What can I use?* A strip of tape would be best, but I didn't have a roll on me. *Baby diapers have sticky tabs to hold them on, don't they?* I turned to Kate. "Can I borrow a diaper?"

She looked befuddled but said, "Okay" and pulled one from her diaper bag for me.

When I checked the tabs, they weren't the kind with sticky tapes. They were more similar to Velcro closures. I supposed I shouldn't be surprised. Kate had bought the cushiest, most environmentally friendly diapers on the market. "This won't work. I need something sticky."

I handed the diaper back to her and scanned the area. *Aha!* I hustled over to the table that sold the rolls of tape that resembled roadways. The cheapest roll was $12.99. Though I hated to pay so much when I needed only a couple of inches of tape and had rolls back at my shop down the street, there was no sense in wasting my friends' time or my own. *Should've planned ahead, Hattie.*

While I purchased the tape, Kiki looked over the wares on the adjacent table. "Look." She held up a small plastic bottle. "Paint that looks like water when it dries. First time I've seen that." No doubt the paint was the same used by many of the contestants to create lakes, rivers, and ponds in their model train exhibits. She was intrigued by the miniature foliage pieces, too. She picked up some of the liquid products, like the smoke fluid, and read over the contents. *Smart.* She was looking to see if any contained methanol. When Kate realized what Kiki was doing, she joined in. She held up a bottle of something called weathering mix, that was evidently used on wood and other materials to make them appear old. The bottle said it was alcohol based, but when I examined the ingredient list I saw only isopropyl alcohol, otherwise known as rubbing alcohol. No methanol. I shook my head.

Tape in hand, I led the charge to Bert Gebhardt's booth. Besides the fact that I wanted to inspect the loose granules on the track, it seemed a logical place to start looking for evidence relating to the adulteration of my moonshine. If Bert's jar of moonshine had been tainted by Speer, Wallingford, or Jaffe, it had likely happened at this booth. It was also the place where Bert had keeled over. Once we'd gathered what evidence we could there, we'd work our way outward.

As we turned down row B, I faltered in my step. Dana sat at booth B5 ahead. I'd expected the display to be unattended today, maybe even covered with a drape. *Shouldn't the woman be in her hotel room mourning her husband?* Then again, maybe she was in shock. Or maybe she wanted to be among people. It would be hard to be alone after losing your spouse.

A hand-lettered sign had been taped to the easel with the enlarged Champagne Photo displayed on it. The sign read: EVERYTHING FOR SALE. MAKE AN OFFER. I'd hoped to get a closer look at the sparkling granules on Bert's tracks, to compare them to the raw sugar from the coffee shop, but it would be much harder to do that with Dana at the booth. I couldn't very well share my suspicions with her without solid proof. I didn't like being wrongfully accused of selling adulterated moonshine, and I certainly didn't want to wrongfully accuse someone else of sabotaging Bert's model train display. I also didn't want to be accused in return of trying to deflect attention away from my purportedly poisonous moonshine by faking a scandal.

I slowed and eased up to the booth, unsure what kind of reception I might get. After all, Dana likely considered me culpable for the death of her husband. Bert's toolbox sat open under the table, presumably so that potential buyers could look through his items. Though the two bottles of blue glass cleaner remained, the jar of blackberry moonshine was gone, of course, leaving an empty space between them. After the hospital reported to the police that methanol poisoning was the cause of Bert's death, Ace must have come here to round up the jar of blackberry moonshine, so the police lab could test it.

I ran my eyes over the other jars, tubes, and bottles, searching for antifreeze. I saw none. Bert's bottle of hand sanitizer sat at the end of the toolbox. He'd kept it in easy reach. He hadn't only been a neatnik. He'd also been a bit of a germophobe.

When Dana looked up and spotted me and my friends approaching, she stood from her seat. Though she didn't smile, she didn't scream at me, either. Her eyes bore dark circles under them, telling me she'd had trouble sleeping last night, too. It was no wonder, of course. I'd been unable to sleep on the chance that I might be liable for a wrongful death and lose my business. While I only stood to lose my livelihood, her husband had actually lost his life, and she'd actually lost the man she'd been married to for decades. No matter what I was going through, it was so much worse for her.

"Hello, Hattie," she said softly.

"I heard about Bert." I bit my lip. "I am so sorry, Dana."

She reached out and took my hands in hers. "I know you must feel terribly guilty, hon. But I want you to know that I don't hold anything against you personally. Accidents happen."

I felt myself stiffen at the accusation, but I wasn't about to argue the point, at least not until we had the lab results back and knew for certain whether my moonshine was to blame. Besides, I was lucky she was being civil to me. I wasn't sure I could be so forgiving if someone had killed my husband, even if it was unintentional.

I introduced her to Kiki, Kate, and Dalton, who blinked up at her.

Dana smiled down at Dalton in his stroller. "Aww! He's a cutie. Your first?" she asked Kate.

"Yes," Kate said. "The first of what I hope will be many."

"Bert and I have two sons," Dana said. "They've got five kids between them. The youngest is six months. Such a cutie, too." She pulled up photos on her phone and showed us a dozen pictures of her sons, their wives, and her grandchildren. Dana was in a few of the photos, but Bert wasn't in any of them. I supposed that meant he could have been the person behind the camera, but it could have meant he hadn't attended the family functions, that instead he'd been at home, working on his model trains, obsessing over every detail.

I pointed to the sign she'd made. "You're selling everything off?"

"I am," she said wistfully. "Doesn't seem any point in hanging on to it. It'll just remind me of Bert's death."

With her having multiple grandchildren, it seemed surprising she wouldn't keep the model train equipment for them to play with. You'd think a man would enjoy sharing his love of trains with his boys, and that they might want to pass the hobby on to their kids, as well. "Your sons won't want the trains? For themselves or their kids?"

She shook her head. "None of them was ever interested in the hobby."

Huh. What kid isn't fascinated by model trains?

Ronnie Wallingford wandered up. He gave me and my friends a nod in greeting, and expressed his condolences to Dana. "Sorry to hear Bert didn't make it."

The news must have spread like wildfire through their close-knit group.

"Thanks, Ronnie," Dana said.

He put his hands in his pockets and rocked back on his heels. "I didn't think you'd be here today."

"I didn't, either," she said. "But I just couldn't stay alone in that hotel room another second. It was too quiet, too empty. Besides, I couldn't very well leave all of Bert's train equipment sitting here unattended. I've only got a short time to do something about all of this stuff before I need to head back home."

He eyed Dana's sign. "You're getting rid of the whole kit and caboodle?"

"There's no point in hanging on to Bert's things," she said. "They'll only make me sad. Besides, I don't know how to take care of any of it and we've got an entire basement full of train things back home. I'd be happier knowing someone is enjoying the models. Bert would be, too."

Would he? Earlier, Bert seemed intent on keeping Ronnie from enjoying the caboose he'd wanted so badly.

Ronnie made a face that said he wasn't convinced, either. He pointed through the plexiglass to Bert's display. "Are you going to sell off his Last Spike display, too?"

"Might as well," Dana said. "I'm curious to see how it will fare in the contest. Bert worked so hard on it. He was hoping for an award in the Photo Match category and an overall first prize."

"Oooh." Ronnie sucked air through his teeth. "You must not have heard."

"Heard what?" Dana asked.

"I hate to be the bearer of bad news," he said, "but his train jumped the track during the judging."

Chapter Eleven

W hat?!" Her eyes flashed in alarm. "Are you saying his trains derailed?"

"Just the Jupiter. Looked like some of the sand came loose and gummed up the track."

She turned to the display, deep lines forming between her knitted brows. "How could that be? He knew working with sand was a risk, so he made sure it was glued down tight. He sprayed it with some type of sealant coat, too, to help keep it in place. He kept his tracks immaculate. He cleaned everything thoroughly after he set up the display on Monday." She turned to me. "You were here. You saw him."

I nodded. I remembered Bert wiping down the plexiglass and the tracks, using a tiny handheld vacuum to suck up the loose grains of sand. The man had been fastidious about his exhibit.

Ronnie shrugged. "Don't know what to tell you. A

derailment can be caused by a broken track, or sometimes the wheels aren't running right for one reason or another. Could be operational error, too, going too fast. Far as we could all tell, though, the chief judge was light on the controls, didn't move it too fast or nothin'. Everyone agreed it was a shame. It's a cool model." He gestured at Bert's display case of trains for sale. "My offer still stands on that caboose, by the way. I'll give you two hundred and fifty dollars for it."

Dana turned to look at the caboose and exhaled a long, slow breath. "You know what?" she said, turning back to Ronnie. "You can just have it."

Ronnie gaped. "For nothing? Are you serious?"

She pulled a set of keys from her pocket, unlocked the case, and removed the packaged caboose, holding it out to Ronnie. "It's yours. Take it."

Ronnie took the caboose from her and looked down on it before lifting his face. Worry lines around his eyes and lips told me he was conflicted. "I wanted this caboose," he said. "But not this way. I hope you know that." His words seemed heavy, as if weighted with guilt. I got the sense that, even if he wasn't the one who'd killed Bert, he might've secretly wished the man harm after Bert refused to sell Ronnie the train for a reasonable price.

Dana looked Ronnie directly in the eye. "There's no need for you to feel bad. My husband wasn't always a kind man, but he couldn't help himself. He was born with a mean, competitive streak. That drive served him well when he worked at the brewery. His workers had the highest productivity of any team, year after year. But when it carried over to his personal life? Not so much."

The lines on Ronnie's face relaxed and his shoulders lowered. He appeared relieved, as if he'd served a penance.

His voice cracked as he thanked Dana. "I can't tell you how much this means to me. I've been trying to get my hands on this caboose for years. They hardly ever come available and, when they do, they go fast." He swallowed hard, overcome with emotion. "My set will be complete now."

She gave him a soft pat on the shoulder and he walked away. I was pretty sure I heard the man sniffle.

"Wow, Dana," I said, once Ronnie was out of earshot, "that was very generous of you."

She lifted a shoulder. "I don't need the money. Bert and I have been very fortunate. We're not wealthy, but we've never wanted for anything. I'd call that lucky."

I pointed through the glass to the track. With Ronnie having raised the issue of the loose sand, I supposed it wouldn't matter if I mentioned it, too. "I was here when the judges evaluated Bert's display. I saw the train derail, too. If you look real close, you can see some coarse grains by the rails."

She leaned in so that her nose nearly touched the glass, and squinted to get a better look. "You're right. That sand shouldn't be there. It definitely wasn't there after Bert cleaned his tracks. He tested his trains several times afterward to make sure they were running right. He even ran the trains for spectators who came by the booth on Monday and Tuesday, showed off his model."

I didn't tell her my theory, that what appeared to be sand could instead be raw sugar that was sprinkled across the tracks yesterday morning. After all, I had no proof at this point, and I didn't want to upset her further, to have her think that someone despised her husband enough to sabotage his exhibit. Besides, even if the loose granules were, indeed, raw sugar, I couldn't be certain who might have sprinkled it onto Bert's tracks. It could have been Stuart

because the grain used in beer had fewer methanol-producing pectins than the corn and fruit used to make moonshine. I explained this to Kiki. "Methanol has only a faint odor, and it smells similar to ethanol, the alcohol used to make liquor." The lack of a distinctive odor was part of what made methanol so dangerous. Methanol was difficult, if not impossible, to detect by smell. The taste was similar to ethanol, too, so someone wouldn't be immediately aware they were drinking poison.

As we reached the end of the row, I pointed to the concessions area at the back of the space. "There's tables and chairs over there." I suggested we stop there to compare the raw sugar to the granules stuck to the tape.

We headed over and took seats at a Formica-topped table that could have benefitted from a wipe down. I pulled a white napkin from the dispenser on the table and spread it out on the surface. I pulled one of the sugar packets from the pocket of my overalls, tore off the edge, and sprinkled a little on the napkin. I pulled out the tape, opened it to reveal the granules, and laid it next to the sugar. The three of us leaned in to take a closer look, nearly bumping heads as we did so.

My gaze went from the sugar to my friends. "The grains on the tape look just like the raw sugar to me. What do y'all think?"

"I agree," Kiki said. "I'd put money on it."

"If it's not the same thing," Kate said, "it's something very close."

I pulled out my phone, snapped a photo, and enlarged it to better examine the detail. I held up the screen to show my friends. "It's the raw sugar, all right."

A blur of blue in my peripheral vision made me snap my head to the left. *Oops.* Maybe we should have done our comparison in a less public place. Stuart Speer walked slowly by, only a few feet away. His gaze took in the raw sugar packet on the table and the short strip of black tape. While his eyes went wide and he faltered in his step as he eyed the items, his eyes narrowed to hard slits as he raised his gaze to my face. The look he sent my way was so heated it could have caramelized the sugar on the table in front of me. He turned away and walked over to the counter to place a food order.

Kiki and Kate had noticed the exchange, too.

"Whoa," Kiki said. "If looks could kill."

Kate winced. "Did we just blow it?"

"I hope not," I said, though I feared we'd tipped our hand. With any luck, Speer would think we were just gossiping, and that the trash had already been on the table when we'd sat down.

Kiki asked, "Does he know who you are?"

"Yes," I said. "He does. We haven't been formally introduced or spoken, but he must've seen me making the rounds at the convention, passing out my flyers. He was at the Monday night moonshine mixer event in the bar, too." I'd been dressed just as I was now when I'd taken the mic to lead the trivia contest. Even if he didn't recall my name, he'd know I was the woman hawking the moonshine.

Kiki said, "Maybe you should just confront him, ask him if he threw the sugar on the track. What's the worst that could happen?"

She had a point. What did I really have to lose? Speer might get angry at the accusation, but my livelihood was at stake here. He'd get over it. Besides, even if he'd not only sabotaged Bert's display but also killed the man, it wasn't like he'd murder me right here in front of hundreds of witnesses.

We waited and watched as the worker at the snack bar took Speer's payment and handed the food over to him. When he turned around, he found three pairs of eyes on him. He hesitated a moment before averting his gaze and stepping forward.

I raised a hand and called out loudly enough that he couldn't pretend not to hear me. "Mr. Speer! I need to speak with you, please. It's important."

He forced a smile to his face and walked over. "You're that moonshiner, right? From the mixer?"

"That's right," I said. "Hattie Hayes."

He gave my friends a nod in greeting and made a lame attempt to sound casual. "What can I do you for, Miss Hayes?"

"I was at Bert Gebhardt's exhibit when you and the other judges evaluated it yesterday."

"Fantastic model, isn't it?" he said. "Looks exactly like the photograph."

"It does," I agreed. "Bert seems to really know his stuff. That's why I was shocked to see his train derail."

Speer shook his head. "You and me both."

I have my doubts about that. I pointed down at the packet of sugar on the table, as well as the tape and the granules on the napkin. "We just took a sample from Bert Gebhardt's model and ran a comparison. Some raw sugar was tossed onto his tracks before the judging yesterday." I paused to gauge his reaction.

He cocked his head, his facial features contorting in an expression of confusion, but the dark pink tint that rushed up his neck to color his cheeks told me the look on his face was likely a ruse. "Something was on his tracks, you say?"

"Raw sugar," I repeated. "I saw you with a cup of coffee,

a stir stick, and packets of raw sugar yesterday morning. You walked into the convention center with them before the doors opened for the exhibitors and vendors."

Though his eyes flashed in fury, the forced look of confusion remained on his face. He played dumb. "Not sure I'm following you."

"Is that how you normally take your coffee? With raw sugar?"

He hesitated a moment. "Not always," he said, hedging his bets, maybe even wondering if I'd seen him at the coffee shop earlier today when he'd forgone the sugar. "Depends on my mood, whether I feel like I need the extra jolt." He stopped playing now, seeming to realize there was no getting around my interrogation. He stood straighter, his expression turning both defensive and apprehensive. "What are you getting at?"

"I know Bert Gebhardt has been disrespectful toward you," I said. "I saw it for myself. It would be natural to want to even the score. I'm wondering if you sabotaged his model to get back at him."

Speer's mouth hung open as if in disbelief, but his eyes went wide with fear. "You've got a lot of nerve accusing me of something like that! Especially when you're responsible for the man's death."

My face burned now, too, though my blush was one of humiliation, not guilt. "They don't know that for a fact. The police lab is still investigating."

He scoffed. "They closed your store and told us not to drink your moonshine."

"That was only as a precaution," I said. "I'm sure my 'shine will be cleared."

Kiki joined the conversation. "Let's cut to the chase.

The truth will come out, Mr. Speer, and it's best if you get out ahead of it. Do you admit that you sprinkled sugar on Bert's tracks?"

He shot her an enraged look. "Of course not! This is outrageous! This conversation is over." With that, he stormed off.

Kate watched him go. "I'd bet my firstborn he's lying."

"Me, too," Kiki said.

Kate said, "You don't have a firstborn."

Kiki pointed to Dalton. "I meant I'd bet *your* firstborn, too."

As if he knew his fate was being bartered, Dalton let out a cry. Kate reached down and tended to her son. "We weren't serious, baby. You're sticking with me."

While we were certain Stuart Speer hadn't told us the truth, we were still uncertain what the truth was. Had he sabotaged Bert's model himself? Or had he worked in cahoots with Patrick Jaffe? Maybe he hadn't been part of the sabotage at all but had witnessed Jaffe using the discarded sugar packets to damage Bert's model. I folded the tape back over and returned it to my pocket with the still unopened packets of raw sugar. I crumpled the napkin to contain the grainy mess and tossed the napkin into a trash can along with the opened packet. The evidence of our scientific analysis disposed of, we continued on our rounds.

We stopped to visit Ronnie Wallingford's "Making Tracks: American Cryptids" display, which Kiki and Kate found highly amusing. As my friends looked over the model, I assessed Ronnie Wallingford. He was in a happy mood, no doubt due to scoring his proverbial holy grail in the form of the Norfolk and Western work caboose. His broad smile made his dimples work overtime. Could this seemingly jolly man have killed Bert Gebhardt to get the caboose? It had been clear that Dana would be much easier to negotiate with than her stubborn husband. Bert stood in the way of Ronnie fulfilling a decades-old dream. Maybe Ronnie had determined to get Bert out of the way so he could score the train car. After all, he'd said *I'll get my hands on that caboose one way or another.*

I decided to put him on the spot, like we'd done with Speer. Maybe a direct question would catch him off guard. "I bet you're glad to finally have that caboose, huh? You sure were determined. When you walked away from Bert's booth before, I heard you say that you'd get it one way or another."

To my surprise, he chuckled rather than becoming defensive. "I suppose I was being melodramatic. But, short of stealing it, I was prepared to do whatever it took to leave this convention with that caboose. I figured Gebhardt might change his mind and accept my offer if nobody else expressed interest by the end of the convention."

"Why not just offer him more money and seal the deal right then and there?"

"I'd be in the doghouse when I got home if I spent any more. My wife's always complaining that I pour too much money into my trains. She put me on a strict budget. Never mind that she spends forty dollars on a tiny jar of some miracle face cream or another every time I turn around."

His demeanor was nonchalant. Maybe the threat he'd made had been just that, melodrama. Or maybe he was engaging in a bit of drama now, acting as if his words had been only an offhand remark when they'd actually meant he truly would do whatever was necessary, including kill, to obtain that caboose.

As Kiki and Kate ran their gazes over his model, he eased over to stand between them and pointed out some of the aspects of his exhibit that he seemed especially proud of. "See there?" he said, pointing to a stand of pines. "There's a sasquatch." He moved his finger to indicate a bridge over a river. "That there? That's the Mothman from West Virginia." He went on to point out a number of other cryptozoological creatures, including many who lived in his display's swamps, such as Louisiana's Honey Island Swamp Monster and South Carolina's Lizard Man of Scape Ore Swamp.

While he was busy talking monsters with my friends, I took a close look around his booth. He had a small toolbox, but it was closed. A plastic bin sat on the floor in the back corner. It contained sponges, rags, and several types of cleaners, including a plastic spray bottle with a logo for Gleam Dream Glass & Window Cleaner. Only about a half inch of cobalt-blue liquid remained in the bottle. Wallingford had clearly put the cleaner to use. But had he used it to kill Bert Gebhardt? Did the brand even contain methanol?

There didn't appear to be any other glass cleaners or any antifreeze products among the bottles, either, but I couldn't be certain without rummaging through them. It was also possible that if he'd poisoned Bert with antifreeze, he'd disposed of the bottle somewhere rather than be caught with the incriminating evidence. But maybe I could get some information out of him with the right questions.

"Your foliage is so lifelike," I said. "What's it made of? Fabric? Rubber? Some kind of pliable plastic?"

"No, no, no." Ronnie wagged his finger. "No cheap plastic here. Those plants and trees and grass are the real deal. I collected specimens when I traveled around to train conventions. For the places I haven't visited, I contacted a member of the local model railroad association and asked them to collect some for me and mail it. I want my displays to be as realistic as possible."

"Realistic?" Kiki repeated, her brows lifting. "Dude. You've got monsters in your display."

Ronnie flashed his dimples. "Who says monsters aren't real?"

I pushed a little further. "I'm surprised the foliage hasn't turned brown and dried out."

"Preserving the natural scenery just takes a little work and know-how." He left it at that. No explanation. No elaboration.

And what else does it take besides work and know-how? Maybe a product containing methanol? I wanted to grab the man by the shoulders and shake some answers out of him.

Kiki seemed to pick up on my frustration, as well as the thread of my questions. She said, "So, do you spray it with something? Immerse it in a solution? I'd love to know. I'm an artist. I'm always looking for tips on how to work with different materials."

Rather than tell us how he had preserved his natural scenery, Ronnie replied, "There's lots of options you could try. You can use the spray-on stuff florists use to preserve flowers, or you can use those flower-drying crystals. You girls might be familiar with that stuff. Brides use those crystals so they can hang on to their wedding bouquets. Some people dip their foliage in wax. You can soak the foliage in various things, too."

What various things?! His evasiveness was getting on my last nerve. "Like what?" I asked, my voice coming out far more demanding than I'd intended. I softened it, hoping he'd think he'd mistaken my tone. "What can you soak it in?"

He eyed me for a moment, his dimples changing shape as he flexed his jaw. Was it just my imagination, or did his eyes narrow a bit, too? Did he realize he was being interrogated? Finally, he replied. "Glycerin works best."

"Glycerin," Kiki said. "Good to know."

I strode over to Ronnie's bin, reached down, and grabbed the bottle of Gleam Dream Glass & Window Cleaner. Although I realized I was crossing a line and invading his personal space, I figured the opportunity to collect evidence outweighed the risk of annoying him. I held the bottle up. "How do you like this stuff? The brand of glass cleaner I've been using leaves streaks behind."

"I'm happy with it," he said. "Gets the job done and dries fast."

"I'm the worst at remembering names. I'll snap a quick pic of the bottle so I can remember next time I go to the store." Before he could object, I whipped out my phone and took photos of the front and back of the bottle, strategically ensuring that Ronnie and his model were visible in the background in case I needed to prove I'd come across this bottle at his booth if it later disappeared. I returned the bottle to his bin. "Thanks for the information, Ronnie. Always nice to get pointers from a pro."

"Sure," he said, though he sounded anything but. He'd obviously found our questions and behavior to be odd and didn't know what to make of it.

We left Ronnie's booth and made our way around the corner, where we'd be out of sight. I pulled up the photo of the back of the Gleam Dream bottle and enlarged it to scan the label. I scrolled down the screen. *Bottle made of 25% recycled plastic . . . directions for use . . . hazardous to humans and domestic animals . . . store in areas inaccessible to children* . . . Finally, I reached the ingredients. I hit paydirt. *Cleaner and dirt. There's irony for you.* One of the primary active ingredients was methanol. In fact, the amount of methanol in the product was a whopping forty percent. *Whoa.*

Chapter Twelve

I held up my phone. "Look."

Kiki and Kate leaned in, their blond and black heads coming together like the yin and yang that they were.

"He could be the one, then." Kate grimaced. "Yikes. We may have just been speaking with a killer." In what was probably a subconscious act of motherly protection, she reached down to the stroller to drape a thin blanket over her son, which Dalton promptly kicked off with his crazy karate legs. *Why do babies always look like they're doing ninja moves?*

Kiki made a sound that said she disagreed. "Nyaaaa. It can't be Ronnie. I mean, the guy's a kid at heart. He still believes in monsters."

Kate tried again to cover her son with the blanket. "Maybe *he* is the monster."

"If he were a monster," Kiki said, "he'd be Cookie Monster. Besides, if he were the guilty one, wouldn't he have ditched his bottle somewhere? Gotten rid of the evidence?"

"Maybe," I said. "But maybe he knows other people use the same brand. Maybe he was afraid someone would have noticed his Gleam Dream in his bin, like we did, and that he'd only look more guilty if his bottle suddenly disappeared." I returned my phone to my pocket. "I'll pass this information on to the detective later, see if she thinks it's worth pursuing."

Moving on, my friends and I circled around the end of the row, passing the empty vendor booth. The convention was half over by then. I'd thought before that the vendor might have suffered some type of delay and show up late, but it looked like whoever had rented the stall had decided not to come to the convention at all. My flyer for Monday's moonshine mixer still sat atop the table, a reminder of the happier, simpler time before Bert Gebhardt passed away. I walked over, grabbed the flyer, and folded it to stick in my pocket.

We headed toward Patrick Jaffe's space. When Patrick and Kimberly saw me coming their way, they exchanged looks of surprise and trepidation, as if I were the angel of death approaching. They stood and greeted me hesitantly.

After introducing them to my friends, I asked Patrick about the steam train model contest. "How are you feeling?" I asked. "Confident? Seems to me you're a shoo-in."

He hunched his shoulders. "I'd say I'm cautiously optimistic. I won't know for sure until the awards ceremony on Saturday."

Kimberly offered a slightly different take, as well as a winning smile. "Stop being so modest, Patrick. You know you're on track to win." She turned back to me. "Even the other contestants have said so."

They felt assured Patrick had locked the contest down. But did he beat Bert fair and square, or did he kill the competition?

I watched Patrick closely and said, "Shame what happened to Bert Gebhardt."

A cloud seemed to pass over his face. "Sure is. Totally unexpected." He cocked his head, running his gaze over my face in return. "Gotta say, I'm surprised you're bringing it up. To be perfectly honest, I'm surprised you'd show your face around here. Rumor has it your moonshine is what killed him."

Kiki, being the good friend she was, came to my defense. "The hospital only said he was poisoned. The police haven't confirmed the source. The results aren't back from the lab yet."

Kate piled on. "Hattie's never had problems with her moonshine before."

Seemingly unconvinced, or perhaps trying to divert focus from herself and her husband, Kimberly mused aloud, "Always a first time, I suppose. I poured all our moonshine down the drain, just to be safe. Both of the jars and the jug, too. Such a shame. Your 'shine was delicious."

I grimaced and groaned at the thought of my 'shine being wasted. "You're breaking my heart."

She offered me a small, empathetic smile. "For what it's worth, I hope they figure out it was something else."

"Me, too," I said. "Got any idea what else it could have been?" I was fishing to see what the two of them knew about methanol poisoning, whether something they said might give them away.

Patrick didn't miss a beat before saying, "Sterno, maybe?"

Sterno. That's the stuff Granddaddy mentioned, what killed all those men in Philadelphia years ago. My heart skipped a beat at the coincidence. "What makes you think it could have been Sterno?"

"There was a catered happy hour Tuesday evening at the hotel," Patrick said, "in the concierge lounge. They had a bunch of hors d'oeuvres in metal warming trays. It was college kids setting everything up, and they were too busy flirting with each other and goofing around to pay attention to what they were doing. One of them left an open can of Sterno next to the appetizers. Stuff's gooey, looks a lot like that orange sauce you get at Chinese restaurants. I dunked an eggroll in it and was about to take a bite when Kimberly stopped me."

Whoa. Could Bert have done the same thing? Dipped an appetizer in the fuel, mistaking it for a dip or sauce? If he had, he might have assumed it was simply a foul-tasting food and decided to swallow it rather than spit it back out. But if that's what happened, could he have ingested enough methanol to kill him? And did the fact that Patrick Jaffe seemed to have this explanation at the ready mean he'd thought things through, come up with a plausible explanation for how Bert Gebhardt might have died of methanol poisoning so that he could throw police off his trail if they came looking his way?

Another possible scenario entered my mind. Maybe Patrick had taken the unattended can of Sterno and used it to poison Bert somehow. Maybe he and Kimberly had mixed the fuel in with their own blackberry 'shine, and swapped their jar with Bert's at his booth. Or maybe Kimberly had made the swap in the Gebhardts' hotel room, pretending to stop by for a social chat with Dana but surreptitiously exchanging the jars when Dana was distracted. When I'd reviewed Ace's picture of Bert's toolbox, I'd thought the color in Bert's jar of 'shine looked a little off. I'd assumed the discoloration was an illusion created by the jar being sand-wiched between the two bottles of blue glass cleaner. But if colored fuel gel had been stirred into Bert's moonshine, it would explain the odd color. But just how much of the food-warming fuel would it take to kill a man? I had no idea.

For now, I wanted to learn more about their jar of black-berry moonshine. The fact that Kimberly had allegedly disposed of her 'shine meant she could have been trying to hide evidence that could link them to Bert's death. I was curious where her jar was now. "If you bring me the empty jars and jug," I said, "I'd be glad to issue you a refund or exchange them for bottles from a different batch."

"The jars and jug are likely long gone by now," she said. "I stuck them in the recycle bin in our hotel room."

Given that Bert's cause of death had only been deter-mined late yesterday, the earliest she could have poured out her moonshine was the preceding evening. I checked the time on my phone. "It's barely ten thirty. The housekeepers probably haven't been by your room yet. I'd be happy to go there with you." I'd see if I could sneak a peek into her trash can, too, look for a Sterno can.

"No need." She flung her hand in an unconcerned ges-ture. "I'm not worried about the money."

Though I was curious about the jar of blackberry 'shine she had purportedly dumped out, I didn't think I could push further without the situation growing more awkward than it already was. Instead, I said, "If you change your mind, just come on down to the shop."

Turning back to Patrick Jaffe and the matter of the gran-ules, I said, "I'm curious how these model train contests work. Does the fact that Bert's train jumped the track dis-qualify his model from the competition?"

"No," Patrick said, a cloud seeming to come over his

face. "It won't be disqualified. The judges will mark it down, though. I'm sure he lost a lot of points. Can't imagine he's still in the running to place in the competition, much less win it. Such a shame. It was clear he'd put a lot of effort into the model."

I pushed further. "I saw Bert cleaning his tracks on Monday with a little hand vac and glass cleaner. He made sure those tracks were squeaky clean. Dana said Bert ran the trains on Tuesday with no problem. Any idea what caused the train to derail during the judging yesterday?"

Patrick raised his palms and shook his head. "Beats me."

It was all I could do not to point a finger in his face and holler *Liar!* Either he'd put that sugar on the tracks himself, had his wife do it, or he knew Stuart Speer had done it. I felt sure of it. Why else would he have collected the sugar packets and stir stick from the trash can? Could he be blackmailing Speer? Maybe threatened to expose Speer's sabotage if Speer didn't give his model high scores in the contest?

"You don't have any idea at all?" I said. "I guess you didn't notice those rough granules on the tracks, then."

His head snapped to look at his wife. The two exchanged wide-eyed looks that made it clear they knew something. *Yeah, buddy. Caught you red-handed.*

Rather than say anything else, I merely cocked my head, raised my brows, and looked from one of them to the other, waiting for one of them to break down and reveal that they knew about the raw sugar on the tracks. They didn't, though. Instead, they both averted their eyes.

Patrick shrugged. "I didn't see anything on Bert's tracks."

"Me, neither," Kimberly said, suddenly very interested in examining her cuticles.

Their reactions were unnatural and laden with guilt. An

innocent person would have wanted to know more, would have asked about the granules I'd seen on Bert's tracks, would want to know what they looked like, what they might be, where they might have come from. But they showed no concern whatsoever. There could be only one reason for their lack of interest: *because they already know what was on Bert's tracks.*

I wasn't about to let them get away with lying to me. "It was raw sugar and you both know it. I saw you fish the packets out of the trash can, Patrick."

"Oh, yeah?" He stood up straight and looked me directly in the eye. "That may be, but I know good and well that's all you saw."

He was right, of course. I hadn't seen what he'd done with the sugar afterward. But did that mean he'd done nothing with it? Or did it mean he'd had Kimberly spy on me while he'd sabotaged Bert's display, that he knew I hadn't seen him in the act?

Kimberly cut me a look as sharp as the blond spikes on her head. "It's best you all move along now. We're done talking."

Chapter Thirteen

Having been told we were no longer welcome, Kiki, Kate, and I left the Jaffes' booth.

As soon as we were far enough away that they couldn't hear us, Kiki whispered, "They know something."

"It was so obvious!" Kate agreed.

"For sure," I said. "I wish I knew why they're acting so strange."

Kiki said, "You think they killed Bert?"

I worried my lip with my teeth. "I don't know. I feel fairly confident that either the Jaffes or Stuart Speer sabotaged Bert's model, but I'm not sure whether the sabotage is connected with Bert's death. Methanol takes hours to take effect, so it's clear Bert was poisoned Tuesday night. If they'd already poisoned him then, why would they feel the need to sabotage his model, too?"

Kiki asked, "Did he have to be present at the judging for his model to be eligible to win?"

"Apparently not," I said. "The judges still evaluated and scored his exhibit. Maybe Speer or the Jaffes poisoned Bert, figuring that if he wasn't there to speak with the judges, they'd count off enough points that he'd be out of the running to win the competition. But maybe they later realized that his model was good enough that it could possibly win even without Bert there to present it to the judges. Bert had a display board that contained all the pertinent information about his methods and the model's message. Maybe the killer wanted to hedge their bets, make darn sure Bert would lose no matter what."

Kate crinkled her nose, skeptical. "Would someone really kill just to win a model train contest?"

Kiki said, "I'd believe it. Look around. These people spent thousands of dollars and untold hours on their trains. They're fanatics."

Part of me agreed with Kate. The idea that someone would kill a competitor in a model railroad contest seemed ridiculous to me. But Kiki had a point, too. These conventioneers clearly took model railroading very seriously and might feel different. Besides, people had killed for less. Just because the reasons for the murders seemed senseless to everyone else didn't mean they seemed petty to the persons who committed the heinous acts. Of course, they were objectively not thinking straight. They'd been obsessive, or overcome by emotion—maybe even downright out of their minds. They'd snapped.

I supposed anyone could snap if pushed too far. Bert sure knew how to push other people's buttons. He'd certainly pushed Patrick Jaffe's by measuring the structures in Patrick's model of 1880s Chattanooga and sending the anonymous e-mail to the judges, pointing out that some of the landmarks were not to scale. Could Bert's behavior have caused Patrick Jaffe to snap? Maybe Kimberly had tired of seeing Bert antagonize her husband and she'd been the one to lose it. Both theories seemed viable.

My friends and I continued around the convention center. We spotted Stuart Speer sitting with another judge on folding chairs, listening to one of the seminars. The instructor was discussing the pros and cons of various types of train controllers—traditional, wireless, and smart phone apps. Who would've known there was an app to control model trains? Not me, that's for sure. But it seemed there was a cell phone app to replace virtually every type of controller these days. Televisions could be run via an app. Apps could even turn a cell phone into a video game controller.

Though my eyes stayed on Speer, it seemed there was nothing to be gained by watching him now. Or at least I'd thought so, until I saw him pull his cell phone from his pocket and take a look at the screen. Though I couldn't read his screen from here, it appeared he'd received a text.

Could the Jaffes have texted him? Might Speer and the Jaffes have been in cahoots to ruin Bert's display and derail both his train and his chance of winning the contest? After all, Bert was a thorn in both of their sides. And if they sabotaged Bert's display, might they have killed the man, too?

I realized then that by confronting Speer and the Jaffes, I'd let them know that there was evidence pointing in their direction. *They might want to get rid of that evidence.* I grabbed each of my friends by the arm. "Come on. We need to tell Dana about the sugar. *Now.*"

As I dragged her along, Kiki said, "Are you sure that's a good idea?"

"No," I said. "I'm not sure. But I'm afraid that if I don't tell her, and the sugar is a key to her husband's murder, the evidence could be lost. Stuart Speer or the Jaffes might go by the booth and remove it. Or Dana might sell off Bert's Last Spike model, or clean the grains off the tracks not knowing that they could be a clue. I won't tell her who I suspect or that I saw Speer and Jaffe with the sugar packets. It's probably best I tell Ace about that first. But I'll at least tell Dana that I think the granules could be sugar and suggest she not disturb them until the police can take a look."

We scurried back to Bert's booth, Dalton rolling side to side in his stroller as Kate took the corners fast. Luckily, the baby seemed to enjoy the wild ride. I supposed it felt as if he were being rocked.

Dana looked up from her knitting as we approached. "Back again?"

I pulled the second packet of sugar and the tape from my pocket. "I have something to show you."

Her hands stopped knitting, her brows taking over. She set her yarn and needles aside and stood. "What is it?"

"I didn't want to say anything until I was sure," I said, letting her know why I'd been so secretive when collecting the granules on the tape earlier. "But I think those particles on Bert's track could be raw sugar."

To avoid contaminating Bert's model train display, which could also now be a crime scene, I stayed a few feet back from the table. In my left palm, I laid out the tape with the sugar crystals stuck to it. I had Kiki open a new sugar packet and pour the contents into my other hand. I put my hands together, side by side, so Dana could easily compare the sugar samples. "I collected the grains on the tape from Bert's tracks when we were here earlier. Don't they look just like the raw sugar?"

Dana leaned in to take a look. She huffed in surprise, sending the sugar crystals out in a cloud from my hand. "Oh, my gosh!" She straightened up, her face falling as she realized what the sugar meant. "Someone tried to wreck Bert's model? Why would they do that?"

I couldn't very well say *because your husband was a cantankerous buzzard and they wanted to put him in his place,* though I felt nearly certain that was the case. I shook my head. "I don't know, Dana."

I went over to a nearby trash can and brushed the sugar off my hands before coming back to the booth. Dana, Kiki, and Kate were bent over, eyeing the tracks.

Dana stood. "I should notify the chief judge. Whoever did this should be barred from competing ever again."

"I agree," I said, "but I think it's important that we let Detective Pearce know what we've found first. I'll give her a call." I whipped out my phone, dialed Ace, and explained what I'd discovered, the raw sugar on Bert's tracks. "The sugar made his train derail when his entry was being judged." Although I could hear Ace perfectly, I pretended that I was having trouble. I stepped away from the booth, put a finger to my ear, and turned away from Dana so that she couldn't hear me. I kept my voice to a whisper. "I saw two people with raw sugar packets yesterday morning. One was a contest judge named Stuart Speer. The other was a contestant in the steam engine category, a guy named Patrick Jaffe." I told her how I'd seen Speer enter the convention center with a coffee, stir stick, and packets of raw sugar. "A little while later, my grandfather and I were at the vendor tables, looking at trains, and Speer threw his stir stick and sugar packets into the trash nearby. As soon as Speer was gone, Jaffe came around, reached into the garbage can, and dug them out."

"Hmm." Ace sounded skeptical. But who could blame her? My moonshine had yet to be ruled out as the source of the methanol, and we weren't even sure we were dealing

with a murder. All we knew was that Bert died from methanol poisoning. "Even if someone sabotaged Bert's tracks,"
she said, "it would be a civil matter, not a criminal one, and
would not necessarily have anything to do with his death."
She asked me to repeat the names, probably so that she
could jot them down with her ever-present pen and notepad.
"I've got a couple of things on my plate that I need to deal
with right away," she said, "but I'll send Marlon down there
to cordon off the area and keep an eye on things until I can
get by to take a look. And, Hattie?"

"Yes?"

"Watch yourself. There's a fine line between assisting
with an investigation and meddling in it."

"Understood."

We ended the call and I stepped back to the booth to
inform Dana that a police officer was on his way to secure
the scene. "He'll string some police tape around your booth
and protect the display so the sugar can't disappear. Whoever did this might come around and try to get rid of the
proof." As Dana's exhale had shown, all it would take to
disperse the sugar would be a well-placed stream of air.
Someone could fake a sneeze or wave a program to fan
themselves and the evidence would be blown away, especially now that Dana had removed the plexiglass barrier
from around the exhibit.

Shortly thereafter, Marlon arrived on foot. He must've
left Charlotte in her trailer in the parking lot, along with his
helmet, though he still wore his black riding boots. He appeared part cowboy and part cop, but totally handsome. He
cast me a sour look as he strode up. "Ace says you found
some potential evidence. Can't imagine how." He scratched
his head in a mocking gesture. "I thought I'd asked you not
to insinuate yourself in the death investigation."

"I can't help it if clues pop up right in front of me!" I said in my defense. "Besides, the sugar is only evidence that someone tried to wreck Bert's display. It could have nothing at all to do with his death."

Marlon only grunted in reply.

Dana wrangled with the plexiglass. "Should I put this back up?"

"That's a good idea," Marlon said. "It'll protect the display."

He helped Dana erect the see-through barrier around the model, then strung yellow and black crime scene tape across the front of the booth to keep people out.

Dana pointed to the sign announcing her sale. "Can I still show people Bert's things if they're interested?"

Marlon considered for a moment. "I don't suppose there's any problem with that. But take the items to them rather than letting them come inside the tape."

To that end, they rolled the sales display case up to the front of the booth. Dana closed and latched Bert's toolbox, and Marlon grabbed the handle on top to move it to the front of the space as well. Lastly, he repositioned her chair just outside the cordon tape.

She pointed to Bert's chair, which remained at the booth. "Feel free to take a seat, Officer Landers."

As Marlon repositioned Bert's chair as well, Dana turned back to me and my friends. "Thanks, girls," she said, her voice warbling with emotion. "I hope this sugar leads to some answers. I'm leaving town on Sunday morning and I'd hate to return home without my husband and without an explanation for how this stuff got on his tracks. If someone tried to ruin his chances of winning the contest, I owe it to Bert to figure things out." She swallowed hard and fresh tears filled her eyes. "I only wish I'd realized sooner why he was feeling and acting strange yesterday. Maybe I could've gotten him some help, saved his life."

"You had no way of knowing," I said, hoping to assuage her guilt. "Besides, with his model scheduled to be judged yesterday morning, I doubt you could've convinced him to leave the convention."

She emitted a soft, sad chuckle and wiped an errant tear from her cheek. "You're right about that. After all the time and effort he put into his Last Spike model, he'd insist on staying even if it killed him." Which, in a sense, it had.

My friends and I decided it was time to leave the convention altogether. We'd done all the reconnaissance we could do here without a badge, gun, and law enforcement credentials. There was nothing left to be gained by hanging around and, from the irritated look on Marlon's face, he'd just as soon I was gone. I only hoped I hadn't jeopardized our personal relationship. We bade both Dana and Marlon goodbye and aimed for the exit.

Dalton had been a perfect little angel all morning, spending most of his time napping in his stroller or staring up at the overhead lights, listening to the train sounds and songs, and sucking on his fist and fingers. By then, his patience had run out and he began to fuss. Kate whipped a pacifier from her diaper bag and plugged it into his mouth, immediately silencing him.

Kiki said, "Too bad they don't make those pacifiers in adult sizes. I'd love to have one to stick in my mother's mouth the next time she nags me about my hair or clothes."

As my friends and I made our way to the doors, we stopped at a booth where Kiki and I insisted on going half-sies on an old-fashioned wooden train set for Dalton.

"He was a great distraction while I was collecting the

sugar from Bert's tracks," I told Kate. "He deserves a reward for that."

According to the package, Dalton wouldn't be able to enjoy the toy until he was eighteen months old, but it would give the little guy something to look forward to.

Kiki grabbed a tunnel piece made to look like stone. "He'll need this cool tunnel, too."

"And this neat bridge." I chose a long red suspension bridge that looked similar to the famous Golden Gate.

"You two are going to spoil him!" Kate lamented, her smile telling us her complaint was completely insincere. If we honorary aunties wanted to spoil her son rotten, she'd happily let us.

Luckily, Dalton was still so small he hardly took up any space in his stroller and we were able to situate the smaller boxes in the seat with him. We slid the larger box for the train set into the basket underneath.

My friends and I left the convention center and discovered Marlon's police SUV parked at the curb with his horse in the trailer behind it. As we came up behind it and Charlotte's muscular haunches became visible, Kiki burst into the Sir Mix-a-Lot song in which he detailed his admiration for big buttocks.

Marlon had left the windows open at the front so that Charlotte could get ventilation. I stepped up to the window to greet her. "Hi, Charlotte."

She turned my way and I reached up to scratch her chin, just as I did with Smoky. Her chin covered a lot more area, though. She nuzzled my hand, as if looking for an apple or carrot.

"Sorry, girl," I said. "I don't have a snack with me right now."

She blew out a huff of air, as if disgusted by my lack of forethought. I hoped she could find it in her big horse heart to forgive me.

Having checked in with Charlotte, we started across the parking lot to Kate's minivan. While gray clouds still scuttled overhead, we'd missed the rain shower. Evidence of it remained on the wet sidewalks and ran along the gutters, finding its way into the storm sewers.

As we made our way, Kiki said, "What did you think about that Sterno theory? You think Bert accidentally ate the stuff at the happy hour?"

"I'm not sure," I said. "Ace told me that as little as a tablespoon of methanol can potentially be fatal, but the concentration of methanol in Sterno varies by product." I regaled them with the horrific tale my grandfather had told me.

They found the story as upsetting as I did. Kate put a hand to her heart and Kiki closed her eyes for a moment, as if sending up a silent prayer for the victims.

When Kiki opened her eyes, she said, "The Jaffes said the college kids working the happy hour weren't paying much attention. Maybe they mentioned it to deflect blame, to make the staff look guilty when, in fact, they snitched a jar of Sterno from the event themselves and mixed it into the jar of moonshine Bert drank from."

"Could be," I said. "Patrick sure came up with the theory fast, almost as if he'd thought it out in advance."

Kate concurred. "Seems like the happy hour gave them a chance to get their hands on methanol in a way that couldn't be traced to them."

Hands . . .

I stopped in my tracks. "What if hand sanitizer killed Bert Gebhardt?"

Kiki and Kate had continued on and were several steps ahead of me now. They stopped and turned around.

"Ace said that methanol can be introduced to the body by ingestion, inhalation, or dermally," I said. "There were news reports a while back. A bunch of people got sick from hand sanitizer that had methanol in it. They absorbed the poison through their skin." There'd been warnings on the television news and articles that came across my cell phone newsfeed. I remember looking over the list and comparing it to the products I'd purchased to make sure I wasn't inadvertently using a tainted sanitizer. "Maybe Bert's hand sanitizer is what killed him."

"I remember that, too." Kiki pulled out her cell phone and searched for hand sanitizers, but the products were supposed to contain only ethanol, not methanol. Kiki looked up from her phone. "Even if he used a lot of tainted hand sanitizer on his skin, do you think he could have used enough to kill himself?"

"Maybe," I said. "I saw him apply it two or three times. Who knows how many other times he put it on during the day?" The potential sources of methanol seemed endless, which led me to have another thought. "I wonder if Bert might have been exposed to more than one source of methanol, and the cumulative effect is what killed him." Maybe he'd used some tainted hand sanitizer but also ingested some methanol at the buffet. But, even then, would it have been enough to kill him? I was no doctor or scientist. The best I could do was share my theories with Ace later.

We climbed into Kate's minivan, buckled ourselves in, and she headed up Market Street.

"Bollocks!" Kiki hissed under her breath as we drew near. She pointed to the front stoop of the Moonshine Shack. "You've got problems, Hattie."

A news van sat at the curb in front of my shop. The raven-haired reporter I'd seen at the convention on Monday was standing outside the front door. She'd put her face to the glass and cupped her hands around her eyes to see inside, probably looking for me or an employee she could interview. Her cameraman stood behind her, waiting. Looked like the news outlets who'd been so happy to hail me as a hero only a short time ago couldn't wait to expose me as a killer now.

Chapter Fourteen

Kate pulled her minivan to the curb across the street. Though the sidewalk was public property, it nonetheless galled me to no end that this reporter was standing outside my store. My absence would make me look guilty, as if I'd gone into hiding. She should have waited until she spoke with me before recording her segment.

Ughhhh . . . I sighed. "Good thing I'm not at my shop." Until the police gave me permission to reopen the Moonshine Shack, it would remain closed. "What would I even say to the media?" I had no idea how to handle a nosy television reporter.

Kiki, who'd spent a summer in London during college, tended to go cockney when riled up. "You'd tell the prats to piss off! You had sod all to do with that man's death. I know it."

I chewed my lip. "How'd they even know my moonshine was suspected?"

Kate offered some guesses. "Maybe someone associated with the train convention contacted them?"

"Could be," Kiki said. "Maybe someone who's trying to draw attention away from themselves."

Kate backtracked. "Or maybe she just overheard someone talking about it at the convention. You said that all the convention participants were notified not to drink your 'shine, right?"

"They were," I said, adding another sigh. "It wasn't exactly a secret. I just hope my business can survive a poisoning scandal."

Even if it was proved that my moonshine wasn't at fault, the seed would have been planted in people's minds, and the public would still associate my brand with a death. Guilty or not, I might have to rebrand after all, like Kiki had suggested earlier. Lightning Bug Moonshine might not be such a bad moniker. Neither would River City 'Shine.

Kiki glared at the woman through the windshield. "You should play hardball, Hattie. Threaten her and her station with a defamation suit if she wrongfully reports that your moonshine caused Bert Gebhardt's death."

"Wouldn't threatening her with a lawsuit make me sound defensive?"

"Of course, it will!" Kiki rolled her eyes. "But you're in a tough spot, Hattie. You have to be on the defensive, whether you like it or not."

Kate agreed. "Better to nip this in the bud, right?"

They were right. I had a lot to lose, and the only way I could slow things down was by standing up for myself. Once the horse was out of the barn, it would be impossible to put it back.

Worried about those unnipped buds and empty barns, I whipped out my cell phone. When I'd launched my shop,

I'd invited owners of nearby businesses and firms to my grand opening celebration. Heath Delaney, a local lawyer, had attended my party. After tasting my delicious fruit moonshine flavors, he later returned to my shop to buy 'shine. I'd also met with Heath at the behest of the young woman who'd taken over the Irish pub across the street from my shop. She'd asked me to serve as her mentor and, together, Heath and I had helped her get her business launched. I looked up the phone number for the law firm of Delaney and Sullivan and called the office. When the receptionist answered, I asked to speak to Heath. "It's a very time-sensitive matter," I told the receptionist. "An emergency, actually. Any chance I can talk to him right now?"

"Let me check. Please hold."

The reporter was now facing her cameraman with her mic at her lips. Given that it was 11:37 local time, I surmised that she wasn't making a live report but rather recording a video clip to play later, maybe even on the noon news that would begin in a few minutes.

Fortunately, Heath was between meetings and was able to take my call right away. I gave him a quick rundown. "Bert's wife said the only things he'd ingested since Tuesday evening were meals at the hotel and my moonshine. The detective seized several jars from my store last night. The police lab is testing them now, but we don't have the results yet." I told him how careful I was with my moonshine. "I always throw out the foreshot. Every. Single. Time. I know how dangerous methanol can be. I just don't see how my 'shine could have been the source of the methanol."

"Gotcha," he said. "Put me on speaker and carry your phone over to your store. Other than identifying yourself, don't say anything. Understand?"

"Okay."

"By the way," Heath added, "my rate is three hundred dollars an hour."

It was a good thing we were on the phone so he couldn't see my jaw drop.

Kiki said, "Talk fast, counselor. Summon your inner auctioneer."

My friends and I continued down the sidewalk, standing nearby until the reporter ended with, "Could the wild black-berry moonshine purchased here at the Moonshine Shack have killed model railroader Bert Gebhardt? Will it be lights out for this 'shine shop? More as this story develops."

When she lowered her mic and stepped toward the van, I raised my hand to stop her. "I'm Hattie Hayes, the owner of the Moonshine Shack. My lawyer would like to speak to you."

Her brows arched. I wanted to hear the conversation, so rather than hand her the phone I kept it in speaker mode and simply held it out flat between us.

Heath's voice came through the speaker, all professional and cordial. "To whom am I speaking, please?"

The reporter identified both herself and her cameraman.

Heath's disembodied voice came back. "I'm sure your station has warned you about the risks of wrongful report-ing and the potential for costly defamation lawsuits."

"Of course," she said, rolling her heavily made-up eyes.

"The police lab is in the process of analyzing the moon-shine from the Moonshine Shack for possible methanol contamination but has yet to render a report. Any statement about the products sold there, or the store itself, would be premature, mere conjecture. If you mention Miss Hayes, her store, or any of her products in a news report before the police lab releases its findings, I will file suit against you, your cameraman, and the station."

The woman hesitated a moment in a move that seemed a power play. Finally, she said, "It's a fact that the moonshine is being tested at the police lab. I could easily get away with stating that simple fact. But I'll agree to hold off submitting this clip so long as you agree to contact me right away when Miss Hayes hears the results from the police lab. Good *or* bad."

I wasn't sure the reporter and I agreed on what result would be good or bad. Good for me would mean my moonshine was determined to be blameless, but that wouldn't make much of a story for her.

She clarified her statement. "When I say contact me when you hear the results, I mean *the instant* you hear them. Understood?"

So, she's going to play hardball, too, huh? I suppose I should've expected it.

Heath agreed to the condition on my behalf. "We can do that."

She said, "Great. I'll look forward to hearing from you." She turned and signaled her cameraman. The two returned to their van without another word.

I waited until the van drove off before asking Heath why he had agreed to her condition.

"I know her type," he said. "Big egos. They won't back off unless they feel like they got something in return. The news would get out at some point anyway. But at least we've kept the wolf at bay for now."

Even so, I could only wonder if we'd merely whacked one mole, whether other news outlets had come by here earlier, if this reporter was just one of many. But I also knew she was from a station not known for being particularly careful with their reporting, more tabloid fodder than well-researched investigative journalism. Maybe the rest of the stations would have more integrity and wait until the police lab had issued its findings before making a public report.

Once I'd completed my call with Heath and calculated how much our short chat would end up costing me—*fifty-five dollars*—my entourage split up. Kiki set off to do some work on a graphic arts gig, while I followed Kate back to her place in my van. Kate and I rarely had a chance to spend time together, and things had been even more difficult recently with me being busy setting up my store and her being wrapped up with her pregnancy and then her new baby. It would be nice to get to hang out for a while.

Two hours later, Kate was catching up on chores she'd been forced to ignore due to the demands of motherhood, while I sat on her couch with Dalton on my lap, his big floppy baby head supported in the crook of my elbow. I'd been reading the little guy some books. We'd just finished *The Little Engine That Could* and were nearly done with the classic *Mike Mulligan and His Steam Shovel*. Of course, I added my own observations to the story. "Mike is such a typical guy. He just starts digging his hole without thinking how he's going to get his steam shovel out when he's done. Then he leaves Mary Anne in the cellar she dug because she's old and he'd rather try a newer model. Don't be like Mike. Okay, Dalton? Don't be fickle, and plan ahead so you don't cause yourself unnecessary headaches."

Even while I criticized Mike Mulligan for not planning ahead, I had to admit I found the guy's situation relatable. I, too, felt like I'd dug a hole for myself and was now trying to figure how to get out of it. Maybe I should've stayed with my previous steady job at the headquarters and factory of Chattanooga Bakery, Inc., maker of the world-famous

MoonPie, rather than starting a moonshine business. People might get chubby eating too many MoonPies, but the tasty treats could never accidentally poison anyone. At any rate, Dalton didn't seem to appreciate my words of wisdom. He opened his tiny mouth and issued a big yawn.

I began to read him another picture book, *Where the Wild Things Are*. A few pages in, he lost interest in my commentary and the story, and fell asleep in my arms. He wouldn't know how the picture book ended, but he also wouldn't know the difference. Everything I'd read had been gibberish to his little baby brain. I kissed his head. "I'll finish the story next time. I promise." Moving as slowly and smoothly as possible so as not to wake him, I carried him down the hall to his nursery and placed him in his crib. I gave his cheek a soft caress and whispered, "See you next time, cutie patootie. Sweet dreams."

I returned to the living room and addressed my friend. "What can I do to help?"

"The fridge needs to be cleaned out. I haven't had a chance to get to it since we got home from the hospital."

"That was weeks ago."

"I know," she said. "You might want to don a hazmat suit."

As she folded laundry at the kitchen table, I methodically went through the refrigerator, shelf by shelf. I opened a plastic container to find a thick green liquid inside. I held it up. "I can't tell if this is fresh split pea soup or rancid pancake batter."

Kate said, "I've never made split pea soup."

"Out it goes, then." I poured the scary substance into the sink and turned on the faucet to wash it down the drain.

She folded a pair of her husband's underwear and said, "So. You and Marlon. Where do you think it's going?"

"I'm not sure yet," I said. "It feels like things are headed in a good direction. Or at least it did until Ace called him to come to the convention center today. I don't know how angry he is at me for ignoring his advice not to get involved in the investigation." I headed back to the fridge and opened it again.

"You're not the type of woman to sit idly by and wait to be rescued," Kate said. "You're not some doormat Cinderella waiting for Prince Charming to show up with a glass slipper. You're driven and smart and tenacious. If he can't cope with that, he's not the right guy for you. Better to find out now."

"You're right." Even so, it made me a little sad to think our relationship could end almost as soon as it began.

"There's another way to look at it, though," Kate said.

"Oh, yeah?" I said, reaching for another food storage container. "How?"

"Maybe he warned you off not just because he's a cop and doesn't want you interfering with police business, but because he's falling for you and doesn't want to see you put yourself in harm's way. He's worried about you."

"I like that idea much better." I opened the container to find a fuzz-covered chunk of something that had turned an unusual shade of greenish-brown. I held it out for her to see. "This creature would be right at home on Ronnie Wallingford's cryptids' exhibit." I'd just dumped the whatever it was into the garbage, when my ringtone sounded from the front pocket of my overalls. I reached in to retrieve my phone. The screen told me it was Ace calling. "It's the detective!"

Kate put a trifolded towel on top of the stack she'd created and raised her hand, fingers crossed. "I hope she's got good news for you."

I would've been more encouraged if Kate's tone hadn't

sounded so anxious. I jabbed the phone to accept the call. "Hello, Ace."

"You're in the clear," she said. "The lab found no trace of methanol in the moonshine from your store. Methanol was only found in the jar of blackberry 'shine Bert Gebhardt drank from. It was too little to be the foreshot. Looks like it was added after Dana purchased it at the Moonshine Shack."

Thank the stars. I closed my eyes and sent up a thank-you to every deity in existence to make sure I had my bases covered. When I opened my eyes, I gave Kate a thumbs-up so she'd know it was good news.

Ace said, "I'm heading over to the convention center to interview folks. If anything pans out, I'll let you know."

"Thanks." We ended the call and I immediately texted Kiki and Marlon. *My 'shine's been cleared.*

Their responses were just as immediate, and reflective of each of their personalities.

Kiki sent a GIF of an orange tabby in a sombrero who appeared to be dancing in celebration.

Marlon's response read: *Good. I'd hate to think I've kissed a killer.* He followed it up with the lips emoji followed by the winking face emoji.

I returned my phone to my pocket. I gathered up my purse and pulled out my keys.

Kate stopped mid-fold on a hand towel. "You're leaving?"

"The detective is heading over to the convention center. I want to be there if she learns something and makes an arrest. I also want to tell her my other theories, about the antifreeze and the glass cleaner and the hand sanitizer."

"Darn." Kate sighed. "It's been nice having an adult to talk to. I mean, I love Dalton, but he's not much for conversation. It's all waa-waa-waa, gurgle-gurgle blurp."

"Anytime you need adult conversation," I said, "come on

down to the shop and hang out with me. Bring Dalton with you." Like my grandfather, the baby slept most of the time anyway. Dalton would be no trouble. I couldn't say the same about my Granddaddy, though. He didn't always behave as he should.

"I'm going to take you up on that," Kate said. "I'm also going to look for a playgroup, so Dalton can make some friends."

I wasn't sure what use a tiny infant who couldn't move on his own would have for friends just yet, but I supposed it was never too early for a child to start learning social skills. "You'll make some mom friends that way, too," I said. "But don't forget me and Kiki when you do."

"Never!" she said as if the mere thought were ludicrous.

I gave Kate a hug and headed out to my van.

Once I was seated, I placed a quick call to Heath Delaney to notify him that my moonshine had been cleared.

"Good," he said. "I'll call the reporter right away."

I could feel his bill increase with each syllable we spoke. "Thanks!" I said, quickly clicking off the call.

I started my van and aimed for the convention center. Marlon's SUV still sat at the curb, Charlotte taking a standing nap in her trailer behind it. I drove past and spotted Ace, who was walking through the parking lot. I drew closer and beeped my horn to get her attention. As I rolled up, I rolled down my window and raised a hand. "Hi, Ace!"

She gave me a look as sour as the one Marlon had given me earlier. "I should've known you'd show up."

I'd hoped for a warmer welcome, but maybe she'd change her tune when she realized I was here to help. "I have some thoughts I'd like to share with you, some potential sources of methanol."

She pointed out the obvious. "You could have just told me on the phone."

"I thought if I came here I could help move things along," I said, "save you some time. The convention center is a big place, but I know the people and where their booths are located."

"And you figured it would be easier to ask for forgiveness for butting into my investigation than to get my permission to tag along."

Busted. "Well, yeah." I winced in contrition.

She glowered at me for a second or two before giving in. "All right," she said. "Meet me at the doors."

I rolled up my window, zipped into the first available parking space, and sprinted to the entrance.

Ace wasted no time getting down to business. "Fill me in."

I pulled out my phone and showed her the photo I'd taken earlier that compared the granules on the tape to the raw sugar from the packet. "I've got the tape and a fresh packet of sugar on me if you want to see them."

"I do."

I pulled both things out of the pocket of my overalls and handed them over to her. She repeated my earlier analysis, tearing off the corner of the sugar packet, dumping a few granules into her hand, and comparing it to the grains that were on the tape. She even pulled a magnifying glass out of her tote bag to take a closer look. From my vantage point, her eye grew huge and distorted as she looked through the glass. "Looks like the identical substance to me," she said.

"Do you think Speer or Jaffe could have tossed the raw sugar onto Bert's tracks to sabotage his model?" Had Jaffe taken the used packets from the trash in order to sprinkle the remnants on Bert's tracks? Or could Speer have flung the sugar over the top of the plexiglass out of outrage? I told her my alternate theories, that Kimberly Jaffe might have acted on behalf of her husband or that Stuart Speer and Patrick Jaffe might have worked together to wreck Bert's display and his chances of winning the contest. "Do you think maybe the two were in cahoots?"

"Whatever way it happened," she said, "it was a clever ploy. But an action like that smacks of petty vengeance. Someone who's thinking on that scale doesn't seem like the type of person who'd be contemplating murder." But then Ace inhaled deeply and contradicted herself. "On the other hand, someone who'd interfere with Gebhardt's exhibit obviously had an unsettled beef with him. They might have sprinkled the sugar on his tracks before they realized they had a chance to take things even further. They might not have even intended to kill him. Maybe they only meant to make him sick. Until we collect more evidence, it's impossible to say."

My mind went in all different directions, too, like the tracks fanning out from a train station. Just when I'd thought one theory made the most sense, my mind would do a one-eighty, as if on a turntable, and take me in another direction. We were dealing with a complicated whodunit, where there were two "duns" having been done. But were there also two whos? Were those two whos in cahoots—or in this case were the two in toot-toot cahoots to kill the model railroader?

Chapter Fifteen

Ace angled her head. "How'd the wife seem when you pointed out the sugar on the track?"

"Dana?" I said. "She wasn't happy about the thought that someone tried to sabotage her husband's model."

"She's supportive, then?"

"To a degree," I said. "She joked about these model train conventions being the only place her husband would ever take her on vacation, and I think she resented that he put more focus on his hobby than his family, but she seemed to have fun with the other wives and had accepted her lot in life, tried to make the best of it. She's selling off her husband's train paraphernalia—both the Last Spike display he built and the collector trains he had for sale."

"Depending on what he's got, his trains could be worth something."

"I have no idea," I said. "But I don't think Dana's trying to make a buck as much as just trying to unload it. Her sign says 'Everything for sale. Make an offer.' She'd mentioned what a pain it is to transport the large train displays, and she'd have to handle it on her own now that Bert's gone. I also know she gave away one of the valuable collector trains."

"She did? To whom?"

"A guy named Ronnie Wallingford." I told her how Ronnie had coveted the Norfolk and Western caboose Bert had for sale, how he repeatedly returned to Bert's booth to inquire about it and increase his offer. "Ronnie's offers were generous, but Bert wouldn't budge on the price, tried to gouge the guy. Dana tried to talk Bert into accepting the offer, but Bert got angry at her, too, and refused. Today, Dana let Wallingford have the caboose for free."

"In other words, Bert was no longer an obstacle to Ronnie obtaining the caboose."

"Exactly." The only question was, had Ronnie removed the obstacle by poisoning him? "My friends and I stopped by Wallingford's exhibit earlier. He had a bottle of Gleam Dream Glass and Window Cleaner in his toolbox. I snapped photos." I pulled them up on my phone and showed them to her. "See? The label shows that it contains a high concentration of methanol."

She looked at the photos for a moment before forwarding them to her own device. She handed my phone back to me. "Did the Gebhardts know Ronnie Wallingford before this convention?"

"I don't think so. I didn't get the impression they'd met before. But many of the others seemed to have crossed paths at earlier events. The spouses are familiar with one another. They seem to hang out together at these conventions."

Her head bobbed as she considered this fact. "You've

spent some time at the convention center and hotel with the model train folks. Your shop, too. Anyone stick out to you as the most viable suspect?"

I was flattered that she'd asked my opinion. Unfortunately, I'd been unable to pare down the list. "I wish I could tell you." I shared the thoughts that had crossed my mind. That Dana might have killed her husband because he was a self-centered jackass. That Ronnie Wallingford might have tired of Bert's aggressive sales tactics related to the caboose. That Stuart Speer had clearly been annoyed that Bert second-guessed his decisions, and that he obviously suspected that Bert had been the one to send an anonymous e-mail to the association pointing out size discrepancies in scale in Patrick Jaffe's steam train model. That Patrick Jaffe and Bert Gebhardt had a heated argument when Jaffe's display was being judged, and that things would have likely escalated had my grandfather not forced the men apart by driving his scooter between them.

I'd already listed quite a few potential suspects, and I wasn't even done yet. "There was a housekeeper at the hotel, too. A woman named Martha. Bert chewed her out for going into his room Monday morning when he'd hung the do not disturb sign on his knob." I explained about the pizza flyer obscuring the sign. "Bert told Martha he was going to complain to the hotel manager. When he stormed off, she picked up a bottle of glass cleaner from her cart and pretended to shoot him with it. I thought she was just blowing off steam, but who knows. She'd have a key to Bert's hotel room, too. That would have given her access to the Gebhardts' jars of blackberry moonshine. It's possible the glass cleaner she used contained methanol. Or maybe one of her other cleaning supplies has methanol in it. She came to the convention, too. Yesterday morning. I saw her here." It crossed my mind that she might have come to spy on Bert, to see if he had succumbed to the poison she'd slipped into his jar of moonshine. "She stopped and talked to that judge I told you about. Stuart Speer. He left his coffee cup at the empty vendor booth where they'd been talking, and she picked it up and carried it off."

"Could you tell whether there was anything in it?"

"No," I said.

Ace gave the woman the benefit of the doubt. "My guess is she picked it up out of habit. Housekeepers are neat people. They see trash, they pick it up and dispose of it."

Ace could very well be right, but . . . "You don't find it suspicious that she came over here to a model train convention?"

"Not really," Ace said. "You said she's an older lady. Maybe she's got grandkids and thought she'd come check things out, see if the convention looked like something they might enjoy. Maybe she plans to bring them here tomorrow or Saturday to see the model trains. Or maybe she came here to buy one of them a birthday gift." She shrugged. "You might have heard this Martha woman call Bert a nasty name and seen her pretend to shoot him with a spray cleaner, but my guess is she considered that to be retribution enough. Housekeepers tend to be thick-skinned. They're constantly talked down to and blamed for stealing property from hotel rooms when ninety-nine times out of a hundred it's the guest who lost their property or it's a bogus claim. They learn to roll with it. If nothing else pans out, I'll look into her. But I think it's a better use of my time to focus on the out-of-towners before they leave Chattanooga. Once they're out of my jurisdiction, it'll make my investigation all the harder."

Her priorities made sense. I had no idea how difficult it

was to extradite somebody from another state, but my guess was there would be a lot of paperwork and lawyers involved. It would be expensive, too, to have to transport a suspect all that way. Ace would have to be able to show very solid proof, and her best bet of getting that proof was for her to try to round it up now, while the convention was still going on and the suspects from out of state were still here in Chattanooga. If nothing panned out with the out-of-towners, my guess was that she'd check out the hotel's security camera footage, verify which housekeepers had entered the Gebhardts' room. A part of me still wondered about Martha. She'd sure looked smug after she saw Bert get chewed out by Patrick Jaffe and the judge.

Ace raised the issue of the methanol again. "The other sources of methanol you mentioned. What are they?"

"Sterno, for starters." I repeated what I'd learned. "One of the other competitors, a guy named Patrick Jaffe, said there was a jar of pink Sterno on the table at the hotel during a happy hour event that was held early Tuesday evening. The catering staff had set it out, but they'd forgotten to light it and slide it under a food tray. Jaffe mistook it for a type of orange sauce and dipped an egg roll in it. Fortunately, his wife caught him before he put it in his mouth. Bert might have done the same." Frankly, I hoped that this theory proved correct. If Bert had to die, I'd much rather think it was due to negligence rather than murder. Of course, there was another potential source we had yet to discuss. "Bert used a lot of hand sanitizer gel," I said. "I saw him apply it several times. I've heard that people got sick from tainted hand sanitizer products a few years back. You think the hand gel could be the source of the methanol? That he absorbed it through his skin?"

"It's something to consider."

"His hand sanitizer was still in his toolbox when I went by Dana's booth earlier."

"Good," Ace said. "I can round it up to be tested in the lab."

"I have another idea, too." I went on to tell her about the class my grandfather and I had sat in on earlier in the week, how the instructor had mentioned that antifreeze could be used to preserve natural materials in model train displays. "It keeps the foliage from drying out and turning brown."

She issued a curt hmm that said the information was news to her, too.

"I'm wondering if the methanol might have come from antifreeze. Blue or pink antifreeze could have been added to my moonshine without changing the color much. Ronnie Wallingford has a lot of natural foliage in his model. He was evasive when I asked him how he'd preserved it, wouldn't give me a straight answer."

Ace considered what I'd told her. Evidently, she decided the Sterno theory seemed to be the most viable. She gestured to the hotel across the parking lot. "Let's go talk to the head of food service."

We strode across the parking lot and into the hotel. Ace led me up to the registration desk, flashed her badge, and handed the woman a business card. "I need to speak with whoever is in charge of the restaurant and in-house catering."

The woman exchanged curious glances with the other clerk behind the counter before picking up her phone and punching in a two-digit number. "There's a detective from the Chattanooga Police Department here at the desk. She needs to speak with you." She paused for a few seconds to listen. "Okay. I'll send her back with—" She ran her gaze over my overalls and T-shirt, as if trying to determine my role here, whether my hillbilly garb might be an under-cover disguise. She eventually decided to go with "her associate."

Associate worked for me. It sounded better than what I really was, a buttinsky, a busybody, a meddler. But at least my interference was based in good intentions, the desire to help answer the questions surrounding Bert Gebhardt's death.

The woman directed us down a hallway to the left of the check-in counter. "Second door on the right."

I followed Ace to a door with a small square window built into the upper half. The window was lined with reflective film that would allow anyone on the other side to see out but prevented us from looking in. A placard mounted on the wall next to the door read FOOD AND BEVER-AGE. Ace put her knuckles to the door. *Rap-rap-rap.*

A few seconds later, the door was opened by a thin, fortyish man in a basic black suit paired with a white dress shirt and gray tie. He was clean-shaven, his hairline creeping back on his head as if the remaining strands were trying to hide behind it. He held out an arm. "Please. Come in."

We entered the room, which was divided into three cubicles along one wall, two on the other. At the end of the room was a swinging door with another window in it, though this window was round and clear. Through the glass, I could see into the kitchen of the hotel restaurant and hear the sounds of water running and dishes and silverware clinking. The kitchen staff milled about, washing the dirty dishes from lunch service and getting ready for the dinner rush. The savory smell of something simmering made my mouth water. It had been a long time since my morning muffin.

The man directed us into the first cubicle, the largest in

the room. The only seat was behind his desk, but he rounded up two folding chairs for me and Ace and placed them in front of it.

After we'd all taken a seat, Ace said, "I have some questions about your chafing fuel."

He frowned. "May I ask why?"

She watered things down a bit, probably to prevent him from becoming overly defensive. "It's possible the fuel might have made someone sick. I just need to eliminate it as a source of poison." She noted that the heating gel might have been inadvertently ingested at the happy hour Tuesday evening. "I've been told an open jar of it was left unlit next to the appetizers. At least one person mistook it for a dipping sauce. Can you tell me the types of chafing fuel you use? Show me the cans?"

"I'd be glad to." He stood, told us he'd be right back, and disappeared through the swinging door into the kitchen. He returned a moment later with two small cans, which he placed on his desk in front of Ace. Although Patrick Jaffe had referred to the canned warming fuel by the brand name Sterno, these cans were actually an off-brand product, probably a more cost-effective option.

Ace gestured to the cans. "Mind if I open them? Take a look?"

"Be my guest," he said.

She whipped out her keys and used one of them to pry the lids off both cans. I leaned over and looked into the cans with her. One of them contained a pink gel. Though it was brighter than most sweet and sour sauces, and appeared more pink than orange, I could see how someone might mistake it for a dipping sauce if it was placed unlit next to a chafing dish and they weren't paying close attention.

Ace picked up the can and read the label. "Looks like this one contains ethanol."

"That's right," the man said. "The pink fuel is ethanol based. It burns longer and hotter than the other, but it's more expensive. The blue one contains methanol. It doesn't burn as hot, but it's cheaper. We use both types depending on the particular circumstances—whether the event is indoor or outdoor, the type of food being served, how long the food will need to be kept warm, those types of considerations."

Ace picked up the can containing the blue gel in turn and read that label, too. "Three point five percent methanol." She consulted the front of the can. "Seven ounces."

She looked up for a moment, seeming to be performing a mental calculation. When she looked down again, she reached her index finger into the can and lightly tapped it once against the gel to get a minute sample. She held the sample to her nose to smell it but had no reaction. I noticed no obvious, overwhelming smell coming from the can, either, just a faint acrid scent.

Her scent testing complete, she returned her focus to the man and pointed to the cans in front of her. "May I take these with me? The lab might need them for testing."

"No problem," the man said. "We have plenty in stock."

Ace placed the lids back on the cans and pressed them securely back into place before putting the cans into her tote bag. She thanked the man for his cooperation, and we left the room.

Once we were back in the hotel lobby, she said, "I did the math. A single can of the blue chafing fuel wouldn't contain enough methanol to be generally lethal, especially to a man Bert's size. He'd have to consume at least two full cans."

"It's not likely he could ingest much of it without noticing the foul taste, right?"

"Right."

It finally seemed we were making some progress. "That means you can also rule out the canned heat as the source of the methanol in the moonshine then, right?"

"Nope."

"Why not?"

"He could've chugged the moonshine. He might've been drinking so fast that the stuff went down before he even tasted it. Or he might not have been able to distinguish the burn of the fuel gel from the burn of the liquor. The taste and smell of some liquor products isn't that different from rubbing alcohol."

"Not *my* products," I said. "At least not my fruit-flavored moonshine." Granddaddy's Ole-Timey Corn Liquor was another story. I thought back to Monday night, when the wives had come down to my shop after the mixer. Dana hadn't bought a jug of Granddaddy's pure 'shine, but Kimberly had. Might she or Patrick have offered some of it to Bert? Could they have disguised the bad taste of the methanol with the high-proof whiskey?

Before I could even complete my thought, Ace said, "It's also possible Bert Gebhardt swallowed the methanol intentionally."

"Intentionally?" It took a moment for the import of the word to sink in. When it did, my jaw dropped. "Really?"

"It's a theory," she said. "Methanol poisoning is somewhat common in situations of self-harm."

I hadn't even considered the possibility that Bert could be responsible for his own death. Had he done himself in for some reason? If so, why now, after he'd packed up his model train display and driven all the way from Milwaukee to Chattanooga for the train convention? "I don't see why he'd do something like that when he'd spent so much time and money to travel here and planned to participate in the competition. The timing seems strange."

"Maybe," she said. "But it might have been a spur-of-the-moment decision. Maybe he thought he was going to lose the contest. When I talked to his wife at the hospital, she told me that he took his trains very seriously. He might have had mental health issues that were exacerbated by the stress of the travel and competition. I'd hazard a guess that he might have suffered from an undiagnosed case of obsessive-compulsive disorder. Dana told me that Bert followed rigid routines and didn't like to vary from them. He didn't like anyone touching his things, either."

My mind went back to the first time I'd seen Bert, when he was tearing the hotel housekeeper up one side and down the other just because she'd unplugged his model. Of course, I also considered the plexiglass shield he'd erected around his display, the only one in the entire convention center. Though some of the other entrants had signs at their tables reading Do Not Touch, no one else had seen the need to secure their models behind a physical barrier.

Ace went on. "Dana said Bert would constantly check things at home. Doors. The stove. The thermostat. His trains." She exhaled softly. "People trivialize OCD, even make jokes about it, but it's not a laughing matter. People with it have a hell of a time. It's not easy to live in an uncertain, imperfect world when you have a desperate need for things to be certain and perfect."

A mental disorder could explain Bert's demeanor, as well as provide a reason for him to consider ending his own life. I felt guilty now for thinking he was a jerk. Maybe he couldn't help himself. Maybe it was just how his brain was wired.

"Nothing Dana told me was inconsistent or an obvious

fabrication," Ace said. "I had another thought, too. If Bert poisoned the 'shine himself, maybe he wasn't his intended victim." She flattened her lips into a hard line and cast me a dark look.

Again, it took me a moment to process her words and, again, my jaw went slack. "Are you saying Bert might have tried to poison Dana?"

"They had two jars of your blackberry 'shine, remember?"

"Yes." I knew Dana had bought a couple of jars at my shop Monday night after telling me how much both she and Bert enjoyed it. "Was the second jar poisoned?"

"No. We collected that one from their hotel room and tested it, too. Bert might have added methanol to one of the jars with the intention of killing off his wife, and then confused the jars. Or maybe Dana figured things out and swapped the jars herself, treated Bert to a taste of his own medicine, so to speak."

"But if that was the case," I said, "why wouldn't Bert have sought medical attention once he started feeling the symptoms? He'd have to realize what was happening, that he'd accidentally drunk from the wrong jar."

"You'd think so," she said. "But maybe he didn't realize his symptoms were from the 'shine. If he thought he drank the unadulterated stuff, he could've just thought he was coming down with a bug. He might have planned for Dana to drink the poisoned jar after they got back home to Milwaukee. Or maybe he thought he could survive it, that given his size he could tolerate the dose he'd ingested. He might have been afraid that getting help would raise suspicion, and that he'd be found out and charged with attempted murder."

Maybe we weren't dealing with a murder after all, then. Maybe we were dealing with a murder attempt gone awry, one that backfired on the intended killer, turning him into his own unwitting victim. But all we had now were *maybes* and *might haves*. We needed facts. We needed proof.

"If we can determine the source of the methanol," Ace said, "where it originated, we can better determine who might have added it to the jar of moonshine, narrow down the list of suspects. But there might be an easier way. It's possible the security cameras caught something." She angled her head toward the entrance. "Come inside and watch the camera footage with me. As you said, you've spent time with these folks. You'll know who's who and can point them out to me. In the meantime, I'll have the lab run more tests on Bert's moonshine, see if they can determine what other chemical ingredients are in it, maybe identify what type of methanol product was added to the 'shine."

Chapter Sixteen

We walked inside. The enticing smell of fresh popcorn greeted us, making my empty stomach rumble, but crime-solving took precedence over concessions. Through the speakers came Arlo Guthrie singing about riding on the train called the City of New Orleans. The song competed with the *toot-toots* and *chugga-chuggas* coming from the displays. A sizable crowd milled about, having grown larger each day as the word got out about the convention. The entire place seemed to be in motion.

Ace showed her Chattanooga PD detective badge at the registration desk. "I'm here on official business." In other words, *I'm coming in free of charge so don't you dare try to sell me a ticket.*

The guy manning the table said, "Is this about the contestant that was killed with the moonshine?"

Ughhhh!

Luckily for me, Ace corrected the man. "The police lab

determined that the moonshine was not the source of the poison."

"Really?" the man said. "Then we've all just wasted an awful lot of liquor. Everybody poured theirs out."

I forced a smile at him. "I own the Moonshine Shack. It's closed today, but everyone is welcome back to my shop tomorrow. I'd be happy to replace their jars." It would be an expensive exercise, but less costly than the loss of good-will.

Ace glanced around, taking things in, before turning back to the man. "Get me someone from security."

"Yes, ma'am." He picked up a walkie-talkie and said, "I need security to the registration table. We've got a detective here needs to speak with you."

Shortly thereafter, a beefy, dark-skinned man with a nicely trimmed beard arrived at the table. He wore a solid black polo shirt with SECURITY printed in big white letters across the back and again in smaller letters above the breast pocket. After Ace quietly told him why she was there, he led us through the convention center to the administrative offices. As earlier, many eyes were on me as I made my way. Though Ace wore a pantsuit rather than a police uniform, she walked with such an air of authority that many people probably realized she was law enforcement. The fact that a security guard escorted us was a dead giveaway, too. I fought the urge to scream *I didn't kill anybody! Just ask the detective! My moonshine is safe to drink!*

A few minutes later, we were watching footage on four large video screens arranged two over two on the wall, one screen for each of the four cameras mounted in the corners of the expansive convention center floor. The security team member had started the footage when the doors opened at

10:00 on Monday morning, marking the start of the convention. Without the displays yet in place, the space was wide open, only the perimeter of empty tables delineating where the vendor booths would be. I couldn't quite get my bearings. The numbers of the booths closest to the cameras were visible, but it was impossible to tell which one was B5, the Gebhardts' booth. We watched at triple time as the space began to fill and take shape, starting to resemble the way it looked now. On the screen, I saw Bert and Dana enter. Dana carried the folding portable table that the display would be set up on. Bert was rolling what appeared to be the eastern half of his Last Spike model along on one of those flat carts like they have at the home improvement stores for moving plants and bags of potting soil or composted cow manure. It was odd to see Bert alive on the screen, knowing what had happened to him later. As the time stamp progressed in the bottom right corner, it was as if it was ticking away the final moments of his life, counting down.

I pointed at the screen on which they appeared. "There's Bert and Dana."

Ace reached over and slowed the feeds to real time. Bert checked in at the registration table, glanced around, then rolled his display into what I could now tell was row B. Unfortunately, he disappeared behind a wide standup banner now displayed at the back of a vendor booth. He didn't come out the other side. Booth B5 was fully hidden behind the banner.

"Son of a—" Ace growled.

She pulled the feed backward in time a few seconds and we watched the other screens. In light of the fact that the convention center was an expansive place, each camera had to take in a very large area as it was. They couldn't duplicate much of the other camera zones. Thus, Bert's booth wasn't in recording range for any of the others. The value of the video was likely to be very limited.

Ace scrubbed a hand over her face. "Looks like I've got my job cut out for me on this one."

After a few minutes, Bert emerged from behind the banner, rolling an empty cart. He must have set up part of his display. He went outside and came back a few minutes later, rolling the western half of his model railroad along. After several minutes behind the banner, he rolled the empty cart back out to the truck and returned to his booth a third time with his toolbox and the display cabinet for the collector trains he had for sale. Again, he moved out of sight behind the banner. A few minutes later, he rolled the empty cart out to his truck and returned without it.

Ace sped up the feed and we watched people come and go. Few stopped at Bert's booth during the early part of the day, too busy working on setting up their own areas. On the feed, I saw myself heading toward the Gebhardts' booth with Granddaddy rolling along beside me on his scooter. We, too, disappeared behind the banner as we stopped to chat with Dana and Bert and invite them to the mixer. A few minutes later, we reappeared as we left their booth.

Early Monday afternoon, according to the time stamp, Kimberly Jaffe walked up to the Gebhardts' space, her blond spikes looking especially ominous from above, like porcupine quills or a bed of nails. Again, the banner blocked our view, but presumably Kimberly was speaking with Dana behind the curtain of vinyl. I pointed to the screen. "The blonde that just disappeared behind the banner? That's Patrick Jaffe's wife, Kimberly."

It crossed my mind what Kate and Kiki had said earlier, that when someone was murdered, it was often their spouse who killed them. But was it also common for someone to kill another person on behalf of their spouse? Could Kimberly Jaffe have poisoned Bert to get revenge for her husband? If she had poisoned Bert, did Patrick know about it, or had she kept it to herself?

Ace must have had the same thought. "What do you know about Kimberly Jaffe?"

"Very little," I said. "She seemed friendly enough. Even though their husbands are sworn enemies, she and Dana seem to get along."

Ace speculated aloud. "Maybe the two of them were in cahoots. They'd both have something to gain if Bert died."

I hadn't even considered that possibility, but what Ace said was true. Both women would benefit from Bert's demise. Dana would be free of her overbearing husband, and Kimberly could ensure her husband's victory in the steam train competition. Even so, I had a hard time visualizing how either of them would broach the subject with the other. Would Dana say, *Hey, Kimberly, let's get Patrick that first place trophy by killing Bert off. Maybe grab a glass of pinot after?* Or would Kimberly have said, *You deserve better than a bully like Bert. I'd be happy to poison your husband for you. Let's hit that moonshine shop down the street later, maybe stir a little antifreeze into his jar. Bottom's up!*

We continued to watch the footage, seeing people come and go at Bert's booth, including Ronnie Wallingford making his repeated visits. For the most part, Stuart Speer hurried by or steered clear, though he did pass behind the banner early Wednesday morning before Bert's booth was attended. Had he tossed the sugar over the plexiglass as he scurried by? Shortly thereafter, I saw me and my grandfather again, though on a different camera's screen. I glanced over as Patrick Jaffe plucked the sugar packets from the trash can. I pointed his movements out to Ace. The feed continued, showing me, Kiki, Kate, and Dalton making the rounds earlier today, until we reached the current time and Ace and I saw ourselves enter the convention center together.

She groaned in frustration. "I'm tempted to go out on the floor, grab that darn banner, and throw it in the trash."

I couldn't blame her. It might have prevented her from viewing critical evidence that could have resolved this case quickly and easily.

Ace thanked the security staff and we headed back out to the convention center floor. Gladys Knight & the Pips were playing from the speakers now, singing "Midnight Train to Georgia." The Pips sang the train horn sound effect— *hoo-hoo!*

Ace glanced around and impatiently circled a hand in the air. "Get me to Dana Gebhardt."

"Booth B five," I said, motioning with my hand. "This way."

She walked alongside me as I led the way to the Gebhardts' space. Dana sat there, reclined in her zero-gravity chair, her arm crooked back over her eyes. Looked like exhaustion had finally caught up with her. *Is she asleep?*

Marlon was still there, too, sitting just in front of the cordon tape in Bert's lawn chair. He was looking down at his phone, one earbud in his ear, the other dangling at his chest so that he could hear if someone addressed him. He glanced up as we approached, doing a double take when he realized it was me and Ace. He stood and yanked the earbud from his ear. "Ace. Hattie."

After we exchanged greetings, Marlon looked from one of us to the other and quietly asked, "Hattie told me her moonshine was cleared. Any other updates?"

Ace said, "We're working some new angles." She cut her eyes to Dana and then the crowd flowing by, silently communicating to Marlon that she didn't want to discuss things further out here in the open where someone might overhear. "Hattie's helping me out. At least if she's with me, I know what she's up to." She slid her gaze to me now, her expression one of slight reproach, before turning back to Marlon. "You're free to go," she said. "I appreciate your assistance today. Charlotte, too. I owe her some sugar cubes for her patience."

"She'd like that." He slid his phone and earbuds into his pants pocket. "You'll fill me in later?"

"As soon as I can," Ace said.

As he stepped away, he reached out and grabbed my upper arm, giving it an encouraging squeeze. Now that Ace was okay with me being here, he'd also seemed to have forgiven me for ignoring his admonition to stay out of the investigation. I appreciated his support and understanding. I gave him a grateful smile in return.

Dana still hadn't roused. I supposed that after attending model train conventions all these years, she'd learned to catnap through all the noise and hubbub.

Ace stepped in front of her chair and softly said, "Excuse me? Mrs. Gebhardt?"

"Hmm? Huh?" Dana lifted her arm from her eyes and glanced groggily around before her gaze landed on Ace and me. Her voice was hoarse and raspy from sleep when she spoke. "Oh. Hello, Detective Pearce. Hattie." She sat up in her chair, blinking to clear her eyes much as her husband had done—in vain—the day before. "Everything okay?"

"I've got some news for you," Ace said. "It could be upsetting. Would you like to speak elsewhere?"

Her eyes, now lucid, sparked in alarm. She gripped the

armrests of her chair, her knuckles whitening. "We can talk here. If you've got news, I don't want to wait to hear it. What is it?"

Ace said, "It wasn't bad moonshine that killed your husband."

Dana's neck went forward, then back, her eyes narrowing, then widening. She looked like a confused chicken. "What do you mean? Was it food poisoning instead?"

"I mean the methanol that killed Bert?" Ace said. "It wasn't in the jar of moonshine when you bought it."

Her neck went back again, her eyes squinting. "Then how in the world did it get in there?"

"That's what we're here to find out," Ace said. She turned and gave a buzz-off look to a man who'd stopped to gander over the cordon tape at Bert's model, before returning her attention to Dana. "I realize this might be a sensitive question, but I have to ask it. Do you have any reason to believe your husband might have taken his own life?"

"What? Bert?" she said. Her face clouded and she stared at a spot on the carpet for a long moment, shaking her head almost imperceptibly before finally looking up again. "My husband wasn't a happy man, Detective. He could be very intense. Things tended to eat at him. As much as I'd like to say it wasn't possible that he took his own life, if I'm honest I suppose he could have. But if that's the case, he never told me of his intentions. I didn't find a note, either."

"Let me ask you something else," Ace said. "And I mean no offense by it. But is there a chance your husband might have put poison in the moonshine with the intention of harming you instead of himself? Has he ever hurt you, or threatened to hurt you?"

Again, Dana's expression faltered. "He never threatened me with bodily harm or physically hurt me," she said.

"I . . ." She hesitated for a long moment, as if summoning her strength, before saying, "I can't see him trying to poison me, though. I just can't. He might have been a grumpy man, but he wasn't a violent one."

"Understood," Ace said. "Tell me, who's been in your hotel room since you arrived?"

Dana's mouth wriggled as she looked up and thought back. "Me and Bert, of course. I guess that goes without saying. The housekeepers. A few of the other ladies came by Tuesday evening. Bert had stepped out to go visit the local hobby shops and see what they might have for sale. The other wives invited me to have drinks with them on the outdoor patio."

"How long were they in your room?"

"Only a minute or two," Dana said, "while I freshened up in the bathroom."

A minute or two was more than enough time for someone to have surreptitiously exchanged their tainted jar of blackberry moonshine for one of Bert and Dana's jars. Ace must have had the same thought. "Who were the ladies in the group?"

Dana rattled off some names I didn't recognize before hitting on one I knew. "Kimberly Jaffe . . ." She went on to name two or three others.

My mind went back to Kimberly's backpack-style purse, the big one in which she'd stuffed both jars and the jug of moonshine she'd bought at my shop. The purse rivaled Ace's tote bag in size. Kimberly could have easily carried a single jar of 'shine in it to the Gebhardts' hotel room with no one being the wiser.

Dana went on. "We wives sat out on the patio for an hour or so, complaining about our husbands like we always do." She offered a sad smile. "If I'd known Bert wouldn't be my husband much longer, I wouldn't have joined in." She gulped back a sob, closed her eyes for a moment, and fisted her hands.

When Dana opened her eyes, Ace said, "Is it okay if I look in your husband's toolbox, see what he might have had on hand that contained methanol?"

Dana cocked her head. "You mean to say there might be methanol in his cleaners and whatnot?"

"Could be," Ace said. "Methanol is a common ingredient in chemical products."

"You're welcome to take a look." Dana pointed down at his toolbox. "It's right there. I've sold a couple of his tools out of it today. I don't even know what's what in there, but the buyer referred to one of the things as a universal track distance tool and the other was some sort of pliers for removing spike heads."

"Did you only sell the tools," Ace asked, "or have you sold any of his cleaning supplies?"

"Far as I know," she said, "all of his cleaning supplies are still there. Nobody was looking after the booth while I was at the hospital with Bert yesterday, so I suppose it's possible some of his things walked off, but I have no way of knowing. He never let me touch his cleaning supplies. He was afraid I wouldn't do things properly and that I'd break something."

Ace donned a pair of latex gloves, opened the toolbox, and began inspecting the bottles, tubes, and jars of cleaner and other chemical products. As she turned one of the bottles around to check the label, I noticed it was Gleam Dream Glass & Window Cleaner, the same kind Ronnie Wallingford used, a brand that contained methanol.

Ace continued looking through the rest of the items before closing the toolbox and picking it up.

Dana looked startled. "You're taking the whole thing away?"

"Here, I'd be rushed," Ace said. "If I take the toolbox back to my office, I can take my time with it. I know you'd want me to give it my best attention."

"Oh, I do," Dana said. "It's just that I was hoping to sell off more of Bert's tools. I've got no use for them, and I'd hate to be stuck having to take them all back to Milwaukee. I'm trying to get rid of as much of this stuff as I can before heading home. I wouldn't even know how to manage it. Bert normally took care of it all."

"I'll get the toolbox back to you tomorrow morning," Ace said. "That'll give you two days, tomorrow and Saturday, to sell off his tools. Sound good?"

"All right," Dana said.

"Maybe one of the vendors will take them off your hands," I suggested. "I noticed some of them deal in secondhand tools and parts. Or maybe you could sell them online."

"Those are good ideas, Hattie," Dana said. "I might have thought of them myself if I wasn't so flustered and worn out." She shook her head and exhaled an exhausted breath. "I feel like I'm all in a tizzy."

Ace bent down and looked under Bert's display table. While she was bent down, she glanced over at the locked cabinet under the display of collectible trains. She pointed. "Can you show me what's in there?"

"It's empty," Dana said. "That's where the clear panels are stored when the display case isn't assembled and in use. But I'm happy to give you a look." She rounded up the keys from her purse and unlocked the display cabinet. I glanced over at it myself as Ace took a look. The shelves underneath were indeed empty.

Ace stood again and gestured to the track. "Miss Hayes told me about the sugar on your husband's tracks. Do you have any idea who might have put it there?"

Dana shook her head. "None at all." But then she bit her lip and her eyes clouded. "I mean, I didn't see anyone do it, or see anyone with sugar packets. But there are some men here who didn't hold my husband in the highest regard."

That's putting it mildly.

"What men?" Ace asked.

Dana mentioned the same men I'd already told Ace about. Patrick Jaffe. Stuart Speer. Ronnie Wallingford. "Bert had words with each of them here."

"Did any of them openly threaten your husband with harm?"

"No," Dana said. "Nothing like that. They just argued over one thing or another. The judging of the steam train models. The value of a vintage train car." She sighed, weary. "It all seems so pointless now, such a waste of time and energy."

I didn't know what to say to that. Ace didn't seem to know, either. That time was gone. Bert's life was over. It couldn't be undone or redone.

Ace turned to me. "Thanks for your help, Hattie. You're free to go now. Get your shop back open."

The first thing I did when I returned to my van was call Nora to let her know the Moonshine Shack would be saved and that she could return to work the following day.

"Thank goodness!" she said. "I'd hate to have to go looking for a new job all over again."

"And I'd hate to lose you."

Granddaddy didn't answer the phone in his room at the

Singing River Retirement Home, so I drove there, parked in the visitor lot, and ventured inside to find my grandfather. Granddaddy sat in an armchair in the rec room sipping iced tea, which he'd probably spiked with 'shine, and watching the old Western movie *High Noon* with some of his buddies. His face brightened when he saw me walk in, and he used his cane to lever himself to a stand. He scuttled over as fast as he could. "What's the news? They clear your 'shine yet?"

"They did," I said. "I'm free to reopen the Moonshine Shack."

He shook his head. "I told that detective there warn't nothing wrong with your 'shine. If she'd just listened to me, she could've saved everyone some trouble."

There was no point in telling him that law enforcement had to verify things and couldn't just take someone's word for it, so instead I said, "You want to finish the movie or come down to the shop with me?"

"The shop," he said. "I've seen *High Noon* seventy-three times. I could recite the lines in my sleep."

We loaded back into my van and drove down to the Moonshine Shack, where I promptly opened my store and set out my sandwich board. Granddaddy plunked himself down in a rocking chair out front with his tumbler of iced tea and his whittling tools. Though my shop had been closed less than twenty-four hours, it felt like a lifetime.

It was late afternoon by then, nearly dinnertime. I was debating whether to order takeout or make do with a can of soup and saltines from my storeroom, when a familiar clop-clop-clop sounded out front. A moment later, Marlon's voice drawled, "Whoa, girl."

I came out of my stockroom, walked through the shop, and opened the door. "Hey, Marlon."

"Hey," Marlon said as he tied Charlotte's reins to the post. He gave my grandfather a nod. "How's your day going?"

Granddaddy rocked back in his chair. "Fair to middlin'."

Marlon looked from my grandfather to me. "You two eat yet?"

"No," I said. "I was just debating what to do about dinner."

Marlon crooked an arm up on the porch post. "I say we order a pizza. We can even get one with all of those red and green and yellow things on it if you want."

I scoffed. "They're called vegetables. And they're good for you."

"No green pepper!" Granddaddy hollered. "It doesn't agree with me."

"You just say that because you don't like the taste."

He harrumphed but said nothing further.

While Marlon called in our order—extra-large veggie supreme, no green pepper—I rounded up some carrots from the mini fridge in the stockroom for Charlotte and brought them out to her. Her velvety nose brushed my palm as she took them in her teeth. I ran my hand over her neck as she noisily crunched her way through them. Once Marlon had finished his call, we took seats side by side on the porch swing, like an old married couple.

He made a come-here motion with his index finger. "I feel like I only got bits and pieces of the story today. Catch me up."

I told him about my day, how it started with me, Kiki, Kate, and Dalton at the coffee shop, where I stood behind Stuart Speer in line and noticed he didn't get raw sugar and a stir stick today like he had yesterday. I told him how Speer acted strange when he'd spotted us comparing the sugar in the concessions area at the convention center, how he'd subsequently denied that he'd sabotaged Bert's model, how none of us believed his proclamation of innocence. I went on to tell him how my friends and I had made the rounds at the convention center and spoken with Ronnie Wallingford and the Jaffes, how all of them had acted shady and suspect. I told him how I'd pointed out the sugar on the tracks to Dana and notified Ace, which resulted in his being summoned to stand guard over the model until Ace could take over and collect evidence from it, which she presumably did after dismissing me today. I told him about reading stories to Dalton, and what a misogynist creep Mike Mulligan was, how he didn't deserve a new steam shovel after dumping Mary Anne.

Marlon cocked his head. "I think you're getting a little off topic."

"All I'm saying is Mike should have treated Mary Anne better. He shouldn't have made her dig that big hole for him and then left her down in it. That's all."

"Agreed," Marlon said. "He's a jerk." He reached out and twirled one of my curls around his finger, flashing a mischievous grin. "For what it's worth, I'd never leave you down in a hole."

"Careful," I teased. "You might make me swoon." Returning to the more important topic, I said, "Ace had me watch the security videos with her at the convention center. She needed my help identifying folks on the screen."

"Did you two glean anything from the footage?"

"Not much," I said. "The footage was worthless. One of the vendors had put up a huge banner that blocked the view of Bert's booth."

"So, you couldn't tell if anyone switched out his jar of 'shine there? Or doctored it with poison?"

"Nope. We saw some people come and go on the video,

Kimberly Jaffe for one, but whether they exchanged the jars at the booth or poured something in Bert's bottle is anyone's guess. After we watched the security footage, we went to Dana's booth and Ace rounded up Bert's toolbox and looked around. She dismissed me then. That's the last thing I know."

Marlon stopped swinging and instead stretched his long legs out in front of him, his black riding boots crossed at the ankle. "I can guess what Ace did next. She made the rounds of all those folks you mentioned. Rodney—"

"Ronnie," I corrected him.

"Peter and Katherine—"

"Patrick and Kimberly."

"Steve Spare."

"Stuart Speer."

I looked over to see that grin still playing about his lips, even bigger now. I scowled at him. "Stop yanking my chain."

"But it's fun to see you get riled up and feisty."

I rolled my eyes.

Turning back to the investigation, Marlon said, "Ace searched all their booths and hotel rooms, I guarantee you. She'd have seized any of their cleaners that contained methanol so they can be compared to the other chemicals found in Bert's jar of tainted moonshine. They all sound like good suspects. Chances are one of them did it."

"Probably," I agreed. "They all had a motive. But I still wonder about the housekeeper."

"It wasn't her," Marlon said.

"How can you be so sure?"

"Because people always accuse the housekeepers, and it's never the housekeepers."

"You sound just like Ace."

"For good reason. I respond to calls at hotels and

businesses around here all the time, people claiming the cleaning staff took their jewelry or phones or tablets. Half the time I find the stuff fallen down behind the dresser or bedside table."

He could very well be right. I hoped I wasn't wrongfully implicating Martha. But it wasn't like my suspicion had no basis at all. She had brandished a bottle of glass cleaner behind Bert's back, called him a number of choice words under her breath. *Maybe I'll have to explore this angle on my own.* I told him what Kiki and Kate thought. "They're sure it's Dana."

"Could be," Marlon said. "Some people take 'till death do us part' a bit too literally. But most often it's the husband who kills the wife, not the other way around."

"My friend Kate said the same thing. Besides, there's no evidence pointing to Dana." Bert had made a lot of enemies, but there were no clues clearly pointing to any of them, either.

Marlon intertwined his fingers and rested his hands on his belly. "In the time I spent with Dana Gebhardt today, she didn't act like everything between her and her husband was peaches and cream. When a spouse is guilty, they sometimes act like they're so heartbroken they can hardly go on. They overplay their hand. Their melodrama gives them away."

I concurred with his assessment of Dana's behavior. "She's been fairly forthcoming about her husband's faults. Not in a mean way, but in a realistic way. She wasn't openly crying today, but she looked tired, like she hadn't slept much, if at all, last night."

"Either she's very pragmatic," Marlon said, "or he didn't mean a whole lot to her."

"I got the impression their marriage derailed years ago

but, like a lot of people, she hung on for other reasons. Financial maybe. Maybe because they shared children. Maybe because being alone didn't sound much better than putting up with a curmudgeon."

"Speaking of being alone," he said. "Let's not do that Saturday. How about we get together instead and go on another trail ride? Charlotte would love to see some different scenery. What say we take her up to the equestrian trails at Summit Knobs?"

Nora was scheduled to work Saturday and Kiki had offered to help out, so the store would be covered. "I'm game if Charlotte is."

Marlon looked to his horse. "What do you say, Charlotte?"

She raised her head and issued a nicker.

Marlon gave her a nod. "We'll take that as a yes."

Chapter Seventeen

Marlon, Granddaddy, and I enjoyed our pizza together on the porch of my shop. As we did, I glanced over at Marlon, wondering where things between us might lead. What kind of ticket did we have to this romantic ride? Would we stay on track for a long-distance trip, or would we split off at some point, recouple with other people, and head off in different directions?

I wondered whether he was seeing anyone else besides me, who I might be competing against for his attention and affection—besides Charlotte, that is. He'd made it clear she'd always be his number-one girl, and I was okay with that. Smoky would always be my number one guy, too. Though I was tempted to ask Marlon whether he was seeing anyone else, I wasn't sure it was wise to put my cards on the table yet. I wasn't seeing anyone else at the moment, but he didn't need to know that. Not unless he asked. Yep, the only thing around my shop that had been labeled was the moonshine.

Even so, it would be nice to establish a mutual understanding of where we stood. If he didn't bring it up soon, I just might have to.

Granddaddy fell asleep in his rocker and proved he could, indeed, quote lines from *High Noon* in his sleep. He mumbled and muttered. "'Don't try to be a hero. You don't have to be a hero, not for me.'"

I n a rare act of affection, Smoky met me at the door of our cabin when I arrived home after work late Thursday evening. He'd become used to me taking him to the shop. I supposed it now felt extra lonely to be up here all by himself all day, especially when I'd left so early this morning to meet my friends for coffee and hadn't returned until well after dark. I heaved the hefty cat up into my arms. He stiffarmed me with a paw to my chest, as usual, but he did let me smooch his furry cheek and carry him to the kitchen without putting up too much of a fuss.

After spooning a can of shredded tuna cat food into Smoky's bowl, I poured myself a couple of fingers of my peach moonshine. I sipped the 'shine straight while Smoky and I curled up on the couch and watched the nightly news. I used the remote to circle repeatedly through the local stations, trying to catch any news about the murder. My shop didn't seem to be mentioned in connection with Bert Gebhardt's death on any of the channels as far as I could tell, thank goodness. In fact, there was only a brief mention in one of the broadcasts about an out-of-towner who'd been visiting Chattanooga for the model train convention and had succumbed to a suspicious methanol poisoning. *The source of the methanol has yet to be determined, and the investigation is still underway.*

As soon as the police lab had determined what other chemicals and ingredients had been in Bert's 'shine, they could determine exactly what product had been mixed in. I was curious what it would turn out to be. Antifreeze used by Ronnie Wallingford? The chafing fuel Patrick Jaffe mentioned? A glass cleaner? It dawned on me that maybe someone had used windshield wiper fluid. All those rental trucks in the parking lot of the convention center would contain enough fluid to poison dozens, if not hundreds, of folks. It would be easy enough to siphon the fluid out of the receptacle in the engine by using a syringe or turkey baster or even those small pipettes that a few of the vendors had for sale at the convention. The tiny gadgets were intended to be used to apply thin lines or small dots of glue to a model train display, but they could have been repurposed for murder. *Who knows?*

Smoky slept curled up against my chest, and even deigned to purr softly for a few minutes before he dozed off, another rarity for the usually aloof feline. I supposed it was true that absence makes the heart grow fonder, even if that heart was a furry one. *Maybe I should ignore him more often.* I dismissed the thought nearly as soon as I'd had it. No way could I intentionally ignore my little guy, make him feel desperate for my attention. I adored him too much. Yep, he had me wrapped around his furry padded paw.

Now that my moonshine had been cleared and I was off the hook, I slept much better. I woke on Friday feeling refreshed. But I also woke feeling curious. Were Ace and Marlon right about Martha? Did the housekeeper have nothing to do with Bert Gebhardt dying? Or was I right to suspect there could be more to her story? I found it odd she'd come to the model train convention after having it out with Bert Gebhardt. Why would she purposely put herself in a position where she might end up in a confrontation with the man again? She'd have to have a compelling reason.

I decided to find out for myself. After all, whoever had killed Bert had the nerve to implicate my moonshine and could have put an end to my business and my dream. They'd used me for their own gain. My backside remained thoroughly chapped by that fact. If I could help put that person behind bars, I could even the score. This fight for justice was my fight, too. Or maybe I was just a busybody who enjoyed solving puzzles and was trying to justify my butting into the investigation. The truth was probably somewhere in between.

At any rate, I fed Smoky, ate my breakfast, and showered in record time. Rather than my usual overalls and logo-imprinted T-shirt, I put on the baby-blue A-line dress with white polka dots that I'd bought to wear to Kate's baby shower months before. I paired it with white sandals, slathered my face with three times my usual amount of makeup, and pulled my curls up into a bouncy bunch atop my head in a poor girl's attempt to look like Shirley Temple back in the day. The final piece of my disguise was a pair of cheap red plastic reading glasses that had belonged to my granny.

When I took a look at myself in my full-length mirror, I hardly recognized myself. Part of that was because I looked nothing like the everyday Hattie, but part of that was because the reading glasses distorted my vision. I removed the glasses, used my thumb to punch out the lenses, and put them back on. Yep, I definitely didn't look like the woman in denim overalls everyone had seen around the convention center complex the past few days. *Good*. I'd have an easier time spying on Martha if I could do it incognito.

I gave Smoky a peck on the head and ruffled his ears. As I removed my hand, he reached up to swipe at it. "Be good while I'm gone. Don't be lazy. Maybe chase a bug or do some squats. It'll be good for you."

He gave me a dirty look that said he thought he was perfect just the way he was, cinder block physique and all.

I grabbed my purse, went out to my van, and drove down the mountain, finding myself sitting in rush-hour traffic, creeping along at a snail's pace as I made my way into the riverfront area. *Thank goodness I don't have to deal with this every day.* Working irregular hours at my shop definitely had some benefits.

Finally, I arrived at the hotel. As I parked and turned off my van's motor, I checked the time on the dashboard clock. It was half past eight. The housekeepers should be starting their rounds soon, if they hadn't already.

I grabbed my purse and headed into the hotel. As I made my way across the lobby, my ears detected the unmistakable cadence of Kimberly Jaffe's titter. *Hee-hee-HEE-hee!* I turned toward the sound to see a group of the model railroaders' wives sitting at a long table in the restaurant seating area in the atrium. They were having breakfast together, plates of half-eaten waffles and pancakes sitting on the table in front of them. Dana Gebhardt sat among the ladies. While she wasn't giggling like Kimberly, she did have a smile on her face, seeming to also find amusing whatever had set Kimberly off.

While it might appear that she was unaffected by her husband's death, her mood might have been lifted by the mimosa sitting in front of her. Plus, I had to consider that, even if losing her husband might have brought her grief, it might have brought her some relief, too. Bert had been overbearing and controlling, treating her like his trains, expecting

her to follow the course he alone had laid out for them.
People could have mixed feelings about their spouses. Re-
lationships could be complicated and contradictory. Smoky
was proof of that. Many times he ignored me, as if I was
unimportant and didn't exist. Other times he grabbed my
fingers in his teeth when I tried to pull my hand away after
petting him. *Moody little mongrel.*

I continued on, making my way into the hallway where
I'd seen Martha on Monday, taking a tongue-lashing from
Bert. A housekeeping cart sat in the corridor up ahead,
pulled over in front of an open door on the opposite side of
the hall from the Gebhardts' room. It would be the perfect
opportunity for me to figure out which cleaning products
the hotel staff used and whether any might contain methanol. It would also be a chance for me to speak with Martha.
At least, I hoped the person cleaning the room would be
Martha. I'd noticed hotels seemed to assign the same staff
to certain floors, probably so that their faces would become
more familiar to guests and make the guests feel more at
ease with them going in and out of their rooms. Or maybe
it was for ease of internal accountability, so that they knew
who was or was not doing a good job on certain floors
based on the appearance of the area.

As I tiptoed toward the cart, the sound of a vacuum
started up inside the guest room ahead. *Good.* It would
provide some cover for me. I scurried up, careful to stay out
of sight of the open doorway, and pulled my phone from my
purse. I quickly snapped a series of photos of the cleaning
products lined up on the cart. Citrus-scented furniture polish. Bleach-based bathroom disinfectant spray. And *aha!*
The bottle of cobalt-blue glass cleaner. According to the
label, it was the Gleam Dream brand, the same type Ronnie
Wallingford used, the brand that had been sitting in the bin

at his booth with a bunch of other cleaning supplies. I knew from looking at its label earlier that, despite its benign-looking bright blue color, the brand contained copious amounts of methanol. The product was a spray bottle of potential death.

A reusable steel water bottle sat beside the cleaning products. Although I had yet to actually see the woman vacuuming in the guest room, the name Martha Grissom was written on the bottle in permanent marker.

I'd been so focused on the cleaning products that I hadn't seen a guest come up the hall. The man wore a train engineer outfit, pegging him as one of the conventioneers. He cast me an odd look, clearly wondering why I was so interested in photographing toilet and glass cleaners. Fortunately, he didn't ask. He might have figured we'd have to shout over the sound of the vacuum. I gave him a quick smile and tapped on my phone's screen, hoping to make him think he'd been mistaken, that I'd merely been sending a text rather than snapping pics of the housekeeping cart.

The whir of the vac stopped. Realizing I'd appear suspicious hanging out right here by the cart, I turned around and scampered back to the beginning of the hall. I walked slowly toward the cart, retracing my steps, trying to time my arrival at the cart with Martha's return to it with the vacuum.

A hand reached out through the open door and pushed the housekeeping cart out of the way. Oddly, the hand did not appear old, frail, and papery, like Martha's should. *Huh.* Then again, maybe I was too far back to get a good look. Besides the hand had shot out and then been pulled back into the room, providing me only a quick glimpse.

The vacuum emerged from the room next, reared back at an angle on its back wheels. A woman in a housekeeping uniform walked out behind it. Unfortunately, this woman was portly, middle-aged, and ginger haired, rather than thin and elderly with a maple syrup–colored coiffure. Maybe Martha had the day off. With the hotel being open 24/7, the cleaning staff probably rotated shifts. Or maybe Martha was cleaning on another hallway or floor.

By then, I was coming up on the cart. The woman looked my way and said, "Good morning."

"Hi." I stopped. "I'm looking for Martha. Is she around?"

"Martha the housekeeper?" the woman asked.

"Yes," I said. "I saw her here earlier in the week." *And now I want to spy on her, see if I notice any dubious behavior.* The only dubious thing I saw at the moment was this woman's expression. She squinted, her focus roaming over my lens-less glasses. I whisked them off my face and tucked them into my purse before she could realize they were merely part of a disguise.

"Something I can help you with?" she asked flatly. She might have assumed I was going to be like those people Ace and Marlon had mentioned, the guests who made baseless accusations of theft against the cleaning staff or derided them for moving the guest's personal belongings out of the way to accomplish their tasks.

I realized I'd have to get on this woman's good side if I expected to get very far with her. I lowered my voice to a whisper. "I saw a man yell at her in this hall on Monday morning. He was relentless. I just wanted to see how she was doing."

The woman's face and shoulders relaxed. "Oh. That's nice of you. But that man?" A hot rage flashed in her eyes. "He got Martha fired."

"Fired?" Whoa. I pointed to the steel water bottle on the cart. "But I see her bottle right there."

The woman glanced over. "Yeah. I wasn't sure what to do with it. I got reassigned to this floor after she was let go and they gave me her cart to use. I guess she forgot to take it with her."

"Do you know what happened?" I asked. "Why she got fired?" Her excuse for having entered the Gebhardts' room despite the do not disturb sign being hung on the knob was reasonable. The sign had been fully hidden behind the pizza flyer and easy to overlook. She hadn't intentionally disregarded the sign. It seemed unfair to fire a worker under those circumstances.

The woman glanced around as if to make sure none of the guests could overhear her gossiping about one of their own before leaning in to whisper to me. "The guest you talked about? He insisted that the manager call Martha to his office right then and there. Rumor has it that the conversation got ugly and Martha called the man a really insulting name, right to his face. If she'd kept her mouth shut, she might have just gotten a verbal reprimand."

In light of what I'd heard Martha mutter on Monday morning, I didn't have a hard time believing she'd called Bert an offensive name. Even so, the guy had earned it, decorous or not.

The housekeeper sighed. "The manager had no choice but to terminate Martha on the spot. When the manager asked her to sign a form acknowledging she'd made the mistake, she supposedly told the manager to stick the paperwork where the sun doesn't shine." The woman's expression turned wry. "Martha does have a potty mouth, but she's not one of those nasty people who's rude for no reason. All of us liked working with her. She was fast and she'd always do more than her fair share to help the rest of us out. Anyway, after the manager fired her, she walked right out the door. One of the other housekeepers was sweeping the lobby at the time and saw her go. She didn't even turn in her uniform."

If Martha had been fired on Monday, she wouldn't have been working Tuesday morning, and couldn't have taken advantage of her time cleaning in the Gebhardts' room to poison the jar of blackberry moonshine. Then again, if Martha had walked out with her uniform, she might have also walked out with her housekeeping key card. But had she subsequently used it to sneak into the Gebhardts' room and poison Bert's jar of moonshine with a cleaning product?

She certainly had a good motive now. Bert had cost the woman her job. But she had to realize Bert's wife was in the room, too. Would she have poisoned the 'shine knowing it could hurt or kill Dana? Would she be willing to accept that kind of collateral damage to get revenge on the man who'd cost her a job? Besides, wouldn't the hotel management have immediately deactivated Martha's key card so that she wouldn't be able to get back into the guest rooms? Seemed that voiding the card would be part of the usual termination process. But if Martha had walked out and not followed usual procedures, maybe the management had forgotten about her card and failed to cancel it.

I offered a sympathetic smile. "I'm sorry to hear that Martha was let go. She didn't deserve to be terminated."

The woman glanced anxiously across the hall to the Gebhardts' room. "I'm terrified to go in there. I'm afraid the man will get angry about something again. I can't afford to lose my job."

They haven't heard. "You don't need to worry about that," I said. "The guy passed away."

"Passed away?" Her jaw went slack and a line of confusion formed a gulley between her brows. "What are you talking about?"

"Did you hear about the guy from the train convention who died?"

"The one they say was poisoned?"

"Yes. That's the one. He was the guy who got Martha fired." In a sense, both Bert and Martha had been terminated. Now, he'd be stuck where the sun doesn't shine.

The housekeeper had been leaning toward me as we talked quietly, but she eased back now. "We didn't know that. We've all been running around here like deer in headlights." She exhaled a long breath. "Wow. I'm going to let the others know. Maybe we can talk to our manager and see if he'll give Martha her job back."

"I hope it all works out." I gave the woman a final smile and turned to leave the hotel. As I made my way back through the lobby, I heard Kimberly Jaffe's giggle again. *Hee-hee-HEE-hee!* I had to hand it to her. That woman knew how to have a good time.

Chapter Eighteen

I exited the hotel and walked back to my van. Once I was seated, I pulled up the pics I'd taken of the cleaning products I'd seen on the cart and enlarged them so I could read the ingredients.

The aerosol furniture polish was chock-full of toxic and risky ingredients. Turpentine. Propane. Something called cyclopentasiloxane which, according to a quick Internet search, had endocrine-disrupting properties. Though methanol did not appear in the list of ingredients, the list did contain three long words with "meth" in them: octamethyl-cyclotetrasiloxane, methylchloroisothiazolinone, and methylisothiazolinone. *Cheese and grits!* I couldn't have pronounced those chemicals if someone pointed a gun at my head. Science had not been my forte, and what little chemistry I'd learned all related to the moonshine-making process.

I ran a second search, this one on the bathroom cleaner.

This cleaning product was not much better as far as health risks, though it, too, contained no methanol. Like the furniture polish, it contained chemicals that could kill you slowly over time, after repeated exposures, not relatively quickly with a small dose like methanol would.

I slumped against my seat and thought back. Bert, too, had used the Gleam Dream brand of glass cleaner. So had Ronnie Wallingford. That meant Martha, Ronnie, and Bert all had the lethal substance in easy reach. By implication, so would Dana, since she'd presumably have access to Bert's toolbox—which he'd forbidden her from touching. But Bert's bottles of cleaner had been full. I had the photo Ace showed me as proof. I pulled it up on my phone and took another look at it now, once again noting the off color of the 'shine before verifying what I already knew to be true. Bert's bottles of cleaner were full to the brim. Still, something swirled in my mind, a dark wisp of an idea that dissipated before it could take shape, like a puff from a train's smokestack.

I knew the police lab was trying to determine what substance had been added to the moonshine to kill Bert Gebhardt, and I knew Ace would have to figure out which of the suspects had possession of or access to which toxic products. *Might as well help her along, right?* I e-mailed her the photo of the cleaning products on the hotel's housekeeping cart. Rather than tell her that I'd been snooping and sleuthing again on my own, I told her a little fib: *I was taking a shortcut through the hotel this morning and happened by this housekeeping cart. Took a quick pic. Thought it might be helpful to see that the hotel also uses Gleam Dream.*

My nerves began to buzz. *Could Martha have used the hotel's glass cleaner to kill Bert?* She seemed to be the most likely suspect right now. Not only did she have easy access to a product that contained methanol, but she could have used her housekeeping uniform and master key to access the Gebhardts' room to poison the moonshine. She also had the greatest motive among the suspects. Bert had taken away her livelihood. She might easily feel justified in taking his life in return.

Now that I knew Martha had access to a methanol product, my curiosity was further stoked. She'd cussed out Bert. Her manager, too. She apparently wasn't someone with a lot of self-control. Or maybe she was, but she'd thought they'd deserved to be called the names and she was willing to accept the consequences. Maybe she felt that she had to take a stand. If only I knew her better, perhaps I could figure things out.

What was her last name? I couldn't recall, but it had been written on the water bottle I'd seen in the cart. I pulled up the pic again on my phone and enlarged it so I could read the name scrawled on the bottle. *Grissom.*

With all the talk of privacy policies and data breaches these days, it was also easier than ever to find private, personal information about people. All it took was me typing in her name along with Chattanooga, TN, and the mylife. com website spit out an address for her. It was scary, really, how easy it had been.

I typed the address into maps and set off to perform surveillance, a spy in polka dots.

Fifteen minutes later, I pulled slowly past Martha Grissom's home. Though her house was of modest size and had only a carport with an aluminum roof rather than a garage, it appeared to be well maintained and the yellow paint was bright and cheerful. Pink dianthus surrounded the base of the post to her mailbox at the curb. A Nissan Versa sedan sat in the driveway, the orange paint reminiscent of a monarch butterfly.

But while Martha's house showed pride of ownership, some of the others on her street did not. Shutters were missing on the house next door to hers, and one of the front windows was patched with plywood and silver duct tape. Three houses down, children's outdoor toys lay broken and fading among tall, patchy grass in desperate need of mowing. All in all, the neighborhood was a mixed bag.

I don't know what I'd expected to gain by driving by, but I'd learned little. Nevertheless, I circled the block and eased slowly by again. Once I'd passed it, I glanced back at her place in my rearview mirror. *Wait. Did the car's reverse lights just come on?*

I slowed, shifting my focus between the road ahead of me and my rearview mirror. *Yep.* The orange Nissan backed out of the driveway and into the street, its rear visible as it headed off in the other direction. I decided to seize the opportunity and follow her. At the next intersection, I wheeled around in as tight a circle as my van could manage and headed after her. Or at least I hoped I was heading after Martha. After all, I didn't know for certain whether the Nissan sedan belonged to her or someone else who might be living in the house with her. For all I knew, I was following a family member or roommate, or maybe even someone who'd merely stopped by for a visit.

But when the car stopped at a traffic light at the exit to her neighborhood and I pulled up behind it, I was able to verify that it was indeed Martha at the wheel. Her maple-syrup hair poof stuck up an inch or two above the headrest. What's more, I could see part of her face in her rearview mirror.

When the light turned and she hooked a left, I waited for

a few seconds before heading out after her. I didn't want her to realize she was being followed.

We were on a four-lane road. While she stayed in the far-right lane, I drove in the one to the left, intentionally trying to stay in her blind spot, the exact opposite of what I'd been taught to do by my driving instructor when I was fifteen and learning the ropes. With my van in the other lane, Martha wouldn't see me in her mirrors and know I was trailing her.

When she slowed and turned on her right blinker to signal an upcoming turn, I eased over into her lane and took the turn a few seconds after her. She drove up the block and turned on her right blinker again, this time turning into the parking lot of a low, single-story brick building. *The post office.*

I turned in, too, driving past the back of her car as she took a space near the door. I parked my van at the very end of the lot and climbed out. After she went inside, I gave it a few seconds and ventured inside, too.

A couple of people were in the lobby. One was pulling a pile of mail from his post office box. Judging from the thick stack, it looked like he hadn't checked the box in a while. Another patron stood at a counter, addressing an envelope. Martha had taken a place in line for the service counter. I walked over and got in line behind her. I supposed I could buy a book of stamps. With bill paying being done mostly online these days, I hardly ever used stamps anymore, but it couldn't hurt to have a book around, just in case.

Only three people stood in line before Martha, and none of them had an abundance of packages or anything else that appeared to be particularly time-consuming. I had to act fast before the line progressed and the housekeeper was called to the counter to conduct her transaction.

"Excuse me?" I said.

Martha cast a glance back over her shoulder. "Are you talking to me?"

"I am," I said. "I'm almost certain I recognize you from the hotel near the convention center. You work there, right?"

She grunted and turned sideways to better address me while also being able to keep an eye on the line ahead of her. "You're partially right," she said. "I did work there. Don't anymore."

"I don't know if you remember me, but I saw you in the hall Monday morning, when that big jerk was shooting off his mouth."

She ran her gaze over me, squinting, as if trying to place me but having no luck. The dress and makeup I'd put on to disguise myself had not only proved to be a moot endeavor but had also thrown her off. In retrospect, maybe I should have worn my usual overalls and sneakers so she'd have recognized me.

I went on. "I hope that you no longer working at the hotel has nothing to do with him."

She pursed her lips sourly. "It has *everything* to do with him. That arrogant bastard got me called into my manager's office. When I said that I thought he was overreacting, he blew his top. My manager told me to apologize. At that point, I wasn't about to bow down to either of them. I told them both what I thought they were in no uncertain terms, and my manager fired me." She shrugged. "No big loss. I'm tired of cleaning hotel rooms anyway. The hours aren't as good, but commercial cleaning is easier. I'll probably go back to that. I know my supervisor at the hotel will give me a good reference."

"I'm glad to hear that you'll land on your feet." I gave

her a smile and leaned in conspiratorially. "By the way, it's kinda funny what happened to the guy, huh?"

Her expression didn't change. "What do you mean?"

"You didn't hear? Right after the judges arrived to evaluate his model, he keeled over dead, right there in front of everyone." It felt slimy to speak so callously of the incident, but I was trying to create a rapport with this woman, and it seemed the best way.

She snorted. "What do you know. Wishes do come true."

Whoa. She'd just admitted that she'd wished Bert Gebhardt dead, didn't she? But did that mean she might have taken steps to help her wish become a reality? And had she really not known that Bert had been taken off by ambulance? She'd tossed that smirk over her shoulder when he'd been on his way from Jaffe's booth to his own after their screaming match. He'd been discovered unconscious only minutes later. The arrival of the EMTs and them subsequently hauling Bert away on the gurney had created quite a hubbub. Was she being disingenuous with me? Had she really not seen all the commotion? Perhaps she had left the convention center in the meantime.

We moved forward as one of the customers before us left the counter and another from the line took his place.

I pushed the issue. "I saw you at the model railroad convention," I said. "I was going to say hello, but I couldn't get through the crowd. It was right before Bert passed out."

She turned her face toward the counter and said, "Guess I must've missed it."

Had she turned her head to monitor the progress of the customers ahead of her, or was she trying to avoid my prying gaze? As another customer left the window and Martha became the next in line, I knew my time to grill her was

bought a book of stamps, choosing a pretty variety from among the options, one with flowers on them. When her transaction was complete, she turned and walked out without so much as a glance in my direction.

As I stood there, watching her go, the postal worker called out again. "Next!"

Chapter Nineteen

After spending so much time dolling myself up that morning, it would seem a waste to change into my overalls, T-shirt, and sneakers. I decided I might as well keep the dress and makeup on. Maybe the new image would give the conventioneers a renewed sense of faith in my moonshine and bring them out to my shop tonight to try some samples and buy some new jars.

With Nora watching the Moonshine Shack, I swung by Singing River and picked up my grandfather. He'd had such a good time at the convention center on Wednesday—prior to Bert Gebhardt passing out, anyway—that I thought it would be fun to bring him back again.

I strolled up and down the aisles once more, Granddaddy rolling along beside me on his scooter. I'd printed out new flyers on my home computer while I'd been getting ready that morning. The flyers not only reminded the

conventioneers of their twenty percent discount on all pur-
chases at my shop, but it also offered them one jar at half
price. I figured I needed to up the ante to get them down to
my shop after everything that had happened this week. Of
course, I was here with dual goals: sell some 'shine and do
some snooping. *Could there be some clue here that I'd
overlooked before?*

As we approached Patrick Jaffe's booth, both he and
Kimberly eased back behind his display and busied themselves. Patrick looked down at his controller and moved
his hands among the knobs as if adjusting them, but it
didn't appear that he'd actually moved them one iota. Kimberly put her phone to her ear as if she'd received a phone
call and turned away, putting her other index finger to her
ear as if to block out noise. Obviously, they were avoid-
ing me.

Were they afraid that I was on to them, that I knew they
had something to do with the raw sugar that had been sprinkled on Bert's tracks? I wondered what Ace had said to
them, what products she'd found in their possession. A glass
cleaner with methanol? Antifreeze? Could be. After all, Patrick had quite a bit of natural foliage on his display, too.
Maybe he'd used antifreeze to preserve it.

At this point, with Ace on the case and my moonshine
exonerated, I knew it was best that I merely observe and
report than perform my own interrogations. I walked past
the Jaffes' booth and ignored them just as they were ignoring me. *Two can play this game.*

My grandfather had me stop at several of the vendor
booths so he could take a look at their wares. We bought a
few more things to include in the model layout at my shop.
A dog that looked like one he and my granny had when

they first married. An old-fashioned sheriff's car and sheriff figure. A man that resembled his daddy, my great-grandfather. A horse that looked just like Charlotte, her head held high, her mane tossed.

As we passed the empty vendor table, I stopped to examine the tag. I'd noticed it before, but hadn't taken the time to read it. There'd seemed to be no reason to do so. But now I was curious about the conventioneer who'd seemingly gone up in smoke. The tag read RESERVED FOR ELLIOTT AVERY. *Hmm.* Assuming a man had flirted with Martha at the hotel as she'd claimed, could Elliott Avery have been that man? Could something have happened to him between Monday morning and the start of the convention approximately an hour later? It seemed unlikely anything could have changed in such a short period of time, but it couldn't hurt to see what I could find out.

"Wait here," I told my grandfather, leaving him at a presentation on using 3D printing to create scenery. "I'll be right back."

He was a good sport. He'd never be able to figure out how to do three-dimensional printing himself, nor did he own the equipment that would be needed. Nevertheless, he'd find these newfangled ways of doing things interesting. "Are you telling me there's a printer that knows how to whittle? Don't that beat all!"

While he was listening to the lecture, I ventured over to the registration table. I'd told a little fib in my text to Ace earlier, pretending I'd just happened upon the hotel housekeeping cart, and I told the man working the table a little fib now.

I pointed in the general direction of the empty booth. "Elliott couldn't make it?" I said, insinuating Elliott Avery and I were on a first name basis. By pretending to know the vendor who hadn't shown up, I thought it might loosen the man up a little, encourage him to give me more information. "I see his booth is empty."

The man thumbed through some paperwork remaining in a manila folder before pulling out a sheet of paper. "You're referring to Elliott Avery?"

"Yes, that's him. He's a friend of my grandfather's." Each fib rolled off my tongue more easily. I was getting pretty good at this.

The man held up the sheet. "Says here he notified the desk that he had to go back home to prepare for a hurricane." He took a closer look at the sheet. "Makes sense. His home address is in Hatteras. That's in North Carolina, on the Outer Banks."

The information explained why Avery hadn't attended the conference after all. It also brought back to mind the gusty weather and scattered rain we'd had on Wednesday. But it didn't tell me for certain that Avery was the man Martha had allegedly spoken with at the hotel. After all, there were other hotels nearby. While most of the conventioneers were staying at the hotel right next door, a few of the more budget minded might have secured rooms at one of the less-expensive inns.

I thanked the man for the information and left the table. On my way back to claim my granddad, I glanced down row B and saw Dana sitting at the booth, knitting. Bert's Last Spike display was gone. So was the table it had been resting on. Looked like Dana had unloaded them. Apparently, she'd even sold her and Bert's zero-gravity chairs. She was now sitting in one of the cheap metal folding chairs provided by the convention center.

Curious, I ventured down to her space. I gestured at the

empty spot where the display had been. "You sold Bert's Last Spike model?"

She nodded. "There's a guy here who runs a steam train in Alabama. One of those tourist traps. They're expanding their facility and adding a museum. He said the Last Spike would be a great addition. He dismantled it and carried it out to his truck this morning."

"That's wonderful," I said. "Bert's legacy will live on."

She continued to work the yarn. "Lots of people will get to enjoy it, too. Many more than if he'd just taken it home and put it down in our basement, like he planned."

"I hope you got a good price for it."

"Good enough," she said. "I'm sure Bert spent more in total on all the parts than the guy offered, but no sense dickering over it. I'm not up to it. I'm happy to recoup even part of the expense."

While she said she wasn't up to haggling, she appeared well rested today, the circles under her eyes gone. They weren't bloodshot from crying, either. She'd fixed her hair and makeup, and put on a cute blouse with her blue jeans. I chastised myself for assuming these things meant she wasn't grieving. Maybe grooming herself had been a calming routine, a ritual that brought her life some sort of normality when it had taken off like a runaway train. She could be trying to put on a brave face, not wanting to be a downer for the others at the convention. She might be waiting to fall to pieces when she returned to their house in Milwaukee. It would likely seem quiet and empty without Bert around.

Still, now that the police had determined Bert's death was not caused by improperly produced moonshine, but rather by someone intentionally adulterating the jar, shouldn't she be more upset? Shouldn't she be fearful and angry and suspicious of the others at the convention? Or even upset with Bert, if she'd thought he'd done this to himself? Maybe she was, and she was simply good at hiding it. After all, what could she really do to solve the case? The Chattanooga police were working on it. She probably trusted that they would get to the bottom of things, and she was simply waiting for answers.

I noticed Bert's toolbox was back. It stood open beside the display of collectibles, which contained only a single train now. Looked like Dana's liquidation sale had been a big success.

The return of Bert's toolbox told me that Ace had taken from it everything she considered relevant. I was dying to know what she'd found, not only here but at the other booths as well. Unfortunately, for me anyway, our sharing of information went primarily in one direction only, from me to her. Ace tended to be very tight-lipped, unless sharing something could help her case. I knew better than to ask her outright. Still, maybe I could learn something with a few apt questions posed to Dana. "I see the detective brought Bert's toolbox back."

She glanced nonchalantly over at the box. "She had Officer Landers drop it off here this morning."

It wasn't surprising Ace had asked Marlon to return the toolbox. He'd guarded Bert's booth earlier in the week and knew where it was located within the convention center. He'd met Dana, too. Besides, Marlon and Ace had been close since working a horse theft case together a while back, before I'd met him. They'd ended up at the wrong end of a shotgun but managed to survive the ordeal. I supposed going through something like that gives you an unbreakable bond. I knew she trusted him. But I had to admit it was a little awkward when he knew things about investigations that involved me and he couldn't share what he knew. It put him in the middle, made for an awkward triangle.

Dana nodded and smiled. "Officer Landers made all the wives go crazy again."

"He makes me go crazy, too," I said, "but I'll never let him know it."

She pointed a knitting needle at me. "Smart girl. Letting Bert know I had a hopeless crush was my first big mistake with him. He realized he had the upper hand. You never want to let a man know that."

I stepped closer to the box and looked down. "Have you sold many of Bert's tools?"

"Quite a few," she said.

"That's what I thought," I said. "His toolbox looks much emptier."

"The police kept Bert's cleaning supplies. I told Detective Pearce to take what they could use at the station. The glass cleaner was brand-new, full to the top. Bert had only used a few drops of it."

"That was nice of you." I gestured toward the lecture area. "I better go round up my grandfather. It was nice seeing you again, Dana." I decided not to give her one of my discount flyers. Even though it hadn't been my moonshine that had killed her husband, my 'shine had nonetheless been used as the delivery device. I didn't want to seem insensitive. I realized then that this was the last time I'd see her. Marlon and I had planned an early trail ride with Charlotte in the morning, before the day became too warm, and then I'd be working at my shop all day. "Have a safe trip back to Milwaukee."

"Thanks, Hattie. You take care now."

I passed Ronnie Wallingford's booth on my way to get

my grandfather. Like the Jaffes, he didn't seem happy to see me. Unlike them, though, he didn't ignore me. Instead, he stared me down, his dimples looking like angry slashes in his cheeks rather than a jovial facial feature. Ace had probably asked him about his heated haggling with Bert over the collector caboose. Though Dana would have mentioned the interaction, too, Ronnie must have known that my report of the events would add credence, point fingers in his direction. Obviously, I didn't bother giving him a flyer, either. In fact, I gave his booth a wide berth.

I arrived back at the lecture area to find that my grandfather had dozed off on his scooter, his arms crossed over his chest, his head down. When I put a hand on his shoulder, he reflexively threw up his gnarled hands and exclaimed, "Hey!"

A few people turned around. I gave them a contrite smile for interrupting their session and mouthed *Sorry!*

I bent over and softly said, "Time to go, Granddaddy."

He scrubbed a hand over his face and shook his head to fully wake himself up.

As we rolled away, he said, "Everything they was talking about was so confusing, I couldn't tell if it was just over my head or if I was having a stroke. I did that whole F.A.S.T. test they told us about at Singing River. I checked my face in my scooter's side mirror, but it wasn't drooping, and I could raise both of my arms. My speech wasn't slurred, neither. I said 'Old McDonald had a farm, E-I-E-I-O' with no problem. Course a few people looked at me like I'd lost my mind."

I wasn't above teasing him. "You sure you haven't lost your mind, Granddaddy?"

As we left the convention center to return to the car, I glanced over at the hotel. "Mind if we take a detour?" I asked my grandfather. "I've got a question for the hotel desk clerk."

"Okey doke," he said, turning his handlebars to aim for the hotel.

My grandfather waited out front in the fresh air by a potted plant, while I went inside and headed over to the registration desk. I knew the hotel staff were told not to share private guest information, but if I pretended to already know about a guest, they might be more forthcoming. I stepped up to the counter and gestured to my granddad through the front window. "My grandfather has a good friend attending the model train convention. A guy named Elliott Avery from Hatteras, North Carolina. Could you place a call to his room for me? I want to let him know we're here."

The woman typed on her keypad and leaned in to consult her screen. "I'm sorry." She flashed an apologetic smile. "Looks like Mr. Avery checked out early. He was originally booked through Saturday night, but he left on Monday morning."

"The hurricane." I slapped a palm to my forehead. "I hadn't thought much about it since it didn't affect us too bad here. I'll bet he had to go back home to batten down the hatches."

Maybe Martha's story about the disappearing flirt wasn't a ploy. Maybe she had been telling the truth, after all. The fact that Elliott Avery had been both a guest at the hotel and a registered vendor at the train convention matched up.

As I thanked the woman and turned to go, I saw Ace come out of a door behind the registration desk marked STAFF ONLY. A man in a business suit was with her, probably one of the hotel's managers. He held a key card in his hand. Either because she was focused on her mission or because I didn't look anything like my usual self in this flouncy dress with my hair up, she didn't seem to notice me. They strode across the lobby to the elevator bank and pushed the up arrow button.

Whoa. Was Ace going to search someone's room?

Chapter Twenty

Ace and the hotel manager were clearly on their way to a guest room. But whose? Dana and Bert's room was here on the first floor, so it couldn't be theirs. The fact that she was going up meant she was likely going to take a look at the Jaffes' room or Ronnie Wallingford's or Stuart Speer's. I wondered which piece of evidence had led to this search, what she might find in the rooms. But she wasn't likely to tell me what she was doing here now and, besides, it was time for me to get to my shop and relieve Nora so that she could pick her children up at school.

I walked back outside, and Granddaddy and I returned to my van. After driving back to my cabin to retrieve my lonely kitty, I drove us all to my shop, parking in one of the two spots by the back door. Granddaddy left his scooter in my van, and instead used his cane to hobble into the dimly lit stockroom. Meanwhile, I lugged Smoky in his carrier, my arm straining with the effort. After setting him down, I locked the back door and released him from his enclosure. He sauntered out, performed a few yoga-like stretches, and sashayed his way into the shop area to take a spot in the front window, where he could keep an eye on the street.

Nora greeted me and Granddaddy with a big smile. "Hi, you two."

"Hi, Nora," I said. "Anything to report?"

"It's been busy!" she said with a smile. "I sold an entire case of wild blackberry moonshine to a woman from the train convention. She said she'd had a derailment at the hotel mixer on Monday night and plans to make them for her book club when she gets back home to Atlanta. They're reading *Murder on the Orient Express,* so she thought it would be the perfect drink option."

I pumped a fist. "Yesss!" With any luck, all of the ladies would then go to their local liquor stores looking for my moonshine, and the liquor stores would place an order with me. Maybe the train convention would take my moonshine nationwide, just like trains did with people and wares during their heyday.

Nora said, "A package arrived for you today, Hattie. I had the deliveryman put it in the back corner of the stockroom." She followed her words with a coy wag of her brows to let me know my grandfather's power recliner had finally arrived.

When we'd come through the stockroom, I'd noticed the cartons seemed to have been rearranged, and now I knew why. I bounced on my toes and silently clapped my hands. *He is going to love it!*

Nora turned to my grandfather. "I sold five of your little whittled critters today," she said, pointing to the shelf where we displayed his small crafts. "We're running low. You might ought to make some more."

Granddaddy smiled, proud that the Moonshine Shack's customers appreciated his rustic knickknacks. "I'll get right on it." He grabbed his whittling tools and a chunk of wood and went out front, where he could work in the rocking chair.

Meanwhile, Nora and I scurried to the back room. She'd pushed the recliner into a corner and obscured it under a soft plaid throw blanket I'd brought to the shop. She'd also stacked several cartons of moonshine around it to make sure Granddaddy wouldn't see it until it was ready. I wrangled the cartons aside, removed the throw, and used a box cutter to slice through the heavy-duty plastic wrap surrounding the faux-leather chair. I put a hand on the seat and pressed lightly. Yep, it felt just as soft and cushy as it had on the furniture showroom floor.

I unlocked the wheels so that we could move it easily. As quietly as possible, the two of us pushed it into the shop, placing it strategically near the front window so Granddaddy could greet customers as they came in and enjoy the view outside. Once we finished installing the model train, he could sit back in the chair and watch it go around. He'd enjoy that, too.

I folded the throw and draped it over the back of the chair, in easy reach if my grandfather wanted to use it. I plugged the chair into the wall socket, and attached the table tray to the arm so he'd have a place to set his glass of spiked ice tea each day. Lastly, Nora and I wrapped a wide blue ribbon around the back of the chair, and finished it with an oversized bow.

Nora went to the door and opened it, poking her head out. "Ben? Hattie needs you inside."

"What for?" he asked.

Stubborn old coot.

Nora improvised. "She's thinking of rearranging the shelves and she wants your opinion."

It was a good improv. Granddaddy liked to be consulted, to feel relevant.

He rocked hard, getting his momentum going to make it easier for him to stand, and used his cane to push himself up from the rocker. He barely made it out. Looked like the power chair had arrived none too soon. He hobbled through the door, looking down as he made his way to ensure he didn't trip over the threshold. When he looked back up and saw me next to the power chair, my arms spread in invitation for him to sit, he nearly fell backward in surprise. "What in the world?"

"Ta-da!" I called.

He smiled so wide it was a wonder his dentures didn't drop out and hit the floor. "Is that fancy chair for me?"

"It's my way of thanking you, Granddaddy," I told him. "You deserve the best. Without you teaching me how to make moonshine, the Moonshine Shack wouldn't exist."

"Well, I'll be darned!" He hustled over, turned around, and plopped down in the chair, crushing the bow behind his back. He picked up the remote and tested each of the buttons in turn, first laying the chair all the way flat, then pushing the button forward until the chair rose and leaned forward, gently setting him on his feet. He tried the footrest and back independently, too. "This is perfect!" he cried. "I can take a nap in it without falling out, and it'll stand me right up after, too." He stood himself up and stretched out his arms. I stepped into them for a warm hug.

After Nora's shift ended and she headed out, I took a quick inventory of the stock in the shop, happy to see so many shelves in need of replenishing. I restocked the supply in the hopes that more people from the train convention would venture into the Moonshine Shack this evening. With it being Friday night, more of them were likely to come down Market Street to enjoy the restaurants and entertainment. Between customers, I also prepared my sample table, lining up shot glasses and jars of moonshine topped with pour spouts so I'd be ready to serve a taste or two to help customers decide which flavors to purchase. *Might I suggest a jar of each variety?*

Around 4:30, Marlon clop-clop-clopped up to the shop on Charlotte. I rounded up a bucket of water for her, as well as a Granny Smith apple, and carried them out front.

"Hoo-ee." Marlon ran his gaze from the top of my pulled-up curls, down over my dress, to the tips of my toes in my white sandals. "You clean up good, little filly." He followed his words with a wink that warmed me from those curls to those toes. "Too bad you've got to work this evening or I'd put on my best duds and take you someplace swanky for dinner."

"I'll give you a rain check."

"I'll take it."

I set the bucket down in front of Charlotte, and cupped the apple in my hands. She picked the fruit up with her wriggling lips and long teeth. After crunching her way through the apple, she slurped up water from the bucket, drops dripping from her chin when she lifted it. Having had her snack and quenched her thirst, she shifted around a bit, sassily cocked her back left leg, and closed her eyes to take a standing nap.

I turned to Marlon, who leaned against the porch post, his arms crossed over his chest, emphasizing his biceps as they pulled his police uniform tight around them. The gun show aside, I was dying to know what Ace had found out when she'd spoken with Ronnie Wallingford, the Jaffes, and Stuart Speer, and what all she'd seized from their booths and hotel rooms. In light of the fact that Ace had employed Marlon to return Bert Gebhardt's toolbox to Dana, I was pretty sure Ace had also filled Marlon in on the status of the investigation, what progress she'd made and where she planned to focus her efforts next. Maybe he'd give me the scoop if I played my cards right.

He angled his head to indicate the shop. "I see you've got the sample table locked and loaded. Expecting a big crowd tonight?"

"Not expecting as much as hoping for one," I said. "I made the rounds at the convention center today. I offered everyone a jar at half price. Now that they know it wasn't my moonshine that killed Bert Gebhardt, some of them might be willing to give it a second chance."

I bounced in my sandals, trying unsuccessfully to hide my anticipation and desire to know more.

A grin quietly claimed Marlon's mouth, taking it over until it spread across his face. "You want me to tell you what I know about the case, don't you?"

"Am I that obvious?"

He snorted softly. "You couldn't be more obvious if you'd rented a billboard and one of those inflatable dancing men." He flailed his arms and bent over at the waist in imitation.

"Well?" I snapped impatiently. "What can you tell me?"

He straightened up and spilled the beans. "The police lab ran a more detailed analysis of the adulterated moonshine. They determined that the methanol came from Gleam Dream Glass and Window Cleaner."

"It did?" Instinctively, I stood up straighter, too. "That's big, isn't it? I mean, it narrows down the list of suspects."

"You'd think so," Marlon said. "It seems to point to Ronnie Wallingford. His bottle of Gleam Dream was nearly empty, so he very well could have poured a good amount into Bert Gebhardt's moonshine or bought one of your jars at a local liquor store and swapped them out. Bert's bottle was still full, so that seems to rule out him or Dana. Ace said you'd mentioned a housekeeper at the hotel. She went out to the woman's house to interview her this afternoon."

Uh-oh.

My guilt must have been written on my face because Marlon said, "Yeah. Imagine the surprise when Martha told Ace that the girl who'd been in the hotel with cases of moonshine Monday morning was also at the post office in Brainerd today, asking nosy questions." He narrowed his eyes at me. "What a coincidence that you'd be out that way, nowhere near your home or place of business."

I looked away, averting my eyes just as the Jaffes had done when I passed their booth earlier in the day. Marlon reached out, put two warm fingers aside my chin, and turned my face his way, forcing me to look at him. "You're going to get yourself in trouble one of these days, Hattie. You need to be more careful."

While I appreciated his concern, I didn't like the insinuation that I was putting myself in unnecessary danger. I could perform my own risk assessments. "Martha Grissom is a frail, elderly woman. Short of poisoning someone, she couldn't hurt a fly."

"Oh, yeah? Tell that to the Ruger in her purse."

She'd been packing a handgun? My jaw nearly fell off its hinge. "Okay," I acquiesced. "Perhaps you have a point."

He released my chin, and my skin instantly missed his touch. "You know what the most dangerous part of police work is?" he asked.

"Shoot-outs?" I said. "High-speed chases?" *Chafing on the inner thighs from the polyester uniforms?*

"No," he said. "It's traffic stops. Even if we run a license plate, we don't know for certain if it's the car's owner at the wheel. Could be anyone. It's the unknown that's such a big risk. When we know we're going to round up someone with a long rap sheet and a propensity for violence, we take precautions, we're prepared. It's getting caught off guard that makes things dangerous." He leaned in and skewered me with a look, his amber eyes aflame. "You need to stop taking these crazy chances, Hattie."

I let out a long breath and hung my head. "You're right." I counted to three, hoping to appear sufficiently contrite, before looking back up and resuming my quest for information. "What about the Jaffes? They didn't have any Gleam Dream?"

"No," Marlon said. "Just some Windex. There's no methanol in that. Stuart Speer didn't have any Gleam Dream on him, either. Ace checked their booths, their vehicles, and their hotel rooms. Course there's always the chance they'd already ditched the Gleam Dream they used to poison Bert, if they're the ones who did it. They might have even swiped some from a housekeeper's cart or closet at the hotel. Kimberly Jaffe admitted she'd been in the Gebhardts' hotel room with the other ladies when they swung by to invite Dana to join them for drinks Tuesday evening. Kimberly's prints weren't on the tainted jar, but she could have wiped hers off and swapped them out. Seems like one of the other ladies might have noticed, though. Ace is talking to them now, asking whether they saw anything suspicious."

With any luck, one of them would say she'd seen Kimberly fooling around with the jars of blackberry 'shine, switching them out and this case could be closed. "What about the stuff on Bert's track?" I asked. "Did the lab say it's raw sugar?"

"It is," Marlon said. "They confirmed it a half hour ago. Ace told me I could share that news with you. She wouldn't have had that clue if it weren't for you."

I felt my chest swell with pride. "Glad I could help."

He chuckled. "Not sure it helps that much," he said. "It points the finger right back at the Jaffes and Stuart Speer, keeps them in the running."

In other words, none of the suspects had been eliminated.

Marlon went on. "Ace checked the tainted jar of 'shine for fingerprints, of course. Bert's bottle of Gleam Dream, too. It's still full, so it obviously wasn't used to poison him. But since it was sitting next to his jar of blackberry 'shine in his toolbox, she thought someone might have accidentally left a print on it if they tampered with Bert's jar or swapped out the jars at his booth. The only prints on the glass cleaner and jar were Bert's and Dana's, what you'd expect under normal circumstances."

I thought aloud. "So, either the person wiped their prints off Bert's jar, or wiped them off their own before they swapped them out?"

"Looks that way."

I mulled things over a moment. "You said Dana's prints were on Bert's bottle, too. She had told me he never let her near his cleaning products or trains. I figured that maybe she'd meant it more figuratively, but maybe not. If Bert truly never let her touch his stuff, her prints shouldn't have been on the bottle."

Marlon lifted a shoulder, unconvinced. "She might have touched the bottle after he was gone. She was trying to sell off his stuff, right? Including his tools? She'd have to move the bottle so people could see what's in the toolbox. It's a moot point, really, what with the bottles being full."

His explanation made sense. Still, something had me feeling unsettled.

We heard voices from down the sidewalk as a group of women I recognized from the convention approached my store. Kimberly Jaffe was not among them this time. *No surprise there.*

Marlon backed away and untied Charlotte's reins. "I'll get out of your hair. We're still on for that trail ride in the morning, aren't we?"

"Sure," I said. "I'm looking forward to it."

"Good. Charlotte and I will be by to pick you up bright and early. How's seven o'clock?"

"Could we make it seven thirty? I need my beauty sleep."

His gaze roamed over me again and he said, "No, you don't. But I'll give it to you anyway."

Dang. This guy sure knows how to play a woman.

With that, he swung himself up into the saddle and gave his steed a soft squeeze with his thighs that meant *let's get going.* The two clop-cop-clopped away, Marlon doffing his helmet to the train convention ladies as he passed by. They erupted in giggles and catcalls. One even let loose a wolf whistle. Clearly, these women were ready to party.

I gave them a smile as they stepped up to my store. "Samples anyone?"

Chapter Twenty-One

Friday evening, the Moonshine Shack was bustling, and Kiki and I were hustling. She'd helped me out for free when I'd first opened the place, and she'd discovered she enjoyed the camaraderie and chatting up the customers. While she'd never give up her career as a graphic artist, her one complaint was that it was a very solitary profession. An extrovert like her needed some time with people, and a shopkeeper like me needed some help. Her assisting me at the store was a win for both of us, and it occasionally gave Nora the chance for some time off. Fortunately, I could now afford to pay her so I didn't have to feel guilty about it.

While Smoky chilled out safely in the closed stockroom and Kiki rang up customers at the checkout counter, I poured sample after sample for men in railroad engineer outfits, as well as for tourists and locals dressed in weekend garb. While some people loved my light, lower-proof fruity flavors, others preferred the purer burn of my Granddaddy's

Ole-Timey Corn Liquor. Jars and jugs flew off the shelves
as fast as I could restock them. Meanwhile, my grandfather
sat proudly in his power chair, which I'd rolled out front
and plugged into an exterior socket. He waved his whittling
tools around as he hollered like a carnival barker, inviting
everyone on the street to "Come on in, and getcher free
'shine samples!"

At dusk, I turned on the firefly green twinkle lights that
were twined around the porch posts to draw further attention
to my shop. I also turned up the volume on the bluegrass
tunes to give my shop an even more festive atmosphere.
People tended to spend more time and money in the Moonshine Shack if they felt like they were at a party.

But while I skittered about, pouring samples, rounding
up jugs and jars, and answering questions, something nig-
gled at me. Dana's fingerprints had appeared on Bert's full
bottle of Gleam Dream. Even though she'd mentioned earlier that Bert didn't let her touch his supplies or clean his
equipment, Marlon had pointed out that the presence of her
prints on the jar wasn't necessarily suspicious. Maybe her
words had been mere hyperbole. Maybe she'd moved the
bottle of glass cleaner aside to put the jar of 'shine in the
toolbox next to it. Or maybe Bert had left the glass cleaner
out, and she'd had to move it aside. Or maybe she'd moved
it to show the tools to someone. But with the bottle being
so full, there was less chance the cleaner had been used and,
thus, less chance of this type of interaction. *Hmm.* Still, her
fingerprints on the bottle seemed like a small, easily ex-
plainable fact.

People were still coming in at 9:00, when the store hours
officially ended. I figured I might as well stay open late and
sell all the 'shine we could. *Gotta strike while the iron is
hot, right?* I moved Granddaddy's new chair inside again,

and he joined Smoky in the quieter backroom. He was now napping in the power chair with my cat curled up beside him.

By 10:00, the crowd had gone, most of the revelers having returned to their hotels or moved on to continue the party at the local watering holes. I turned the sign in my window to closed, removed the cash from the register and locked it in the safe, and rounded up both my grandfather and my cat. After bidding Kiki goodbye at our cars out back, I drove to the Singing River Retirement Home and dropped off my grandfather. He raised a hand in goodbye as he drove his scooter through the automatic doors. Once he was safely inside, I pulled away from the curb and headed up the mountain toward home.

As I carried Smoky from my van to the door of our cabin, fireflies lit up in my peripheral vision. But when I turned to look at them, they disappeared. That's exactly how the niggling in my mind felt. Something was attempting to illuminate me, some bright idea, but when I focused too much on it, the thought disappeared.

I fed Smoky a late-night treat and got ready for bed. It had been a crazy, hectic week. I looked forward to spending a lovely morning with Marlon and Charlotte tomorrow, riding the equestrian trails at Summit Knobs.

I woke Saturday morning with that same feeling that there was something I'd missed, but I still couldn't put a finger on it. I wrote the feeling off to mere uncertainty. I figured I must be feeling unsettled because it was the final day of the model railroad convention, the conventioneers would be leaving town tomorrow, and the mystery surrounding Bert Gebhardt's death still hadn't been solved.

The awards ceremony would be held at 4:00 this afternoon. I wondered who would win the steam train contest. I felt pretty sure it would be Patrick Jaffe. His model of Chattanooga was exceptional. Ronnie Wallingford was likely to win the Thumbs award for most humorous model. And if I were placing a bet, I'd put money on Bert's Last Spike model to win the Photo Match award. Given that Dana would be going home with neither her husband, his model, or any resolution regarding his suspicious death, I hoped Dana could at least go home with an award.

Marlon picked me up at half past seven. He wore boots, jeans, and a short-sleeved plaid Western-style shirt with a yoke and pearlescent snap buttons, a modern-day cowboy. I'd donned a striped blouse, jeans, and a pair of sneakers. If my relationship with Marlon continued as I hoped, I'd have to invest in a pair of riding boots with a heel that would help keep my feet in the stirrups.

We drove Marlon's maroon Dodge pickup truck up to the Summit Knob trails northeast of the city, pulling Charlotte in her trailer behind it. As he eased her back out of the trailer, a dragonfly flitted about, hovering and darting, attempting to defend its territory. It was an eastern pondhawk dragonfly, known by its powdery blue color. My mind felt that little niggle again. *Blue* . . .

Marlon got Charlotte saddled up and I climbed aboard, settling in his larger Western saddle. With me being a novice rider and neither of us wanting to overtax the horse, we decided it was best for Marlon to lead Charlotte while I hung on to the saddle horn and enjoyed a ride. We'd swap positions in a quarter hour or so. It was a beautiful clear day, hardly a cloud overhead, though we caught an occasional glimpse of the blue sky through the canopy of shade trees that lined the path. *Blue* . . .

We were a mile down the trail, chatting amiably, when a vibrant eastern bluebird swooped across the trail in front of us and lit upon the limb of a dogwood tree. On seeing his vibrant blue feathers, the thought that had been eluding me illuminated at a million watts as if a spotlight had actually been shone in my face. Bert Gebhardt's bottle of Gleam Dream Glass & Window Cleaner had been full when I'd seen him use it to clean his tracks, and it was full when Ace seized it later. But had it been partially emptied in between?

The liquid glass cleaner on the hotel housekeeping cart had been a vivid blue, cobalt. The fluid in Bert Gebhardt's bottle had looked the same shade of cobalt blue on Monday, when I'd seen him use it to clean his tracks. But when I'd seen it later, it had looked more sky blue, hadn't it?

I sat bolt upright on Charlotte's back. "I think I might be onto something!"

Marlon stopped his horse with a light tug on the reins and a "whoa" before turning to eye me over his shoulder. "What is it?"

I whipped my phone from the breast pocket of my blouse and pulled up the photo Ace had taken of the blackberry moonshine sitting in Bert's toolbox next to his glass cleaner. Sure enough, the liquid in Bert's bottle of Gleam Dream was lighter blue. "The bottle of Gleam Dream I saw in the housekeeping cart at the hotel was bright blue, very colorful. Bert's looked the same when I saw him using it on Monday. But when I saw the bottle in his booth later, the cleaner was lighter in color. Sky blue, or maybe baby blue. See?" I held the screen so Marlon could step back to my side and take a look. "Do you think Dana could have poured some of the cleaner into the jar of moonshine and then added water so the bottle still looked full? She might have figured that if the bottle was full, people would assume it hadn't been used."

I tried to remember what the liquid in Ronnie Wallingford's bottle looked like, but all I could remember was that he had only a small amount left. I pulled up the pic of his bottle on my phone and took a look. It was cobalt. I showed that photo to Marlon, too.

"You're right," he said. "The color is different. We should have the lab run an analysis. If Bert's bottle is less concentrated than the others, Dana will have some explaining to do. I'll call Ace." He retrieved his phone from the back pocket of his jeans and dialed the detective, putting her on speakerphone. When she answered, he said, "I'm with Hattie. She just had an epiphany we thought she should share with you."

Charlotte shifted under me and the saddle creaked as I shared my thoughts on the color of the cleaners. "With the bottles varying in how full they were, the differences in color didn't immediately stand out. But if you compare precise amounts side by side, I suspect the difference in concentration will show."

"I'll take a look right away," Ace said, "and have the lab run a comparison. I'll get back to you as soon as I know something."

Marlon slid his phone back into his pocket. "Should we keep going or turn back?"

"Turn back." I felt certain the lab's analysis would confirm my theory. If Dana Gebhardt was arrested, I wanted to be there at the convention center to witness it. That woman had tarnished my 'shine, made me worry that everything I'd worked so hard to build would be lost. I wanted to see her pay for her crime.

Shortly thereafter, Marlon had loaded Charlotte into her

trailer and we were driving down Still Hollow Loop, making our way back down into Chattanooga. He'd slipped his phone into the dash mount. The ringtone sounded and the screen lit up, showing it was Ace calling.

I reached out and jabbed the button to accept the call, then put Ace on speaker. "What did you find out?"

The detective's disembodied voice came back. "Your hunch was right, Hattie. Wallingford's bottle of Gleam Dream was nearly empty, so neither the lab techs or I had noticed the difference in the colors between his bottle and Bert's. But once we took a closer look, it was clear. The lab ran a test just to be sure. The cleaner in Wallingford's bottle is far more concentrated. Bert's bottle was diluted by half or more. I'm on my way to the convention center now to arrest Dana."

Chapter Twenty-Two

Oh, my gosh! Dana Gebhardt killed her husband! Though I'd known all along it could be possible, I'd hoped it wouldn't be true. I'd liked the woman, at least at first.

Marlon bobbed his head, giving me an awestruck look. "Way to go, Hattie." Turning his attention back to the phone call, he signed off with, "We'll meet you there as soon as we can, Ace."

Unfortunately, we were on a two-lane road with no shoulder, thick woods on both sides, and a horse in the trailer behind us. We couldn't go fast. I only hoped we wouldn't miss the arrest.

Twenty minutes later, we'd reached the edge of the city and were heading toward the convention center when Ace called back. "I'm at the hotel. The Gebhardts' booth at the convention center was empty. The man at the adjacent booth told me Dana sold off the display case this morning and gave him everything she couldn't sell. There's no sign of her at the center, so I came over here. The desk clerk told me she checked out ten minutes ago. I just missed her. The Gebhardts' registration indicates they were driving a U-Haul truck with Wisconsin plates when they checked in. I've issued an alert. The fastest route to Milwaukee would be via Interstate Twenty-Four, but there's a chance she's taking State Highway Twenty-Seven north."

I'd had an inkling about the colors of the glass cleaner, and now I had an inkling that Dana wasn't planning to drive back to Milwaukee. She'd told me earlier in the week that she would have preferred to fly to the conventions, but Bert had insisted she ride with him in the rental trucks. Now that he was no longer around to force her to do things his way and she wasn't burdened with his train paraphernalia, she might have decided to fly home instead.

"Maybe she's taking neither," I said. "She might be planning to turn in the rental truck here and take a plane back home."

"Smart thinking, Hattie," Ace said. "I'll send officers to the U-Haul locations closest to the hotel and airport."

"What should we do?" Marlon asked.

"We've got it covered. Go back and finish your trail ride."

We ended this second call. As glad as I was that the case seemed to be resolved and that Dana Gebhardt would soon be apprehended, I knew I wouldn't feel completely at ease until the woman was behind bars where she deserved to be. It was one thing for her to kill her husband—*one very bad thing*, of course—but it was another for her to nearly ruin everything I had worked so hard for. I was furious that she'd used me and my moonshine in such a terrible way.

We were headed west on Bailey Avenue, looking for a place to turn around again, when an orange and white

U-Haul truck approached us from the opposite direction. I sat up and leaned forward to get a better look as it rolled past. Dana sat at the wheel. Her eyes met mine and our gazes locked as we passed each other. Her eyes went wide with recognition and alarm.

"It's her!" I cried.

Marlon muttered a curse. We'd have to turn around quick. Poor Charlotte. The horse was going to get dizzy if we kept having to reverse course. Marlon pulled into the parking lot of a prep school and circled until we faced out. Unfortunately, there was quite a bit of traffic on Bailey Avenue.

"C'mon! C'mon!" Marlon growled, willing oncoming traffic to hurry up.

Finally, after waiting nearly half a minute, we were able to pull back out onto the road. By then, the U-Haul was nowhere in sight. But at least we now knew the general area where Dana was. Marlon grabbed his police radio from the console of his truck and called in the information. "We've spotted murder suspect Dana Gebhardt eastbound on Bailey Avenue in a U-Haul truck."

As we drove along, Marlon kept his eyes on the road and I looked for our quarry. Although she could simply be so far ahead that she was out of sight, I glanced down the side streets to see if Dana had turned off and tried to ditch us. She had. She'd turned down South Watkins Street. I pointed. "There she is!"

With the trailer behind us, Marlon wasn't able to brake and turn in time, but he took the next right onto Buckley Street. She'd made a left turn on Union Avenue and passed right in front of us. Luckily, we were able to pull in a couple of cars behind her. *She won't get away now!*

Marlon radioed her current position. "We've got Dana Gebhardt on the run."

When Dana reached the intersection at Dodds Avenue, she sat there so long the driver of the car behind her honked their horn.

Marlon leaned his head toward his window. "I can see her reflection in her side mirror. She's panicking. She can't decide where to go from here."

It was no wonder. She wasn't from Chattanooga and wouldn't know where the roads would lead. If she'd been using her phone's maps app, it was likely set to take her to a U-Haul facility and had been rerouting, giving her orders like her husband had when he was alive. I wondered what would happen if she said *Hey, Siri. Get me an escape route!*

Hooonk! The driver's patience was gone.

Dana turned right. When we reached the intersection, we did the same. She hooked a sudden left on Kirby Avenue, probably thinking she could lose us. With a heavy horse behind us, we hadn't yet been able to gain enough speed for the turn to be a problem. Marlon hooked an easy left onto Kirby, gaining on her. We were directly behind her now. After a couple more turns, she took a left onto McCallie Place. The road was flanked by a greenbelt with a railroad track running through it.

Marlon shook his head and issued a soft snort. "Dana's going to be real surprised when she realizes this road is a dead end."

A few seconds later, the U-Haul rolled to a stop where the pavement ended.

"We've got her," Marlon said as we pulled in behind her. He reached over to his glove compartment in front of me and retrieved a gun.

I shrunk back against my seat. "You really think that's necessary?"

"Uh, yeah," Marlon said. "She killed her husband, remember?"

"But not in a violent way."

"You're right," he said. "It was just poison, the kind killer."

"Okay," I acquiesced. "You've got a point. I just don't like the idea that this arrest could lead to a shoot-out. There's been enough bloodshed."

"Actually," Marlon said, "there's been no bloodshed. The lack of bleeding is one of the few positive aspects of death by poisoning. It's cleaner than an attack with a knife or gun or blunt instrument."

Now he was just pushing my buttons. "You've got another point," I said through gritted teeth. "But can we agree that there's been metaphorical bloodshed?"

"All right," he said. "I'll give you that. Stay here, and keep your head down. If she resists, things could get ugly."

I lowered my head, but as soon as Marlon slid out of the cab and closed his door, I raised it again, just high enough that I could see over the dashboard. I had not put so much effort into helping Ace solve this case to not watch the arrest go down.

From behind me came a *woo-woo*. After hearing the same noise all week at the model train convention, it almost didn't register with me. But then a steam engine appeared in my side mirror, approaching from behind on the adjacent track, a gray combination of smoke and steam belching from its smokestack. The Missionary Ridge local. The same train I'd ridden on that long-ago birthday celebration. Soon the *clackety-clack-clackety-clack* of its wheels joined the horn noise.

Ahead, Marlon stuck close to the U-Haul truck, sneaking up along the driver's side. As he approached the cab, he hollered, "Chattanooga Police! Put your hands up where I can see them!" Marlon stood back from the window, reaching a hand forward to open the door of the U-Haul, but finding it locked. He used his knuckles to rap on the driver's door. "Open up, Dana! Now!" When that didn't work, he reached out to adjust the truck's side mirror to give him a better view into the cab without him having to take the risk of looking in the window directly.

Clackety-clack-clackety-clack. Woo-woo!

What he couldn't see from his perspective, but what I could see from mine, was Dana Gebhardt sliding out of the passenger door. *She's making a run for it!* She turned my way, intending to escape back down the dead-end road. She ran toward Marlon's pickup in an odd tiptoe, as if trying to be quiet. It must've been instinct. With the noisy train approaching, there was no way Marlon could have heard her footsteps on the opposite side of the truck anyway.

Dana's eyes met mine again through the truck's windshield. We stared frozen at each other for a beat, then she took off, bolting past my window.

Not so fast, sister.

I thought of the words Granddaddy had muttered in his sleep, the quote from *High Noon. Don't try to be a hero. You don't have to be a hero, not for me.*

I decided that, while I didn't need to be a hero for anyone else, I owed it to myself to be one for me. I shoved my door open and hopped out of Marlon's pickup. I hollered, "She's back here! She's running away!" but the chances of Marlon hearing me were slim to none. By then, the train was upon us. With the entrance to the narrow Missionary Ridge Tunnel just ahead, it had slowed somewhat, but it was still moving at a decent clip and making a lot of noise. *Clackety-clack-clackety-clack.*

I bolted after Dana. Though the woman was in okay shape, she was clearly not a regular runner, and the loafers she wore were not made for sprinting. I had my age and my sneakers on my side, and quickly gained on her. With the moving train forming an effective wall on the left, I vectored to the right, both with the goal of caging her in and so that Marlon might see me running back here if he turned around, and he'd realize Dana had come this way.

Soon, I'd caught up with Dana and was running directly parallel with her. I wasn't trained in police tactics, and I had no idea what to do. *Should I tackle her?* We were on hard asphalt. I really didn't want to risk either of us getting hurt. If I was momentarily incapacitated, what might she try to do to me? She'd already killed her husband. Would she be willing to claim another life? She just might, given her desperate situation.

When she saw me next to her, she tried an evasive maneuver, stopping quickly. I'd sprinted a few steps past her by the time I realized she was no longer moving. She headed toward the major street behind me, hoping to escape into traffic. But before she could get there, I'd backtracked and stood between her and escape, my arms out to my sides to block her advance. I must have looked like someone trying to corral an escaped chicken back into its coop.

Clackety-clack-clackety-clack. Still looking at me, she turned her body and began to dash in the other direction. She made it only a few feet before stopping again, the moving train looming in front of her. Passengers looked down at us through the windows above, some of them turning to each other and pointing, clearly wondering why in the world I seemed to be chasing Dana along the road. Though I couldn't see her face, her shoulders slumped. I assumed this meant she'd accepted defeat.

I assumed wrong. She hadn't.

Chapter Twenty-Three

Dana darted forward and jumped up onto the side of the
passenger car, grabbing the handrail that flanked the steps
at the end of it. The door that led from the car to the steps
was closed for safety, so she couldn't get inside the train,
but the lower step stuck out a few inches, giving her a foot-
hold. I watched helplessly as the train carried her away at a
speed I'd never be able to match on foot.

As the next passenger car rolled by, I decided I wasn't so
helpless after all. I ran after the train and did exactly what
Dana had done—grabbed the handrail and pulled myself
up until I was standing on the bottom step, rocking back
and forth along with the train. *Clackety-clack-clackety-
clack. Woo-woo!*

The train carried us down the track, past Marlon, who
stood now on the passenger side of the U-Haul with his gun
pointed down by his side, watching incredulously as first
Dana, then I, rode by on the side of the train. His mouth

flapped but his words were inaudible over the noise of the train. Most likely, he'd shouted something like, *Are you crazy, Hattie?!* But I chose to interpret his moving mouth as saying, *Get her, Hattie! We're counting on you!*

As the train engineer sounded the horn again, unaware that he'd picked up contraband human cargo, Dana turned to look ahead. My gaze followed hers. *Holy caboose!* The entrance to the Missionary Ridge Tunnel loomed only a short distance before us, the light-colored stone framing the narrow, arched entrance. The train slowed, but jumping off would still be dangerous; surely I might break a bone or two, if not a neck. I wasn't a Hollywood stuntperson or black belt in karate. I didn't know how to fall in a way to prevent myself from getting a concussion. And what if I fell wrong and the train ran over my arm or leg and severed it? *Would I still be able to make moonshine with only one hand?*

Dana must have had the same thoughts. Rather than leap from the train, she flattened herself against it. Just in time, too. The passenger car she was hanging on to disappeared into the dark tunnel.

Lest my backside drag along the stone lining the inside of the tunnel, I turned my head to look forward, sucked in my gut, and flattened myself against the train, too. In an instant, I was thrown into darkness. But while my eyes saw nothing, my other senses were on overload. My entire body vibrated and rocked with the movement of the train. My ears filled painfully with the *clackety-clack* of the wheels, the roar of the steam engine, the squeal of the wheels against the track, all of it echoing-echoing-echoing inside the tunnel, threatening to burst my eardrums. The smoke bellowing from the steam engine filled my nose and lungs. *Should've turned my head the other way.* An involuntary coughing fit overtook me, threatening to break my ribs and shake me loose. Droplets of steam scorched my skin like liquid fire.

Though my ears and lungs threatened to explode, I didn't dare take a hand off the rail to plug my ears or pull my shirt up over my nose, and risk falling off the train. Outside the tunnel, there'd been a chance I'd simply roll safely away, but inside the tunnel there was no such chance. Mere inches separated my back from the soot-stained stone and brick walls. If I fell from the train here, I'd end up under it, losing not only limbs but my life as well. I had no choice but to endure the *clackety-clack*, *squeeeeaaaal*, *squeal-squeal-squeeeeaal*, and *roooaaar* that filled my ears.

After a few seconds, my eyes adjusted. Blinking the soot and smoke out of them, I could see a little bit thanks to the light now coming from the end of the tunnel. Or, perhaps I'd died and didn't know it, and my soul was on its way to meet its maker. With only the dim, far-off light source, I couldn't make out much, though I could see the shadow of Dana's silhouette as she continued to cling to the passenger car ahead of mine.

If I'd thought there was room, I'd shake my head. The situation was absolutely absurd. Bonkers. Bananas! What in the world was Dana thinking trying to escape arrest by jumping a train like some Wild West outlaw?

I prayed she'd be able to hold on. She was larger than me, and bore a greater chance of her car rocking and knocking her against the inside of the tunnel, knocking her off the step. If she fell, there was a good chance she could knock me off my step as well. The body count could very likely rise from one to three.

Finally, the train rolled out of the far end of the tunnel, back into the fresh air and sunshine, carrying Dana and me with it. By the time we emerged, my eardrums had taken all they could. I could hear nothing. When the track curved, I gripped the handrail as tightly as I could with my right hand and waved my left arm, hoping to catch the attention of the engineer or maybe even a passenger. I remembered from riding the train as a kid that there was an emergency brake in each car, and that it was marked with red lettering warning an alarm would sound if the handle was pulled.

The engineer glanced back out of his window on the leading car. When he spotted me and Dana hanging on to the passenger cars for dear life, he did a double take, sticking his head farther out. *He's seen us. Thank goodness!*

There was an elongated *squeeeeeaaaaal* that I could only feel but not hear as he applied the brakes and brought the train to a shuddering stop along the curve. The train sat motionless in a semicircle, the smell of hot metal permeating the air. The engineer emerged from the steam engine as Dana dropped from her step and I hopped down from mine. Though his mouth flapped like Marlon's had earlier, I couldn't hear a word he said. All I heard was a soft roar.

Dana tried to run away again, but she didn't make it far before Ace came barreling up from the other direction on the greenbelt that flanked the tracks. I ran after Dana, too. With the two of us in pursuit, she had no chance of escaping. That didn't mean she wasn't going to try, though. We spent a couple of minutes chasing her around the train yard before she tried to run around the turntable. Ace went around one side, while I went around the other. Dana was fifty yards ahead, then forty, then thirty as I gained on her, pumping my arms like pistons. Lifting heavy cases of moonshine had built some muscle in my arms and legs, and I summoned every bit of that strength in my pursuit.

Her twenty-yard lead decreased to ten yards, then five. When Dana attempted to run into the woods, I closed the distance and leaped up onto her back. I'd planned to go for a ride this morning, but not like this. I rode her back like a kid on a pony and was flung forward when she hit the ground face-first on a patch of dirt covered in dried brown pine needles. Luckily, though my skid across the ground dirtied my hair, face, and shirt, it caused no real damage. As Ace straddled Dana and yanked the woman's hands up behind her back to cuff them, I stood and brushed the dirt from my clothing and face, beaming. I'd taken a big risk jumping on the train and felt proud it paid off. A killer was now in custody.

Marlon cantered up on Charlotte, riding bareback. He must've ridden her through the tunnel after us. He slid off her before she'd even slowed to a complete stop and dropped her reins, knowing he could trust her to stick around. He ran over and grabbed me by the shoulders, much as Dana had grabbed Bert earlier in the week. But, unlike Dana, Marlon was sincerely concerned about my welfare. He bent over, looked into my eyes, and asked me something I couldn't hear. I could only see his lips move. The circumstances told me it was something along the lines of *Are you all right?*

"I'm fine," I said. "Just a little dirty." I smelled like smoke, too, courtesy of the steam train's smokestack.

He released my shoulders and cupped his hands over his ears to let me know I had inadvertently been hollering. Given that I was still virtually deaf, I could hardly hear myself speak over the dull roar in my ears. I put fingers to my ears and plugged them for a few seconds in an attempt to clear them. I forced a yawn, opened my mouth wide, and moved my jaw around. "There," I said. "Is that better? It feels better."

Marlon nodded and reached out to pluck a pine needle from my hair. Then, in a surprising act of affection and concern, he grabbed me and pulled me to him, enveloping me in a warm embrace that told me just how freaked out he'd been that I could end up hurt . . . or worse.

"Officer Landers!" Ace called. "Round up your horse and meet me at the station. You come along with me, Hattie. I'll need a statement from you." With that, she grabbed Dana by the upper arm and led her to the waiting cruiser.

Chapter Twenty-Four

A half hour later, Charlotte was lazily munching hay in her trailer behind the Chattanooga Police Department, while Ace, Marlon, Dana, and I were holed up in a conference room. Thanks to me and Dana, the room smelled like a campfire. The only thing missing were the marshmallows for roasting.

Dana's legs were shackled now, too. If she tried to run off again, she wouldn't make it more than a step or two before tripping over herself. A medic from the fire station down the street was checking us out, making sure we hadn't been hurt during our daring train ride adventure. He shone a penlight into our eyes, asked us to follow the beam, and checked our heart rate and blood pressure. Other than temporary hearing loss—and maybe a temporary loss of sanity, too—we both appeared to be fine.

Sobbing, Dana spilled everything, much like a derailed train car spills its cargo, pouring her heart out. I supposed she felt she had nothing to lose at this point and simply wanted to get things off her chest, relieve herself of the emotional burden of her big lie.

She plucked a tissue from the box Ace had set on the table in front of her and wiped her nose. "Bert seemed like a take-charge, responsible guy when we started dating all those years ago," she said. "I thought he'd make a good husband and father. But after we married, he became very controlling and demanding." She said their marriage went off track after only a few years but, when she'd suggested they uncouple, he'd threatened her with a messy divorce, a custody battle, and a life of destitution. "I felt like I had no choice but to stay with him. I tried to make the best of it, but over the years he got worse and worse, and putting up with him got harder and harder." He'd forbidden her from holding a job and made her fear she wouldn't be able to support herself if she left him. "He convinced me it was for my own good and the good of our sons. He said I was lucky I didn't have to work, that most women would love to be kept like I was."

She'd been kept all right. Like a prisoner. Still, it didn't give her an excuse to kill him. I had to admit I felt sorry for her, though. Her situation had been untenable. No person should have to live like that.

She looked down at her lap. "I didn't see any way out." When she looked up again, she said, "Tuesday was our thirty-second wedding anniversary. Bert didn't even remember. When he didn't mention it all day, didn't acknowledge it, something in me just broke. I realized I'd wasted my life with a self-centered husband who cared more about his model trains than me. I was nearly as angry at myself as I was at him." She sniffled before continuing and dabbed at her nose. "A few months ago, we watched an old movie.

It was about trains, of course. But there was a part in it about moonshiners, too. Someone drank some bad moonshine and died. After I bought the jars of blackberry moonshine at Hattie's shop, an idea came to me. I thought I could lace the moonshine with methanol, that maybe I could finally rid myself of Bert and nobody would know it was me." She looked at me. "I didn't mean to hurt you or your business, Hattie. I'm sorry. I just didn't see any other way."

She choked up, closed her eyes, and sobbed for a few moments, her chest and shoulders heaving. Finally, she regained control, releasing a shuddering breath. When she opened her eyes again, she said, "Remember how you asked why I wasn't hanging on to Bert's trains for my sons or grandkids?"

I nodded. "Yeah?"

"The reason they weren't interested is because Bert wouldn't let them anywhere near his trains. You'd think it would be something fun a father and his sons could have enjoyed together and bonded over, but Bert threatened to whoop our boys to kingdom come if they laid one finger on his trains. The boys were heartbroken. They were even jealous of the trains, in a way. Their father paid more attention to his model railroad than he did to his own sons. When they got older and could've gotten their own model train sets, they wanted nothing to do with the hobby. They didn't want anything to do with Bert, either. They didn't want to be anything like their father. They despised him." She closed her eyes again. "I never wanted to raise my kids in a situation like that. I'm so glad it's different for them now. They're such good daddies to their own kids."

I recalled the photos she'd shown me, Kiki, and Kate on her phone, how Bert had been in none of them. I'd wondered at the time whether he'd taken the photos or had simply been elsewhere. I knew now that it was the latter.

Dana gave me a sad, contrite smile as she was led off to the holding cell. Although I didn't condone what she had done, her husband's behavior had been psychologically abusive. She didn't seem to be a threat to the public at large. I hoped she'd get a fair sentence that would allow her to pay her debt to society and enjoy her grandchildren again one day.

Once Dana was put in the lockup, Ace shared some additional information with me. She said that Dana had confessed on the drive from the train to the station that she had not thrown out the bottle of Gleam Dream because, by the time she came up with the idea to poison Bert's moonshine with it, too many people had seen him with the toxic blue glass cleaner, including me. She feared that if she got rid of it, people would wonder where it had gone and she'd look guilty. She'd thought that by diluting it and thus making the bottle appear full, it would throw the police off her scent. It had, but only for a short time.

Now that things were resolving, Ace filled me in on her interrogations of the other suspects. "I had an interesting conversation with the Jaffes. Patrick insists he had nothing to do with any conspiracy or sabotage, though he admitted he was aware of the animosity between Bert Gebhardt and Stuart Speer. Jaffe said he spotted Speer appearing to toss something over the plexiglass at Bert's display Wednesday morning while Bert and Dana were still waiting in line to get inside the convention center. Speer had tried to make it look like he was holding up his cell phone to check his reception, but it didn't look natural. Jaffe went to Bert's display and noticed the sparkling granules on the tracks. He followed Speer, saw him with the raw sugar packets, and guessed that he might have sabotaged Bert's exhibit in retribution for Bert challenging Speer's judging in earlier contests. Jaffe claims he collected the sugar packets and stir stick from the trash as evidence. The stir stick hadn't been used, so it was clear Speer hadn't stirred any sugar into his coffee."

She went on to say that Jaffe had initially intended to submit the empty packets and stir stick to the National Model Railroad Association leadership. "Jaffe said he wanted to win the competition, but that he wanted a real victory, not a hollow one, and that if Speer was biased in his judging, Jaffe believed Speer should be removed from his position." Jaffe also claimed he thought the judging issue was rendered moot after Bert died, and thus did not turn the evidence over to the association. However, when he learned that Bert's death was not from natural causes, he became concerned that he could have evidence of not just improper judging but of murder, too. He'd turned the stir stick and sugar packets over to Ace Thursday afternoon. "We went together to show them to the chief judge."

"Will Stuart Speer be arrested?"

"No," Ace said. "He might have violated the rules for judging the model railroad contest, but I can't arrest someone just for lacking integrity. There was no money at stake in the contest, so it doesn't count as fraud. Speer's actions were sleazy, but they weren't criminal. That said, the association has the right under their own rules to banish him from future participation. As angry as the chief judge was, I doubt Speer will be allowed to show his face at another model train convention in his lifetime."

The two mysteries solved, I provided a statement for the department's records, and Marlon and I were dismissed. By then, it was too late in the day to head back out on a trail ride. Marlon said, "Time to get Charlotte back home."

We drove to the horse boarding facility twenty minutes up the road in Harrison, where both Marlon and Charlotte lived. As I learned, the two shared a barn, with Charlotte living below and Marlon making a home in the converted hayloft above. It was the first time I'd seen his place. After backing Charlotte out of her trailer and setting her free, she trotted over to gossip with a group of other mares. They nickered on seeing her and stepped back to allow her into their circle. They reminded me of the women from the train convention, gathering together to enjoy each other's company. I hoped Dana would find such a group in prison to help see her through her sentence.

Marlon took me upstairs for a quick tour of his place. The space was small and spare, with a sloped ceiling, but it made for a quiet and peaceful bachelor's quarters. A boxy brown couch flanked by end tables sat in the living room, facing a large-screen television. Given the limited space, he'd forgone a coffee table, but a green and tan Southwestern style rug softened the look. The kitchen was square, with a butcher block island that provided two stools for seating. The only things in the bedroom were a dresser and queen-sized bed covered in a striped spread.

"If things go right," Marlon said, "Charlotte and I might soon buy a place of our own."

"Oh, yeah?"

"There's an old house on eight acres for sale next door. I've made an offer. We're waiting to hear back."

Owning the property next door would be a perfect situation for him and his horse. Charlotte would be able to remain with the other horses in her herd, but Marlon could have more space and start building up some equity.

"I'll keep my fingers crossed for you," I said. "And for Charlotte."

"As long as I'm doing grown-up stuff," he said, "there's another offer I'd like to make." A teasing glint played in his eyes.

"What is it?" I asked.

"I'd like to be your boyfriend."

I fought a smile. "What are the terms?"

"Exclusivity, of course," he said. "I like what we've got going. I'm ready to lock things down, slap a label on this relationship."

"Anything else?" I asked.

"A dinner date at least once a week. Maybe you put your hair up and wear that cute dress every so often."

"Liked that look, did you?"

"I won't deny it. Course you look awfully cute in your overalls, too." He cocked his head. "What do you say, little filly? Yay or nay."

I gave him a warm smile and a warmer kiss. "I say yay."

I called Kiki and asked if she could close the store for me. She graciously agreed. I gave her an update of the day's events, culminating in Dana Gebhardt's arrest.

"You jumped on a train?" she cried, incredulous. "Are you crazy?"

"It's a distinct possibility."

Marlon and I swung by my cabin so I could shower, wash my hair, and change into a clean pair of jeans and a fresh blouse. As usual, Smoky followed me into the bathroom. He sniffed at my pile of dirty clothes, his whiskers twitching as he scented the smoke.

Now that I was cleaned up, Marlon and I climbed back into his truck and drove to the convention center. After everything that had happened, and knowing now that Patrick

Jaffe and Ronnie Wallingford were innocent, I wanted to see how things turned out for them.

"You're just in time," said the man working the entrance. "They're about to announce the winners of the competitions." He pointed to the far end of the convention center, where a small platform had been erected. Standing in front of it were dozens of men in striped engineer hats, along with a few women and children.

Marlon and I walked over. I spotted Kimberly and Patrick Jaffe in the crowd. We eased over to stand beside them. They knew I wasn't a killer, and Marlon and I now knew they weren't, either. We exchanged cordial greetings both with them and with Ronnie Wallingford, who stood nearby. Patrick bounced on his feet, clearly anxious to see whether he might win the steam train contest. Marlon and I exchanged a knowing look. We didn't want to spoil this moment for Patrick Jaffe. We'd tell them about Dana's arrest once the awards had been announced.

When the judges ascended the steps to the platform in their blue blazers, one of them was conspicuously missing.

Jaffe shook his head before glancing my way. "Looks like they gave Stuart Speer the boot."

It served the man right. No matter how obnoxious Bert Gebhardt might have been, it didn't make it right to sabotage his display. A judge had to hold himself to higher standards.

After brief introductions, the chief judge said, "Now for the results of the model train competitions." He announced the winners of the Thumbs competition first. "Hands down, the award goes to Ronnie Wallingford for his exhibit 'Making Tracks—American Cryptids.'"

The audience burst into applause. His humorous model had been a real crowd pleaser.

The announcer moved on to the People's Choice award, which Patrick Jaffe won by an enormous margin, before announcing that the late Bert Gebhardt's Last Spike model placed first in the Photo Match category. Although there was no one there to accept Bert's ribbon, his name would forever be listed in the annals of the model railroading association.

The announcer moved on to the awards for the diesel train competition, starting with third place and working up to first. He presented the winners with ribbons, shook their hands, and expressed his congratulations, posing with them as the audience snapped photographs.

"Moving on to the steam train competition." He announced that third place went to the exhibitor of the "well-designed and expertly built Durango and Silverton Narrow Gauge Railroad." Second was awarded to the White Pass and Yukon Route train. "And now, for first place."

Kimberly reached over, took her husband's hand in hers, and gave it a squeeze. *Now that's what a marriage is supposed to look like.* Even though Dana was a killer, I was sad that she'd never been able to experience a loving and respectful romantic relationship with her spouse.

The chief judge paused for anticipation and looked out over the crowd. "The first place winner displayed a fantastic model that not only spoke to the ideas of reconciliation and connection but also featured our hometown location here. Patrick Jaffe, you've won first prize!"

Jaffe threw up his fists in celebration. Kimberly whooped and applauded. Marlon and I clapped along with the rest of the crowd, too.

The awards concluded, the chief judge dismissed the crowd. I noticed Jaffe stop him to ask a question. The two spoke for a moment or two before Jaffe returned to his wife's side, carrying his blue first-place ribbon and a purple People's Choice award ribbon. "I had to know," he said. "I asked the chief judge whether Bert Gebhardt might've won if he'd lived and his train hadn't derailed. He said that the results would have been exactly the same. The judges didn't feel that the Last Spike was particularly unique, and that even though Bert built a good display, it was a fairly easy one to make. There were no complicated structures, and little imagination involved. He also told me that Stuart Speer still denies he tossed sugar onto Bert's display, but they don't believe him. He's been permanently prohibited from judging or entering contests."

"Speaking of being judged," I said, "Dana Gebhardt will be standing before a judge shortly. She's been arrested for her husband's murder."

Kimberly's mouth fell open. "I can hardly believe it. She'd put up with him for so long." She shook her head. "I hope they go easy on her. That man railroaded her into marriage years ago. She deserved better. Heck, we've known those two for years." She hiked her thumb at herself and her husband. "The two of us can be character witnesses for Dana and against Bert."

I suspected that, because Dana didn't seem to pose a risk to the public at large, she might receive a light sentence, but only time would tell.

Marlon and I ended the night with a kiss on my porch. It had been a long, exhausting day, and I slept like a rock now that Bert's murder was solved.

On Sunday, I swung by the Singing River Retirement Home to pick up my grandfather and take him to the Moonshine Shack. Marlon met us there. Kiki did, too.

Between helping customers, Marlon, Granddaddy, and I continued to assemble my grandfather's model train display. Granddaddy barked orders from his cushy new recliner, pointing up at the shelves around the perimeter of the walls and telling us where he wanted the scenery items placed. With our ancestors having been at odds a century before, it was nice to see that members of the Hayes and Landers families could now work together in harmony.

"The train station should be right there," Granddaddy said, pointing to a spot in the center of the back wall. "Put the still next to the cabin. It'll make it look like home." Casting a knowing and narrow-eyed glance at Marlon, he said, "Put Sheriff Landers and my pa over there, by the trees." My great-granddaddy's arrest, at the hands of Marlon's great-grandfather, would be immortalized in miniature. I was glad my grandfather no longer seemed so bitter about it.

When we were done, I climbed atop my step stool to switch the engine on for its inaugural voyage through the layout. Granddaddy grinned like a kid as it set off, filling the air with small puffs of smoke and a delightful toot of its horn. *Woo-woo!* The display made a cute and folksy addition to the 'Shine Shack. It would likely draw in some customers, too.

Kiki had been watching from behind the checkout as we'd set up the train. "You know," she said thoughtfully, circling a ballpoint pen to indicate the walls, "I could paint a backdrop of mountains and trees and sky if you'd like. I could include local landmarks. Rock City. Lookout Mountain. The Incline Railroad."

"Would you?" I asked. "That would be adorable!" Area landmarks would highlight the city I loved and add even more local flavor to the display, which was a definite plus, judging from the People's Choice award Patrick Jaffe had won.

Kiki slid off her stool. "Let me round up my paints."

Marlon took me out for a nice Italian dinner Sunday night, complete with a bottle of red wine and tiramisu for dessert. Afterward, we strolled hand in hand along the waterfront, enjoying the fresh breeze coming off the Tennessee River. The model railroaders had left town by now, but soon musicians and fans would descend on the city for the county's bluegrass festival. Posters along the walkway advertised the festival and announced the lineup of bands. It promised to be a fun event.

"Maybe I'll look into renting a food truck so I can serve my moonshine at the festival."

"That's a great idea," Marlon said. "I bet you'd rake in a fortune. You'd deserve it, too, especially after all you've been put through."

He must have realized how happy I'd been to learn that my 'shine hadn't been the source of the poison. He knew how much my business meant to me, how much it would have hurt me to lose it.

When we stopped to admire the view of the river, Marlon stepped behind me, putting his chest to my back and encircling me in his arms as we stared across the water. He rested his chin on top of my head. I felt safe and protected, all my worries gone. With any luck, my life would stay worry free for a long time to come.

With the murder solved and the model train convention now behind us, things soon returned to normal at the

Moonshine Shack. Fortunately, my customers returned, too. I'd saved my business and restored my good name.

With things calm and routine now, I could focus on managing my shop, expanding my moonshine business, and enjoying my burgeoning romance with Marlon. But even though things were great now, I knew not to take anything for granted. After all, if there was one thing recent events had taught me, it's that one can never know what lies down the tracks . . .

ACKNOWLEDGMENTS

I'm having so much fun writing this series, and I am forever grateful to all the fabulous folks who made it happen. I raise a glass to all of you!

Thanks to my agent, Helen Breitwieser, for finding a home for Hattie at Berkley.

Thanks to Michelle Vega for bringing me into the Berkley fold. Thanks to my editor, Miranda Hill, for the perceptive suggestions and guidance through the revision process. Thanks, too, to the rest of the Berkley team, including Brittanie Black, Natalie Sellars, and Megha Jain, for all of your hard work in getting the book to readers, and to Sarah Oberrender and Auden George for the adorable cover.

Thanks, as always, to you fabulous readers who chose this book. I know you have a lot of options, and I'm honored you've chosen my story. Enjoy your time with Hattie, Smoky, Granddaddy, Marlon, Ace, and the rest of the moonshiners at the Moonshine Shack!

Enjoy Hattie's Train-Themed Moonshine Drinks!

Each recipe makes one serving.
Use 12 ounce or larger glasses. A shot
glass equals 3 tablespoons or 1.5 ounces.

Clown Car

- 8 ounces of ginger ale
- 1 shot of cherry-flavored moonshine
- 1 maraschino cherry

Pour the ginger ale over ice. Stir in the moonshine. Garnish with a cherry and enjoy!

Brass Collar

- 8 ounces of your favorite brand of cola
- 1 shot of unflavored moonshine
- 1 navel orange

Pour the cola over ice. Add the moonshine. Cut the orange in half. Squeeze half the orange, or use a juicer, to extract the juice. Stir 2 tablespoons of the juice into the cola. Slice the remaining orange half into circular slices and use one slice as a garnish.

Derailment

- 8 ounces of lemon-lime soda
- 2 shots of blackberry-flavored moonshine
- Fresh blackberries
- Mint leaf

Pour the lemon-lime soda over ice. Add the moonshine and five fresh blackberries. Stir to mix. Garnish with the mint leaf.

Ready to find
your next great read?

Let us help.

Visit prh.com/nextread

Penguin
Random
House